THE
WRITING
ON
THE
WALL

JENNY ECLAIR

THE WRITING ON THE WALL

Orion

ORION CHILDREN'S BOOKS

First published in Great Britain in 2022 by Hodder & Stoughton

3 5 7 9 10 8 6 4

A CIP catalogue record for this book
is available from the British Library.

ISBN 978 1 510 10828 8

Typeset in Adobe Caslon by Avon DataSet Ltd, Alcester, Warwickshire

Printed and bound in Great Britain by Clays Ltd, Elcograf S.p.A.

The paper and board used in this book
are made from wood from responsible sources.

Orion Children's Books
An imprint of
Hachette Children's Group
Part of Hodder & Stoughton Limited
Carmelite House
50 Victoria Embankment
London EC4Y 0DZ

An Hachette UK Company
www.hachette.co.uk

www.hachettechildrens.co.uk

Dedicated to all the fifteen-year-olds, good luck.

PART ONE

2021

HERMIONE

FRIDAY

It's one of those global-warming days when London is kind of melting, the pavement chewing gum has turned back to goo and the bins outside the flats stink so bad, you have to hold your breath until you're well clear. Hello, climate change.

School finished yesterday and I didn't know whether to laugh or cry. Everyone else was like, 'Finally, let's get out of this dump.' Even some of the teachers seemed to be legging it. I felt a bit choked up clearing out my locker, so many memories, but then I found a Tupperware at the back that was so full of mould, seriously, it was like something out of one of those forensics TV shows that my mum likes watching on Sky and I stopped feeling quite so sentimental.

My mum, Tessa, is mad for true-crime shows. Her favourite thing is stories about serial killers, which is a bit worrying given she's about to drag us both off to live with some bloke she's only been seeing for the last six months. Apparently, he asked her to go and live with him in his big posh house up north and she said yes without even discussing it with me. She's even gone and sublet our flat to some bloke she knows from the pub. When I told her she should hand the keys back to the council because there could be a family that could really do with it, she said, 'It's a crummy two-bedroom flat on the thirteenth floor of a crappy high-rise, it's no good for families.' And I suppose she's right. The lifts are forever out of order and some of the graffiti might be a bit confusing to little kids. Still, my mum says the useless lifts have saved her a fortune in gym memberships and their utter shitness is the reason why she still has the best legs this side of the Elephant and Castle. My mum occasionally suffers from high self-esteem.

I did ask if I could stay in the flat by myself, but she just laughed, and when I said maybe Dad could move back in with me and we could keep an eye on each other, she just laughed even more and said Casper couldn't be trusted with a loaf of bread never mind a fifteen-year-old daughter. I thought the loaf of bread was an odd analogy, but I could see her point. My dad is quite rubbish, although if you were in a lift with him when it broke down, you'd probably have quite a good time.

It's a done deal basically. I'm not legally old enough to live alone, and so in 24 hours I have to go north, to the bit where it's always raining on the TV weather forecast. Mum tries to cheer me up by WhatsApping me photos of the house. It's fucking massive, like something you'd see in Clapham or Dulwich Village, this big red-brick thing with loads of windows – but so what? Our block of flats has got loads of windows, like *loads*, and sometimes when I'm coming home at night on the bus in the dark and I see it in the distance, it looks like a great big cruise ship out at sea. I can't imagine living in a building that no one else lives in, I've never lived in a house before, I've never walked out of my front door and straight on to street level.

I didn't tell Amisha, Millie or Rhiannon for ages. I kept thinking the situation might change, that Mum might meet someone else, preferably someone local, and things would stay the same. Not that I want things to stay the same, not entirely. I love my mates and I love London, even though some days it really upsets me. I think big cities can be quite cruel. There's all the homelessness and too many people out on the street who aren't being looked after properly and everyone talks about mental health, but nothing really ever gets done. Loads of girls in my year have got eating disorders and I know at least two people who regularly self-harm, their shirt sleeves covering up those tell-tale silvery-white blade marks running up and down their arms.

I try and shake off all this negative stuff as I jump on a number 12 bus heading for Peckham. My mum's busy packing everything into bags and boxes and then unpacking everything because 'actually I need the iron'. She's got no method; everything's just chucked in all together. She drives me mad. I can't stay home. If I stay home, she wants me to start packing too and I can't face it. In any case, it's the first day of the summer holidays, and even if I have to leave tomorrow, today I can still hang out with my mates and lie on the grass in the sun, listening to music and arguing over Maccy D's versus Manze's pie and mash. It's too hot for pie and mash really, it's too hot for anything except boy watching, ice lollies and chilled Diet Cokes. I'll pack tonight. Mum's mate Patti's cousin Daryl is

5

picking us up in a van at 9 a.m., though Patti says knowing Daryl, it'll probably be more like midday. I don't have much stuff anyway, just clothes, a box of books, my phone and my charger. We don't need to take towels or bedding, apparently Paul's got everything. My mum smirks when she tells me this. I reckon she thinks she's landed on her feet.

The bus rumbles through Camberwell Green. Up the hill to the right is the hospital where I was born. I'm South London to the belly button; I don't even like to go north of the river. God knows how I'll survive in the actual north of the country. They'll think I talk funny and it's not as if I don't get bullied enough here as it is, and this is where I'm from. Not badly bullied, not like some kids, but there's just a bunch of bitches in my year that make life difficult for me, make me feel like my tongue is too big for my mouth, make me sweat, and I swear when I get anxious, my sweat smells of fried onions.

So yeah, there have been moments when I've daydreamed about getting away from here, living somewhere completely different, but I never meant Lancashire, I meant Melbourne or Manhattan. I mean, who's ever even heard of Lytham St Anne's?

SATURDAY

Patti was wrong about Daryl. He turned up with the transit van bang on 10 a.m. and Mum basically yelled at me until the three of us were strapped in a row on the front seat and Daryl was asking her for the postcode of where we were going. Mum looked blank and called Paul, who had to repeat it about ten times before Daryl could punch it into his phone.

As we swung out into the traffic on the Walworth Road, my mum said, 'That's it, Hermione, there's no going back now. Goodbye, London; hello, new life!'

I told her I felt sick and I noticed Daryl roll his eyes. Mum told me not to be silly and handed me a plastic bag 'just in case'. Suddenly Daryl looked at his phone and said, 'Fuck me, it's two hundred and fifty miles away. No one told me it was a five-hundred-mile round trip. I'm meant to be going out with the lads tonight!' Mum ignored him, reached forward and switched the radio on and tried to sing along to Dua Lipa without knowing any of the words.

* * *

So here I am in my new bedroom, feeling like I just fell down a rabbit hole. Somewhere among all these boxes and bags is a bin liner with all my summer clothes in it, but I can't find the stupid thing. Mum is being useless, wafting round the place with this stupid grin on her face, telling me how lucky we are to be living here.

I mean, don't get me wrong, this house is like mega, seriously. In London it would cost a couple of million. Paul bought it about ten years ago before his wife died and his children left home. Yup, basically Paul is a sixty-year-old widower with two grown-up children. Nice one, Mum. Catch.

His kids, Nick and Lucy, are in their late twenties. Nick lives in Manchester and works in computers and Lucy lives in the Lake District and has a baby. So the man my mother is shagging is a grandfather, which is pretty icky. My mother pretends to be interested in his grandson but believe me, she isn't. She's not great with little kids, and I know this from experience. She just hasn't really got the patience. She likes the *idea* of them, but the reality is something else. She told me once that the day I could put my own shoes on, she felt like she'd been reborn. I mean, that's not a very nana-like thing to say, is it? And she can't knit.

Paul is my mother's knight in shining armour, without the armour. He is big and pink, with a big pink face that looks bigger than it actually is because his pale gingery hair is receding. Paul is everything that my dad isn't. He is sober, solvent and has a clean driving licence. This is probably why my mum has gone running into his flabby pink arms. Honestly, I'm not even kidding, Paul looks like something out of a butcher's shop.

I don't belong up here. I'm a born and bred South Londoner,

which, incidentally, is where my dad still lives. And that's another thing – when am I going to see my dad again? Let's just say his visits weren't exactly regular even when we lived in the same city, and he still hasn't replied to the text I sent him over a week ago, but at least when I lived in London, there was always a chance I might bump into him. Now I've been uprooted, I probably won't ever see him again.

Mum says it's just like repotting a plant and that with all this space and fresh air, I'll be thriving before I know it. Ahem, this is the same woman who killed every plant we ever had on our kitchen windowsill back in our flat in Camberwell. My dad was the one with green fingers, which is of course what got him into trouble, growing skunk with a mate in Streatham. I was only little when that happened and while he was inside, he got my mum to tell me he was on a space mission for the Russians and I believed her. At night I used to look out of the window hoping to see him on the moon. I pictured him in his jeans and denim jacket, wearing his cowboy hat, and I wondered if he'd been allowed to take his guitar with him in the rocket.

I used to draw pictures of him singing on the moon, in Russian, of course. I would make up the lyrics and croon along while I coloured him in: 'Piski poski svetlosko Dobyeski.' See, that's the trouble with being an only child – you've got no siblings to tell you when you're being bat-shit crazy.

I suppose the one and only good thing about being dumped two hundred and fifty miles away from all my mates is that Paul has given me 'carte blanche' to redecorate this bedroom. That's what he actually said – 'carte blanche'. What a wanker. Mum is thrilled. She was all like, 'Isn't Paul generous? Imagine,

Hermione, your very own bedroom and you can paint it any colour you like.'

Paul's usual tomato-coloured face turned several shades lighter – as if he was suddenly slightly unripe. 'Well actually, Tess,' he stuttered, blinking like an idiot owl, 'I've got a few tins of magnolia paint in the garage. I thought maybe that could be put to good use?'

As luck would have it, the tins of hideous magnolia had dried up, because 'someone' hadn't put the lids back on properly. Ha. This meant Mum and I could visit Homebase in Paul's car, which Mum accidentally scraped getting too close to a bollard and we had to patch it up with a red Rimmel nail varnish. 'Don't tell Paul,' she giggled.

I can't wait to get rid of the wallpaper, which is this weird embossed blue and gold striped number and truly hideous.

I chose a bright-orange emulsion, Dulux 'Blazing Sunset', which set my mum off reminiscing about this Greek island she and my dad took me to when I was about three. Apparently, they had this crummy room above a taverna overlooking some dustbins, and I erupted with chicken pox as soon as we landed and the owners wouldn't let me in the bar. So every night my mum just sat with me in the room, while Casper went downstairs, got pissed and forgot to bring us up any dinner. I've still got a scar just above my right eyebrow.

Mine is the smallest bedroom at the back of the house, which is cool with me, because it's furthest from where my mother sleeps with Paul. Sadly, it's also nearest the bathroom and I can hear Paul when he goes for a shit at 7.30 on the dot in the morning. Honest to God, it sounds like an elephant is sitting down for a massive crap and I have to play some music to drown out the trumping. There's an en suite in their bedroom but Paul obviously doesn't feel comfortable stinking it out in front of my mum. Next to the loo is a family bathroom, and then back along the landing towards the front of the house are three other bedrooms.

Mum and Paul have got the biggest. It's got a bay window, and once upon a time someone thought it would be a good idea to paint it a really vile green. I don't think the place has been redecorated since the 1980s. There's a lot of sickly coloured walls and this horrible dark-red carpet running through the house like a river of blood. Apparently, Paul and his wife were going to do the place up, but then she got sick and died about five years ago.

There's a photograph of the four of them, Paul and Melanie, and their kids, Lucy and Nick, on the mantelpiece in the dining room. Melanie looks out of the photo with a suspicious expression on her face, almost as if she knows there's another woman shagging her husband.

Not that Tess would ever admit it, but neither Mum nor I really know how long it's going to take until our new lives feel normal. It's like trying to wear in a new pair of shoes that don't really fit and may turn out to be a terrible mistake.

Thank God I've got 'Project Redecorate Bedroom' to keep me occupied over the next few weeks. Paul was a bit put out when he saw the orange paint I'd chosen. He kind of flinched and said, 'Crikey, that looks a bit loud,' but to give him his credit, he didn't make me change it. He also went back to Homebase and bought a couple of scrapers, some brushes, a sponge paint roller and tray thing – in other words, everything me and Mum had forgotten.

Then he gave me a long lecture about scraping all the layers of wallpaper off before I actually paint the walls – like, obviously.

Scraping wallpaper is dead boring. The trick is to really soak it. Paul gave me the sponge he uses to wash his car with. My dad never had a car. Casper is either a bus or cab boy, depending on how much money he has. Trouble with my dad is that when he does have money, he splashes it about. I remember one birthday he took me and ten girls from my class to Planet Hollywood in a stretch limo for burgers and then to a matinée of *Grease* in the West End. The year after that he was inside, and no one came to my party because I didn't have one.

If you soak the paper for long enough and you get the scraper in at just the right angle, you can peel a big chunk of the paper away from the wall, which is really satisfying, like peeling off nail varnish. But sometimes, the paper seems really glued down and you're chipping away for just a measly little strip. The main problem is that there are two layers of paper to get rid of, the hideous stripy blue one and then, beneath that, this purple and pink floral wallpaper. It's kind of cool actually, but the colours are a bit bleurgh. I think it's from the 70s. I've seen a photo of my nan wearing a blouse in a similar kind of pattern. She was pretty, my nan, back in the 70s. She had my mum when she was really young. That was the trouble with my nana – she did everything really young. She was only fifty when she died.

Once I get down to it, the wall beneath the two layers of paper is that funny orangey-pink plaster colour. There are a few cracks in the surface, but I won't tell Paul because he'll start banging on about getting some filler and I'll be stuck here all summer. Not that I've got anywhere to go. This house isn't really near anything; you have to catch a bus to get to the closest town. It's a number 11 but it's not red, so in my eyes it's not a real bus, it's an imposter. I mean, green and cream buses, what's all that about?

I've sussed out the nearest stop though. It's diagonally opposite a crappy little shopping parade consisting of a newsagent's, a greengrocer's, a chemist and a hairdresser's called Toni's of Switzerland. Honestly, it's like living in Alan Partridge land.

I haven't actually taken the bus to town yet, but I will, soon as I've finished this.

The bus over Waterloo Bridge was always my favourite. On a clear day you can see everything from St Paul's Cathedral on the right to the Houses of Parliament on the left. In London you're in the centre of the universe; here I can't even walk to a fried chicken shop.

My mum offered to help with the wallpaper scraping, but since the sun came out she's been on a sun lounger in the back garden. Mum fancies herself with a bit of a tan. It always annoyed her that my dad used to go brown really quickly. I imagine Paul uses factor fifty and gets funny about wearing a hat. My mum is wearing her bra and knickers, the ones she dyed purple when she was going through her purple phase. We had this big pan and everything she could squash into it, she dyed deep purple. Course, it's a bit washed out now and most of her undies look a dingy grey. She's smoking a fag and I reckon there's vodka in that Diet Coke. Old habits die hard.

I'd go and join her – it's the first time it's been properly hot since we got here – but the wallpaper scraping is weirdly addictive and in any case, I've found something.

Some writing in blue biro on the wall.

I feel a spark of discovery, like finding buried treasure. At last I manage to clear all the wallpaper around it, so I can see what it says, and as I read the words, a jolt of electricity runs through me . . .

Hi, I'm Helena Treace. I am fifteen years old.
    I have blonde hair and two sisters, I want to be famous and I want a boyfriend, I luv David Bowie, Marc Bolan, Roxy Music and spaghetti bolognaise, which isn't a band by the way.
I'm a Pisces, which means I'm indecisive, romantic, imaginative and pleasure seeking – oooer Mrs! At school my best subjects are English and art, but I think I might want to be an actress, yeah right, in my dreams. Anyway, here I am . . .

1975

HELENA

TUESDAY

Helena wheels her bike out of the garage and into the back street behind the Treaces' family home. She'd rather walk to school, which is what all the cool girls do, but Elaine and Gwen insist on cycling. They've been cycling to school together since they were in the upper third, four years ago, when the three of them were eleven-year-old first formers in brand-new brown bowler hats.

But she has known them since before then, since they were five. They were at primary school together.

Immediately Helena conjures up Elaine's collection of miniature china animals on her windowsill and Gwen's film poster of Herbie the Talking Car. She knows the dates of their birthdays, their favourite puddings and what size shoe they wear. She knows that only-child Elaine has a phobia about old men dressed up as Father Christmas, and Gwen, who has one older brother, is allergic to the glue on plasters.

I'm still really fond of them, she reflects (rather maturely in her own opinion) as she pedals her bike up to their usual meeting point outside the post office, *it's just . . .*

Helena feels a bit nostalgic. They're just a bit . . . not *boring*, boring isn't the right word, but Gwen likes Cliff Richard, which is bizarre considering she's not some forty-year-old spinster, and Elaine spends her weekends training her Belgian hare to jump over a mini gymkhana in the back garden, even though she's *fifteen*. Elaine's Belgian hare is called Percy, and the Sandersons' black Labrador is called Nelson, because Mr Sanderson loves Lord Nelson, the weirdo.

While she waits, Helena rolls the waistband of her brown crimplene skirt over three times, so that at least on the cycle to school she doesn't look like the vicar's daughter. If only her legs weren't so big and white and *what is it with her knees?* She's got her father's knees, great hideous turnip-sized things. Seriously, it's embarrassing. Her sisters have got their mother's knees, small and bony. It's not fair, and the school uniform rules are ridiculous. Whose idiotic idea was it to make pupils wear bowler hats right up until the sixth form? At least in the summer they switch to straw boaters, which are a tad more flattering, even if in Helena's opinion they make the entire school look like lady gondoliers.

Life would be so much better if the Queen Anne uniform was a nice dark blue, rather than this revolting dog-poo brown. *No one suits brown*, thinks Helena, who knows that with her blonde hair and blue eyes navy is her colour. Her grandmother told her. Nana Nancy with her leopard-skin coats, chiffon scarves and bright-orange lipstick is a self-appointed fashion and style oracle.

At least in the sixth form they get to wear their own clothes.

Trousers aren't allowed, but apart from that, as long as they stick to the regulation brown-knee-length rule, they can choose what they like, which as far as Helena can see is the only reason to do A levels.

Helena looks at her watch, a present for passing her eleven-plus. She can still remember her mother's relief at the news. 'Oh thank God,' Alicia had sobbed, suspecting Helena might have failed the exam on purpose because she'd wanted to go to the mixed comprehensive rather than an all-girls grammar. And she had; just not enough to actually fail her exams.

They'd celebrated with a special supper. Helena's favourite – gammon and pineapple with peas and chips and a lemon cheesecake for afters. The only person who hadn't been particularly thrilled was her older sister Juliet, but then Juliet has always had a tendency to be a miserable cow.

Probably didn't want me cramping her style, Helena decides, glad that Juliet has finished at the grammar and is currently in the final term of her first year studying English at King's College London.

Not that Juliet living in London isn't almost as annoying as her living in Lytham. Helena can't stand the way her sister comes home for the holidays and immediately starts showing off about all the bands, art exhibitions and shows she's seen. 'Blah blah, Kilburn and the High Roads, blah blah, *The Rocky Horror Picture Show.*'

Even more infuriatingly, from September Juliet would be moving in with three other girls in Chiswick. When Helena thinks about this scenario, she is consumed by jealousy. A fun girl flat-share is wasted on Juliet. She's too quiet, too studious, and she probably doesn't go to half the parties she pretends to, in any case, *what would be the point?* She's still going out with drippy Gareth. Honestly, imagine living in the middle of London and still going out with the boy from three doors down. Speccy, spotty Gareth Morley is studying music at Birmingham. That's why her parents like him so much. Helena's father, Simon, is a music teacher at a private boys' school in Blackpool, and Simon thinks Gareth is gifted. *Well, ya boo sucks*, thinks Helena meanly. *He still looks like a constipated owl.*

Helena's mother teaches in Blackpool too. Alicia is head of ceramics at the college of art, which means that her hands are constantly dry and cracked, which is good really, because it means Helena always knows what to buy her for her birthday: a nice tube of Sally Hansen's hand cream, not that her mother ever uses it. Alicia is vague about her appearance. It's as if she forgets to look in the mirror. Juliet is the same in some respects, so Helena has to compensate for the pair of them, constantly checking her reflection whenever a mirror is available. This morning she noticed the beginnings of a spot on her chin. She'll kill it with witch hazel tonight, and if that doesn't work, she'll zap it with TCP.

At last she sees Gwen and Elaine cycling through the empty Blossoms pub car park on the corner. It's the type of pub frequented by golfers at the weekend, the car park full of Jaguars driven by middle-aged men accompanied by their dolled-up wives, teetering on their slingbacks into the brightly lit saloon bar.

Helena's parents aren't really pub types, but her father Simon makes an evil home-brew cider in the conservatory and her mother likes the occasional gin, while Nana Nancy will 'never say no to a snowball'.

Helena decided recently that she likes Cinzano and lemonade. She remembers the time she and Elaine went round to Gwen's and they all got hammered on the contents of the Sandersons' generously equipped drinks cabinet. It was the Pernod that had done for them in the end. Helena had tried to make it to the downstairs cloakroom, but ended up vomiting in a rubber plant in the hallway.

That was only last year, when the three of them were still inseparable. But something has changed. It's like Helena has moved on and they . . . haven't.

As the girls approach, ringing their bells in greeting, Helena shoves her boater on her head and gets ready to push off from where she's been leaning against the postbox. It's no use her mates slowing down and stopping now, not when they need to build up steam to tackle the hill that goes over the railway line. Once they've freewheeled down the other side, they can slow down and chat. Quite often at this point they cycle three abreast. Kingsway isn't very busy, though once they saw a squashed tortoise in the road, its shell cracked and the insides spilling out like a meat pie.

As Helena stands up on her pedals to tackle the hill, she wonders if she'll get a new bike when her younger sister starts at Queen Anne's. After all, Rosalind has more or less grown out of her two-wheeler so it would make sense for her to have Helena's old one and Helena to have something new and fancy like Gwen's with loads of gears.

Rosalind is still at primary school, but she has a place at the grammar next year, even though she missed sitting the eleven-plus when she was ill. Apparently her academic record spoke for itself, the school had told her parents, which was a huge relief and at least one thing they didn't have to worry about.

Everyone is always worried about Rosalind. Gwen actually told Helena that she had knelt down by her bed and prayed for her back in March when she was so poorly.

Gwen attends St Cuthbert's, the large dirty yellow-stone church at the end of Helena's road. She goes even though no one actually makes her.

Helena pushes down hard on the pedals, past the florist's and the fruit and veg shop, past the pet shop and Raymond's Electric Organ Emporium, until finally they have breached the hill and are flying down the other side.

Some King Alfred boys are crossing the road in front of them, and Gwen, swerving to avoid them, rings her bell. *How embarrassing*, thinks Helena, blushing with shame as Gwen shouts, 'Use the crossing!' like she's some kind of middle-aged lollipop lady.

One of the boys turns round and yells, 'Get off and milk it!'

Oh God . . . it's Jimmy Simmonds.

'Boys are such Herberts,' complains Gwen, once they have their breath back and are able to chat.

'Did you see *Blue Peter* on telly last night?' interrupts Elaine, oblivious as ever to the opposite sex. Basically, if it's not covered in fur and doesn't have really long ears, Elaine isn't interested. Helena wonders why, at the age of fifteen, Elaine is *still* watching *Blue Peter*?

She allows their conversation to wash over her and thinks

about Jimmy Simmonds instead. Jimmy has blue eyes, thick white-blonde hair and contrasting black eyebrows, and Helena fancies him something rotten. Jimmy is number seven in her top-ten list of 'Hunky Boys', which is written down on the back page of her rough book. But there's something about his quick wit today that makes Helena make a mental note to push him up to number five.

Helena is chuffed that she knows ten members of the opposite sex. It's not easy meeting boys when you go to a single-sex school and don't have an older brother like Gwen. Not that Nigel Sanderson appears on the list. Nigel has a double chin and garlic breath. However, because he attends a religious boarding school in the Lake District, he often brings friends home for the weekend and it's thanks to Nigel that Helena has been able to put Ralph on the list. He's in at number six. Not that she's ever actually spoken to him but they have *sort of* met and he did *sort of* stare at her.

The rest of the lads on her list are locals like Jimmy, who is one of five names from the neighbouring boys' school. Jimmy Simmonds, Bailey Greenstone and Trevor Morgan are all in the lower fifth at King Alfred's, while Craig Mitchel and Andy Blake are in the upper fifth, which means they've recently been doing their O levels. Helena met some of them when she was in the Queen Anne's/King Alfred's joint school production of *Le Bourgeois Gentilhomme* just before Easter. Looking back now, those few weeks were some of the happiest of her life. Rosalind was out of hospital too, which had made it even more special.

Steering around a broken bottle on the road, Helena considers who else is on her list.

21

In tenth place is Gareth's French exchange student who came to stay last year in order to improve his conversational French. Juliet invited him round with Gareth one evening to have supper with the family, only of course Juliet hadn't bothered to tell her, so Helena had been caught off guard. Embarrassingly she'd been wearing her purple dressing gown and foul Bri-Nylon pyjamas because she'd been off school with pretend tonsillitis, having forgotten to revise for a history test. Anton Boucher was dark and morose. Her mother had made a crumbly meatloaf with tomato sauce, which Anton had mostly left at the side of his plate. After supper, Juliet and Gareth had taken him for a walk around the lake, but no one had thought to invite Helena.

'I don't know why you're sulking,' her mother commented. 'It wouldn't have been particularly useful . . . you're not doing French, you're doing German, and anyway, you've got tonsillitis, you can't go traipsing around the lake.'

Honestly, her mother could be spectacularly thick sometimes.

Helena doesn't really fancy Anton any more. It just looks good to see his French-sounding name on the list. At least, 'Anton Boucher' had *looked* exotic, until Juliet informed her that 'Boucher' was French for butcher so actually his real name was Tony Butcher, and anyway he was a prat.

Some of the lads on the list are boys whose real names Helena doesn't actually know. Gazza is probably Gary, Jezzer could be Jeremy and Sticks's nickname is no doubt linked to the fact that he is almost skeletally thin. These three are boys that go to other schools but hang out in the same town square and frequent the same coffee shop that Helena has just started going to with some of the cooler girls in her year.

She's still not sure how she's managed to be part of their gang. It all started about a month ago when she was picking her glasses up from the optician's next door to the café and she'd bumped into Sally Winwood, who was in Helena's maths group but not the same form. Sally said she was going to hang out with some mates and would Helena like to come? Helena had stuffed her horrible new National Health gold-rimmed glasses into the bottom of her bag and followed Sally inside the fug of a small café. Through the cloud of cigarette smoke, she recognised a few girls from her year at school – Liza Branwell, who was well known for being 'a bit of a slapper', and Alex King, who was infamously one of the prettiest girls at Queen Anne's. There was also a girl she knew from back in the day when they had both been Brownies. The girl immediately blanked her, so Helena ignored her back. At Brownies she'd been Susan Jones, but now she was at the comp, she called herself Susie and had plucked her eyebrows into thin air.

Everyone was smoking. Helena prayed the smell wouldn't cling to her clothes. Cigarettes were one of the few things her mum really went mad about. Nevertheless, when Sally offered her one from a crumpled ten pack of Embassy, Helena accepted. A boy sitting opposite them in the booth they'd squeezed into had offered her a light. She knows now this was Sticks. At the time she wondered why a boy who looked like he should be lying in a hospital bed was sitting in a coffee bar blowing bubbles through a straw into a strawberry milkshake. He had purple rings under his eyes and she could see the blue veins on his wrist

23

as he offered her his lighter. Back then, she actually didn't know how to use a lighter and was relieved when Sally seized it and held the flame against the tip of Helena's cigarette.

Don't cough . . . for God's sake, don't cough, Helena reminded herself, igniting the cigarette without inhaling too deeply.

I can do this, she told herself, and ever since then, she sort of has.

The girls have reached the turning on to the main road leading up to school. Queen Anne's School for Girls aged eleven to eighteen is an imposing red-brick, two-storey building, with a long smooth tarmac drive leading to the main entrance, used only by parents, teachers and visiting dignitaries. The drive is flanked by immaculately tended green lawns, with marigold-stuffed flowerbeds and a raised round rose garden, just in front of the main doorway.

Rumour has it that the music teacher drove her Mini across the rose garden one morning when she'd forgotten to sober up from the previous night's drinking. 'Poor Mrs Bell,' Helena's mother once said of the incident, 'that divorce has hit her very hard.' *Hit the roses harder*, thought Helena.

Nine hundred girls attend Queen Anne's. Some cycle in, others who live further afield are ferried by coach, while the rest either walk or catch local buses. Only one or two spoilt brats get lifts from their parents.

The coach girls are the most difficult to get to know. They form a separate society and arrive yawning. Helena feels sorry for them – it's bad enough being a Queen Anne's girl without having to get up at sparrow's fart to get there. She heard the phrase 'sparrow's fart' recently and hasn't stopped using it since.

To be fair, anything to do with farting makes Helena laugh. She will happily fart in front of her school friends in the changing rooms before hockey. It makes them all hysterical. Farting is one of the few consolations of attending a single-sex school. Imagine spending your entire school days desperate not to let off in case a boy might hear.

No matter how many guffs are released daily at Queen Anne's, the corridors still smell of cleaning fluid and beeswax, and its only down the short staffroom corridor that the fragrance suddenly switches to the acrid choking stench of cigarette smoke.

Helena needs to practise smoking. She has bought a lighter and rehearses flicking the metal wheel with her thumb, instantly igniting the cigarette without getting all sweaty and clumsy. Fags and lighters are like props in a play – you have to get used to using them.

Not only that but having cigarettes means you get to share them, which means talking to boys, and having a lighter means that you get to lean in close, close enough to maintain eye contact, which essentially is what flirting is all about, that brief intimate moment before the tobacco crackles and begins to glow. It happened just last weekend when Sticks accepted a cigarette and a light from her. There was something in his unblinking pale-grey eyes that seemed to connect with a place tucked deep inside her brown, double-gusseted, interlock regulation knickers and that is why he is number one on her list.

By the time the bell rings for morning registration, Helena is sitting at the desk she bagsied at the beginning of the summer term (back row, left-hand corner). Elaine sits at the desk diagonally to the right of her, one row in front, while Gwen, who worries about getting in trouble, sits more or less under their form teacher's nose, right in the middle on the front row.

At the moment, Helena is on her best behaviour. It's too close to the end of term to risk doing anything that could jeopardise her school report. She's already been given two detentions this term, only one of which she has admitted to her parents. It's not that she goes out of her way to be badly behaved, it's just that when she is, she tends to get caught. Being short-sighted doesn't help. Most people can see a teacher coming a mile off, but Helena, who is too vain to wear her glasses, is always the last to stop talking, or the one doing an impression of the headmistress the longest, or pretending to be Suzi Quatro on *Top of the Pops*.

'Yvonne Swan?'

'Yes, Miss Glenn.'

'Sandra Talbot?'

'Yes, Miss Glenn.'

'Helena Treace?'

'Yes, Miss Glenn,' she replies, wishing that out of all the Shakespearian names her mother could have chosen, she hadn't picked Helena. It's not fair. Trust her to get the worst one. Juliet and Rosalind (or Rosy as she is usually called), are pretty names and they suit her siblings with their middle partings and angelic faces, but Helena is a boring name, just a single vowel more interesting than the even duller 'Helen', of which there already two in her class.

'It's from *A Midsummer Night's Dream*,' her mother had

explained years ago. 'Could be worse,' Gwen once told her. 'The other girl in *A Midsummer Night's Dream* is called Hermia, which sounds like a groin strain.'

After registration, their form teacher Miss Glenn morphs into their English teacher, and the girls remain at their desks for forty-five minutes of metaphysical poetry. Helena struggles to concentrate and rather than listen, she doodles the name 'Lennie Treace' in her rough book. In some ways, it sounds like she could be a boy, but it also sounds cool. After a few times of scribbling it down, she decides it looks better spelt 'Lenni'. Lenni Treace sounds like a pop star. Immediately she surrounds her new name with three-dimensional stars and doodles around the stars with inky hearts, lips and eyes.

'So, Helena, what do you think John Donne is trying to say in this poem?'

Oh God, she hasn't a clue. She doesn't even know if she's on the right page, she zoned out ages ago. Thinking fast, she knocks the poetry book off her desk with her elbow, which gives her the excuse to legitimately ask, 'Sorry, Miss Glenn, what page number was it?' She might not pay attention, but she's certainly not thick.

At lunchtime, Helena finds herself in the queue behind Sally Winwood, who says, 'Oh hi, Helena, are you coming to the Monkey after school, only I'm going if you want to come with me?' Helena swallows hard. She should just come out and say it. *Sorry, Sally, my parents don't like me hanging out in town after school. They think I should cycle straight home and get on with my homework, rather than consorting with hairy louts in coffee bars . . .*

But she can't, so she mumbles something about having to get home to look after her baby sister.

Sally looks both bored and sympathetic at the same time. 'What a drag,' she replies. 'Oh we're sitting over there by the way,' and she nods to a table overlooking the playing fields at the back of the dining room where Liza Branwell and Alex King are tucking into their packed lunches. Immediately Helena decides to inform her mother over dinner that from September she is switching to packed lunches. All these mince and potato dinners are making her fat. It's the obvious solution. But still she nods when the dinner lady offers her a second spoonful of mash.

Feeling slightly awkward, she follows Sally to the far table. Suddenly she doesn't feel quite as hungry. Her lunch looks obscene compared to what the others are eating. Sally has refused the mash and is mostly eating a mound of cabbage. Alex has a packet of Ryvita, a tub of cottage cheese and a small Tupperware filled with celery sticks and a chunk of cucumber, while Liza is tucking into a packet of crisps. Helena imagines what her mother would make of that, crisps for lunch?

The two girls don't pause for breath as Sally and Helena join them. Alex is talking about whether she should finish with Paul Thursby, whose dad has a second-hand car dealership in Blackpool, which means she gets driven around in an old Jag and taken out to country pubs. 'At least you can park up in a country lane and have a bit of how's your father in the car,' Liza comments, 'instead of having to wank lads off round the back of the Co-op.' For a second Helena is tempted to laugh. She is joking, isn't she? But then she realises she isn't and instead she tries very hard not to blush. Gosh, so Alex really is a bit of a slapper, how brilliant. *Watch and learn*, thinks Helena, *watch and learn*, noticing that while Alex is devastatingly pretty, Liza's teeth are quite yellow, and her nose is heavily studded with blackheads.

'I don't like the way he kisses,' Alex announces, wrinkling her perfect little nose. Despite being very blonde, her skin is golden, and Helena can't help noticing that a button has come undone on her school shirt so that when she moves forward to steal a crisp from Liza, she reveals a glimpse of scarlet lace bra. *Where do you even get scarlet lacy bras from?* Helena, coming from a family of flat-chested women, feels destined to wear a training bra for ever. Honestly, she has the tits of a twelve-year-old. Today she is wearing a bra she got from Chelsea Girl. It's made from stockinet and has a picture of a train on each cup. It's meant to be fun and fashionable but suddenly it feels silly and childish. Helena pushes her food around. 'I don't know how you can eat that muck,' Liza announces, and Helena can feel herself colouring.

Suddenly Helena wishes she was sitting with Gwen and Elaine. She'd have wolfed this course down by now and be queuing up for pudding. It's bananas and custard today. Suddenly, her knees feel massive under the table and she's managed to get mince up the sleeve of her shirt. She doesn't belong here.

She pushes her plate to one side and pronounces it 'worse than anything I've ever made in domestic science'.

'Are you going to Karen Elliot's party on Saturday night?' Sally suddenly asks the table and Helena is grateful that she has changed the topic. 'Think so,' says Liza, but Alex shakes her head. 'Paul's taking me to the Cherry Tree out in Wrea Green.'

'Ooh,' Helena interrupts, 'we went there for my mum's birthday. I had the chicken in a basket and the Black Forest gateau.'

'Is grub all you ever think about?' Liza drawls. 'You've got food on the brain, you.'

'I'm going,' Sally interjects. 'To Karen's party, I mean. You can come with me if you want, Helena?'

Helena's heart starts banging in her chest. A party, a proper party . . . She nearly says, *I'll have to ask my mum*, but manages to swallow the words back.

'Yeah, if Karen doesn't mind, only I don't know her.'

'What's that got to do with anything?' sneers Liza bitchily, and Helena decides she's what her Nana Nancy would call a 'hard-faced cow'.

Helena is distracted all afternoon. Not only is the prospect of a party interfering with any other thoughts, but she is also starving, and her stomach makes crazy noises throughout double art. On Tuesday afternoons the usual class of twenty-eight is spilt into two, with the other half doing double games. It's nice, quieter, more intimate.

Today she is sharing a paint-splattered table for four, with Gwen, Elaine and a girl called Anne Miller whose parents are rumoured to be naturists, which is possibly why she has never once asked anyone back to her house. They each have a sheet of grey sugar paper in front of them and a selection of chalk pastels. In the middle of each table the art teacher, Mr Mundy, has set up a still life. On Helena's table is a collection of seaside objects, including a selection of pebbles, some shells and a starfish.

Helena takes an ochre-coloured chalk from the communal box. She's quite good at this sort of thing, definitely the best on this table. In fact, only Kate Rusborough – who wins the art prize every year and is currently tackling a tweed cap and hobnail boot – is better.

'Where did you disappear to this lunchtime?' Gwen asks, cack-handedly attempting the outline of a large conch shell, which within seconds looks exactly like a human ear. Sometimes Elaine and Helena laugh until they are almost sick at Gwen's drawings.

Helena pretends to be concentrating on the starfish. 'Sally just wanted to ask me something,' she mumbles.

'What?' insists Gwen, and suddenly Helena feels bored of her. It's actually none of her business, so she snaps, 'She asked if I want to go to a party on Saturday, if you must know!'

There's a moment's silence before Elaine says, 'But you're both coming to stay at my house on Saturday night, remember? We're having a Chinese takeaway because my parents are going out.' Being an only child, Elaine doesn't like being left in the house by herself. *She can be such a massive baby*, thinks Helena meanly and then she notices how stricken Elaine looks and immediately feels guilty.

Fortunately, before there can be any further discussion, Mr Mundy growls, 'Seaside table, put a sock in it.'

Rumour has it he is seeing Miss Gavin the new music teacher. She has been seen on several occasions getting into his orange Volkswagen Beetle at the end of the day. Meanwhile

31

Miss Sullivan, the RE teacher, who used to be seen getting in and out of that same Beetle, is now reduced to cycling to and from school.

By the time the bells rings, most of the girls have finished their pastel drawings. Helena's is quite good, though she slightly came unstuck on the conch shell, and the whole thing lacks depth. Elaine's is wishy-washy, Anne's is peculiar, while Gwen's starfish manages to have seven arms. Helena can't help herself – she feels a bubble of hysteria rise and within seconds is laughing so hard that her eyes are streaming, and she is making high-pitched hyena noises. Mr Mundy tells her to pull herself together and when she can't, he informs her she can stay behind and help tidy the art room.

By the time she gets to the bike sheds, her trusty maroon Raleigh Rodeo is one of the last bikes left in the racks and her friends have gone. Helena cycles home morosely on her own. *The bloody bitches*, she thinks. Just because she didn't have lunch with them. God, they're so babyish. Even her little sister Rosalind is more mature than Elaine and Gwen, she decides, suddenly remembering that the excuse she'd told Sally about not being able to go to the Monkey is actually a reality. Today is a Tuesday and on Tuesdays her mother works late and Helena has to pick up Rosalind from Tania's.

Tania's house is on the street behind the Treaces'. She has nine-year-old identical twins at Rosy's school and doesn't mind an extra child tagging along at the end of the day. As far as Helena can tell, there is no Mr Tania.

'She might be as common as muck,' she once heard her mother say to her aunt on the phone, 'but she's got a heart of gold and that place of hers is spotless.'

The twins are chubby red-haired boys who mostly play out in the back street. 'I think Tania would rather they were run over than dirty the house,' her mother once remarked. By contrast Tania treats Rosalind as if she were an extremely precious Fabergé egg.

By the time Helena rings Tania's bell, Rosalind and the twins are sitting down in front of the television eating spaghetti hoops on toast. It looks delicious. Alicia tries not to use convenience foods, which is a shame because sometimes her resentment over cooking from scratch 'every bloody day' affects the quality of the meals she produces. 'Ah, one of your *bugger the patriarchy* pies,' her father once remarked over a spectacularly watery quiche, and her mother looked quite murderous for a moment.

Rosalind looks almost translucent compared to the scarlet-cheeked Colin and Roger, whose names always sound to Helena as if they should be a couple of old accountants. Helena sits down on the sofa, waiting for her sister to finish her spaghetti while the boys proceed to demolish their tinned rice pudding and take turns to spoon jam directly from the jar and into their mouths.

'How was school?' Helena asks Rosy, who has one eye on the television.

'Fine,' she responds, then, without being asked, she puts her knife and fork together neatly and says, 'Thanks for having me, Tania, ta-ra, lads,' and follows Helena out of the door.

She's no trouble really, thinks Helena fondly, although she does have a tendency to snoop, which is why Helena has had to hide her diary, cigarettes and the note Craig Mitchel sent her when they were rehearsing for the play.

Written on a scrap of paper obviously torn from an exercise book, Craig had written, 'Looking extra fit today, Nicole,' which was the name of the character Helena was playing. Honestly, the cheek of him. Everyone knew he was going out with Anna Gould from the year above.

When they get home, Helena leaves her little sister to her own devices and goes upstairs to her room.

The Treaces have lived in the same large, red-brick Victorian house ever since Rosalind was born eleven years ago, when Juliet was seven and she herself was just four. She remembers the little bundle of white blanket being carried into the hall, she and Juliet on the stairs, Nana Nancy racing from the kitchen to get her hands on the new baby.

Up in her room, Helena pretends to do her homework. She has some particularly vicious maths that needs tackling and a Latin test to revise for, but all she can think about is the party.

What will she wear? Helena spreads her schoolbooks out on the desk and then slopes off to her older sister's room. By rights, she should have moved into this room by now. It's bigger and airier than her cramped back bedroom, but Juliet went spare over the idea and Helena was forced to back down. 'I wouldn't mind if I was dead,' her sister had said, which was quite dramatic for her, 'but I'm not.'

By contrast to Helena's 'rat's nest', Juliet's bedroom is pristine. Alicia hoovers Juliet's carpet, 'because I can see it'. The walls are plain white, save for her sister's Fleetwood Mac and

Lindisfarne posters. Helena would quite like Fleetwood Mac, if only Juliet didn't.

A small silver cup engraved with Juliet's name sits on the neatly arranged bookshelves. She won the English prize in her final year at school. Of course she did, the swot.

Most of the clothing left in Juliet's wardrobe is heavy and wintery. She took all her good summer stuff back to uni after Easter. Helena takes a pair of purple velvet bell-bottoms off a hanger. *Hmm, these could look great with a cheesecloth shirt*, she thinks, and ditching her school skirt, she attempts to wriggle into her sister's trousers.

Sadly, Juliet is both four inches taller than Helena and a size ten to Helena's twelve. 'It's not fair,' rages Helena, yanking and pulling at the fabric until she manages to squeeze the flares over her hips. For some reason, she refuses to allow the trousers to defeat her. By sheer force, Helena squeezes the button into the button hole, and proceeds to tug at the zip. *The buggering thing WILL close, it will close, dammit* . . . and as she yanks the metal clasp upwards, she is suddenly conscious of a searing pain as a roll of pale-pink flesh gets caught between the teeth of the zipper.

Oh God, Oh God, what if she has to go to hospital and get cut out of her sister's velvet trousers? As Helena begins to whimper in pain, she hears the kitchen door bang shut and her mother call, 'Girls . . .'

Shit, now her parents are home. Helena squeezes her eyes shut and forces the zipper down again, hardly daring to look. Once the pain subsides, she opens her eyes. There is no blood, but her stomach is bruised purple and there are puncture marks on her belly. *Bloody hell.* Quickly she hurls the trousers back into the wardrobe and tiptoes out of her sister's room, throwing a casual 'Hi!' over the bannister rails as she retreats back into the sanctuary of her own bedroom. By the time her mother comes upstairs and pokes her head around the door, she has her Latin textbook out and is writing out the verb 'to love'. *Amo amas amat.*

For supper that night, Helena's mother has thrown together a spaghetti bolognese. It isn't one of her best and when Helena's father asks if he could have some Parmesan cheese, Alicia snaps, 'No, because I didn't buy any.' Simon then suggests that 'a splash of Lea and Perrins might do the trick'.

'Do what trick?' her mother snaps, but nobody dares reply.

'Anything exciting happen at school?' her father asks, changing the subject.

It's on the tip of Helena's tongue to say, *'Well, yes, actually I've been invited to a party at this girl's house. I don't know her very well, she doesn't go to my school, but I've seen her around and she's having a massive sixteenth birthday party and loads of boys will be there.'*

But she doesn't. She says, 'Elaine's invited me and Gwen for a sleepover on Saturday night.' After all, it's the truth, she just doesn't bother to add, *but I've got absolutely no intention of going.*

And so it begins, the fibs and the half-truths; the secrets and sneakiness. She doesn't mean to lie. It just happens.

'Oh that's nice,' her mother responds cheerfully. Alicia likes it when she 'plays' with her old friends, girls whose mothers she recognises in the local supermarket. She's forever bumping into Gwen's mum. Last week Alicia came home and said, 'I saw

Lorraine Sanderson at the wet fish counter, we had a lovely chat, why aren't you in the choir like Gwen?'

Bloody Gwen. She's so shaping up to be head girl, thinks Helena, taking the dirty plates through to the kitchen and scraping leftover spaghetti bolognaise into the bin.

Telling her mother that she is staying at Elaine's on Saturday is just phase one of her plan for the weekend. She still has to decide what to wear and, more importantly, where she's going to stay.

She could ask Elaine if she could come back to hers after the party. Perhaps they could leave a key out? She wouldn't wake them; she could sleep on the sofa. But even as she tries the request out in her head, she knows it sounds rude, or as her mother would say, 'the height of bad manners'. She'd be exploiting Elaine and relying on both girls to keep their traps shut. She could always ask Sally if she could stay at hers, but she doesn't actually know where she lives, and the thought suddenly makes her feel shy. There are other options, of course. There's Elaine's garage, where Elaine's Belgian hare Percy lives in his specially adapted hutch, or her own garage for that matter, which is occasionally locked but can always be accessed via the back garden gate and through the side door, which doesn't even have a lock. If she took the spare keys to the Maxi, she could spend the night curled up on the back seat.

Feeling more positive now that she has a choice of options, Helena puts the kettle on to make herself a cup of tea, but as she opens the fridge to grab some milk, she spies a bottle of wine between the Gold Top and the orange juice.

Helena eyes the wine. She doesn't really like the taste, if she's honest, but if she's going to get invited to parties, she'd better start getting used to boozing.

She removes the cork from the half-empty bottle and slops a good inch into the bottom of the Radio 1 Roadshow mug.

That had been a good day, Helena recalls. Thousands of them on the prom in St Anne's. She'd gone with her sister, because at the time she'd only been fourteen and her mother didn't trust her not to do 'anything daft'. She'd managed to lose Juliet and her drippy mate Caitlin in the crowd and proceeded to shove and push her way through the seething mass towards the stage where the DJ was throwing T-shirts and stickers into the hordes of teenage girls. It was a hot day, the air smelt of BO and antiperspirant, of Kiku talcum powder and Charlie Girl scent. But there was something else more potent in the atmosphere, a kind of hysteria. The screaming came in waves. Helena couldn't really hear what was being said from the stage; the mic was distorting, there was no point listening, the only reaction that seemed to make sense was to scream. So she had screamed and pushed and eventually wormed her way to the very front where a local group from Blackpool (scream) were going to play their latest hit (scream).

No one had ever heard of 'Buzztime' but as they trooped on stage and into position, a rumour spread that they were due to be on *Top of the Pops* next week and the screaming grew louder. The lead singer opened his mouth and was immediately drowned out. He could have been singing 'Old MacDonald Had a Farm'. For a moment he looked shocked and almost missed his cue to start singing. He was tiny, Helena remembers, with a face like a little face-powdered Chihuahua. Around the stage stood burly blokes in Radio 1 Roadshow T-shirts whose job it was, as far as Helena could see, to pick up girls who tried to mount the stage and casually throw them back into the crowd. Helena hadn't managed to get close enough to climb on to the stage, but as the band left the podium, she found herself standing directly on their exit route to a waiting transit van. A wave of bodies behind her almost sent her flying, she remembers, relishing the memory of being, for once in her life, in the right place at the right time. The little doggie-faced singer was within grabbing distance, so Helena had launched herself at him and as she landed a kiss on his sticky orange cheek, she remembers realising that despite his towering metallic platform boots, they were exactly the same height.

What happened next wasn't what she expected. The orange-faced man turned to see where the kiss had come from, picked out Helena from the mass of sweaty, screaming females and made a grab for her. Somehow his hands found either side of her face as he pulled her to him.

'Let's have a proper kiss,' he breathed into her face, and suddenly she realised he was quite old and his tongue darted into her mouth like an adder. Oddly enough, it was one of the bouncers that pulled the man away, more or less throwing him into the van, before slamming the door behind him and muttering something that sounded like 'fucking nonce'.

It had sort of been her first kiss, and truth be told there hadn't been a *lot* more kisses since. Helena takes her wine upstairs. She will drink it slowly and think about all the kisses to come. But first she has to work out how she can best suck up to Gwen and Elaine so that they agree to go along with her plan.

WEDNESDAY

Helena leaves the house first thing in the morning armed with a secret weapon, and cycles to her usual position by the postbox. As soon as she sees Gwen and Elaine cutting through the pub car park, she waves enthusiastically and flags them down.

In a squeal of brakes, the girls pull up and Helena immediately offers them a crumpled paper bag containing a quarter of Kola Kubes, pinched from Rosalind's anorak pocket.

'Kola Kube, ladies?' she asks innocently

'No thanks,' says Gwen, pulling a face. 'I've just cleaned my teeth.' *Of course she has*, thinks Helena, but Elaine takes two. She has a hopelessly sweet tooth.

Helena pops the last cube in her own mouth and they cycle off. Gwen's right, it tastes weird after a mouthful of Colgate.

She doesn't refer to yesterday; she isn't going to sulk. She is bouncy and cheerful. She tells Gwen her hair looks great and Elaine that her mum is totally fine about her staying on Saturday night.

'Oh,' says Elaine, suddenly remembering to be a bit miffed.

'We thought you were too busy, what with that Sally Winwood and her lot.'

'Yes,' Gwen reiterated. 'We thought you had better things to do with your precious Saturday night.'

It strikes Helena that they'd probably spent the entire cycle ride home after school yesterday bitching about her.

'Oh no,' she responds airily. 'I mean, it's nice to be asked and all that, but sweet and sour chicken and cod balls, girls! I mean, there's no competition.' They eye her warily, but she can feel them thawing and by the time they get to school the three of them are back on an even keel.

There must be a way, thinks Helena, *to please everyone including myself*. In an ideal world, she would smuggle Juliet's purple flares out of the house in an overnight bag, go to Elaine's, grab an early Chinese takeaway (obviously taking care not to stuff herself silly – those trousers are seriously tight) and then around 8 p.m. she would bugger off to the party. She might even take a taxi. After all, she has some birthday money left over.

The first lesson of the day is maths. The year are split into four sets depending on ability. Gwen is in the first set, Helena in the second and Elaine languishes somewhere near the bottom of the remedial class.

Sally Winwood has saved Helena a seat, right at the back of the class. Helena feels a bit guilty. She's promised her mother to try and concentrate a bit harder this term, especially since her last report was full of teachers' comments all echoing variations on the same 'noisy and silly' theme.

Mr Matthews, her maths teacher, had been one of the most scathing. In the space marked 'behaviour', he had written, 'If

41

Helena could be bothered to apply herself, she might be quite an able student. Sadly, she is content to squander her intelligence on idle chit-chat and inane giggling in class.'

Just then, Helena notices that Sally Winwood has what looks to be a lovebite on her neck. When she was thirteen, Helena had tried giving one to Elaine. It was impossible. Mind you, she *had* been wearing braces at the time. Maybe now her teeth have been fixed, the suck and bite process might be easier?

They open their exercise books on Mr Matthews's instruction, but as soon as he turns his back to draw a shape on the board, Sally starts writing Helena a note. 'Are you all fixed for Saturday?'

'Reckon so,' Helena writes back

Mr Matthews wheels back round. 'So, girls, what is a quadrilateral triangle?'

About three hands shoot up. It's always the same three hands. One is covered in plasters. Angela Harris has terrible warts.

There is some discussion about what this mysterious triangle might be, but Helena has zoned out. Sally is writing in tiny letters on a piece of paper she has torn from her rough book. When she has finished, she shoves the piece of paper over to Helena's side of the double desk. It says:

Who do you fancy? I fancy Woody, Gazza and Griff.

Helena has no idea who Woody and Griff are, but in equally tiny handwriting, she writes back:

I fancy Gazza, Sticks, Jimmy Simmonds and this
French lad called Anton who is really fit.

Checking that Mr Matthews still has his back to the class,
Helena adds a series of hearts around the boys' names.

Sally's eyes widen when she reads Helena's list and in slightly
larger, although still very small capital letters, she writes:

Liza fancies Sticks, so hands off

Game on, Helena thinks.

Will he be at the party?

Yup, responds Sally.

If Helena was writing a note to Elaine or Gwen, she would
now draw one of her evil little troll-people with a speech bubble
coming out of his mouth and in the speech bubble she would
write, Hmmmm, and who will emerge victorious?!!!!

But she's not sure Sally would understand the evil troll
language she shares with her old primary school friends. She
might think it was immature.

She hesitates for a moment and makes the mistake of looking
up at the board.

What on earth is going on? Mr Matthews is pacing the raised
dais that his desk is perched on. He is a thin, stooped man with
a nicotine-yellow moustache and a terrible temper. Oh God,
they are meant to be doing something. Dammit, she might

43

have to put her bloody glasses on; she can't see a thing. Helena squints just as Mr Matthews turns to survey his class, and their eyes meet. Instantly she can feel herself colour.

'What is it, Miss Treace? You look somewhat perplexed, dumfounded, befuddled?'

'No, no, it's fine,' she insists, but it's too late – he's making strides towards the back of the class. She can smell the cigarette-whiff of him. She is transfixed, her brain frozen. Mr Matthews is unpredictable. She stays stock-still, eyes down. She just needs to hide the note under her textbook, quickly, quickly. Her hands are sweating under the desk. *Now*, she thinks, and reaches for the paper, but she is too late and Mr Matthews grasps it before she can. He walks off with it to the front of the class.

The tension in the room is unbearable. Helena looks beseechingly at Sally, who has a glazed, slightly bored expression in her eyes. *We are going to get done for this*, thinks Helena, expecting Mr Matthews to issue a couple of detentions and throw the note in the bin. But he sits down, pushes his glasses to the top of his nose and proceeds to read out the note in a stupid falsetto girl's voice. It's excruciating.

'*I fancy Gazza, Sticks, Jimmy Simmonds and this French lad called Anton who is really fit*,' he trills.

Helena knows her face is beetroot. Sally, by comparison, looks completely unfussed. She still has that faraway look in her eyes and her colour is completely normal.

There are titters now around the class. Claire Chambers is actually laughing out loud. Quick as a snake, Mr Matthews reaches behind his back and, without looking, picks up a piece

44

of chalk from the rim that runs beneath the blackboard and throws it overarm in Claire's direction. Hard. It hits her on the ear and immediately they are all silent again.

Mr Matthews stands up and strides over to the bin, where he proceeds to shred the note of shame. Then in his normal baritone he says, 'You have no idea how much it depresses me, day in, day out, year in, year out, watching how girls with perfectly decent brains allow them to atrophy. I don't care if it's hormonal. Let me tell you something. You are boring. You are boring and shallow and stupid and most of the time I cannot stand the sight of your ridiculous bovine faces. Oh yes, and some of you smell.'

And with that, he walks out of the room and slams the door.

There is still ten minutes of class time left. For five minutes, the girls sit silently, expecting their teacher to return, but he doesn't, and slowly the whispering and sniggering begins to build and Alice Higgins does the honking laugh that occasionally gets her sent out of assembly. By the time the bell rings for the next lesson, a noisy hysteria pervades the room. Even Sally is sitting on the desk laughing and chatting, as if the incident had absolutely nothing to do with her. Only Helena sits mortified and silent. Suddenly she cannot wait for the day to be over.

By lunchtime, the news that Helena fancies Sticks has obviously reached Liza's triple-pierced ears and she is giving Helena filthy looks from the far corner of the dining hall.

Safely flanked by Gwen and Elaine, awaiting her helping of liver and onions in the dinner queue, Helena tries not to look in the direction of Liza's lunchtime clique, but an accidental glance is all it takes to convince her that Liza is bitching about her.

Feeling the heat rise again from the collar of her school shirt, Helena forces herself to tune into Gwen and Elaine's inane chatter. It's all so uncomplicated with these two.

'Guess what I'm doing?' imparts Gwen self-importantly. 'I'm learning to play the theme tune from *The Sweeney* on the piano. I was up at 6.30 this morning practising.'

'Well, guess what I have to do every morning before school?' counters Elaine. 'I'm having to administer special medicinal eye drops to Percy because my poor furry baby has got conjunctivitis.'

Helena sighs. Neither of them ever really talk about boys or make-up or how they really feel. Sometimes Helena has a feeling that there is someone special missing from her life, someone she could really share things with, a soul mate who wouldn't be shocked whatever she told them. Someone she could discuss masturbation and periods with, someone who could tell her whether her pubic hair was completely normal and what colour eyeshadow really suited her. Maybe Sally had been on the brink of being that special best friend, but now with the note being read out in class, things had got complicated.

Helena is so distracted she forgets to say no to boiled potatoes, even though she is on a really strict diet this week. To compensate, she will refuse pudding, even though she can see trays of pink sponge being taken out of the ovens. It usually comes with matching pink custard and is one of Helena's favourites.

Suddenly Helena is really pissed off. There's no point even being on a stupid diet if she can't go to that party on Saturday. A tiny voice from the back of her head reminds her that at least if she doesn't go, she won't have to try and squeeze into her sister's tiny velvet trousers, which means she can have pudding if she wants, but she immediately silences it. There's got to be more to life than pink sponge and custard and playing Ouija boards with a bloody rabbit at Elaine's house on a Saturday night.

She is silent during lunch, batting off Gwen's request to spill the beans about exactly what happened in the maths class and Elaine's insistence that if it were her, she'd be dead with embarrassment and anyway, what is it about this Sticks boy and how does she know him?

'I don't really want to talk about it,' Helena mutters both tragically and mysteriously, and much to her annoyance, the other two couldn't seem to care less and are soon deep in conversation about whether Elaine should buy her father a Parker pen for his birthday.

Helena cuts up her liver and pushes it to the side of her plate. For once, she's really not hungry. Suddenly she is aware that Sally is behind her and tapping her on the shoulder. Refusing to meet Helena's eyes, Sally looks slightly flustered as she hands Helena a slip of folded paper.

Oh God, not another note, thinks Helena. Haven't there been enough bloody notes today? Sally scuttles off and Helena unfolds the scrap of paper and scans the message:

Meet me in the Geog wing toilets in
5 min - Liza. PS just you!!!

Helena looks at her watch. Five minutes to get to the loos,

47

see what Liza wants and then make a dash to the sports hall to get changed into her pleated skirt, orange Aertex blouse and hockey boots by 1.40 p.m. or risk a detention. Christ.

Helena pushes her chair back and tells Gwen and Elaine she's just got to sort something out and would they clear her dinner stuff?

'And what did your last slave die of?' jokes Gwen, but Helena ignores her. Usually, she makes up some fictional disease to make them laugh, like Japanese fungal infection of the vagina or Bubonic septic herpes, but right now she's not in the mood and she marches out of the dining room, cheeks on fire.

The toilets by the geography wing are a throwback to the 1930s when the school was first built. They are wood-panelled and dank, the basins cracked, and the toilet seats are rumoured to be riddled with woodworm. No one uses them if they've got time to go anywhere else, though sometimes Helena visits them when she needs a poo in privacy. Why is she thinking about this now? Oh God, because her stomach is churning with anxiety and she feels as though she might crap herself like her uncle George once did on the golf course. It's family folklore now, about the brown stain seeping through his cream golf trousers, and they all laugh about it, but what if it happens to her? Well, she'd have to kill herself, it's as simple as that.

Pushing open the solid wooden door, Helena checks her watch – thirty seconds to spare. She is breathless and desperate to pee but there's no time. Liza, Sally and Alex are already in situ.

Liza is plucking her eyebrows in the huge fly-spotted mirror

48

that is screwed into the cracked wall tiles, and rather than stop what she's doing, she addresses Helena through the glass.

'Ah, here she is.' There is an ominous pause. Alex leans against the wall chewing gum with her arms folded, while Sally is perched on the pipes at the far end of the cubicles looking miserable.

What can she say to make this better? Helena takes a deep breath. Here goes. 'Listen,' she begins, and then everything just tumbles out. 'I'm really sorry, Liza. I know you fancy Sticks and I do too, but I swear I didn't know until today and I know I don't stand a chance anyway, so you don't need to worry.'

Liza laughs, a slightly cartoonish laugh. 'I'm not worried. Why should I be worried? No one even knows who you are. I've been going to the Monkey for months. You've been about twice and now you're getting all pushy and full of yourself and you want to watch it.'

Helena mumbles, 'I know, I got carried away. It was just meant to be a bit of fun in class, I'm sorry. I didn't know . . . Um, are you, like, going out with him?'

'She will be after Saturday night,' Alex chips in. 'Won't you, Liza?'

'That's the plan,' grins Liza, smirking, adding, 'Oh yeah, about Saturday. Sally said she'd invited you to the party. Well, consider yourself uninvited. I don't want to see your face at Karen Elliot's house, not even in the garden, do you get it?'

'I get it,' mutters Helena, but inside she is raging. Who is Liza to tell her what to do? How come she's deciding who is on the guest list and who isn't? What's it even got to do with her?

49

'Can I go now?' she blurts.

'No one's keeping you,' shrugs Alex. *God, why is she so stupidly pretty*, thinks Helena, glancing at Sally, who is staring at her knees.

It's over. Liza is already attending to her eyebrows again in the mirror. She is dismissed. Helena leaves the toilet block, making sure the door slams behind her.

The bloody cheek of it. Honestly, what a load of bitches. *Not Sally, Sally is just a bit weak*, thinks Helena. She doesn't want to fall out with Sally. She's OK. She laughs at Helena's jokes and they both like Roxy Music and David Bowie. Even Alex is OK really, but Liza?

Liza is a nasty piece of work, thinks Helena, borrowing a phrase Nana Nancy uses.

Nana Nancy is Helena's favourite old person. She is gossipy and quick to find fault with anyone apart from her son and his daughters. She doesn't even have much time for Alicia, who she thinks is a bit stuck up.

Helena channels her inner Nana Nancy and slags off Liza in her head all the way from the geography toilet block to the sports hall at the opposite end of the school.

Nasty piece of work, uppity cow, face like a slapped arse . . . she thinks, adopting her grandmother's Lancashire accent in her head and getting broader with every step.

By the time she gets to the sports hall, she is in such a fury, she is weirdly looking forward to getting out on the hockey field with her stick. Stripping off and changing into her games kit, Helena realises she is already sweating, and they're not even on the playing field yet. Tying her studded boots tightly in a double bow, Helena clacks out on her plastic studs to the pitch, where the PE teacher is already pacing with a whistle clamped between her teeth.

Miss Carew is small and sinewy and despises all but the fittest and the fastest. She is prone to calling her pupils 'lumps of suet, wet lettuces, drippy no marks' and she once told Sheena McKay she was a 'criminal waste of legs'. Today they are quickly divided into two teams and sent out to run around the playing field to 'warm up, you lazy toads'. Helena decides to run her fury off and sets off at a feverish sprint. For a while she and Yvette Norcross, who competes for the county, are running side by side, until Yvette suddenly seems to click into another gear, leaving Helena heaving on the side of the track.

'Oh,' yells Miss Carew in her most sarcastic voice. 'For a moment I thought we had a new Olympic hopeful in school, but then I looked again and it's Helena Treace running like a potato. You're a waste of synovial fluid, Treace.'

Oh, this is a new one. Helena doesn't even know what synovial fluid is and she continues limping around the track, wishing a bolt of lightning would strike Miss Carew dead.

The rest of the afternoon's lessons pass in a blur of fury and disappointment, and she doesn't join in when Gwen and Elaine suddenly burst into a chorus of 'we're all going on a summer holiday' as they're cycling home, then look at each other, stop and fall into an embarrassed silence.

What's that about? thinks Helena.

At home that evening her mother picks up on her mood and, in a vain attempt to cheer her up, reminds her it's her grandmother's birthday at the weekend and that Nana Nancy will be coming for lunch on Sunday and won't that be nice?

Great, thinks Helena, even though she loves her grandmother. This weekend is shaping up to be really dull. Saturday night at Elaine's, then a 75th birthday party on Sunday.

Of course, Juliet won't be there. She rang to say she'd posted a card and a gift and then gloated to Helena about how she'd be spending Sunday afternoon at a friend's barbecue near the river in Hammersmith.

Lucky bloody Juliet. Honestly, thinks Helena, who had been relieved when Juliet ran out of two-pence pieces to put in the phone box and the pips had signalled the end of their chat.

However, the conversation wasn't completely in vain. Thinking about what her sister had said in bed later that night had sparked an idea.

THURSDAY

'Mum,' she begins at breakfast the next morning. 'I was thinking, I'd really like to go into the square after school today and buy Nana Nancy a card and a present, just something small from me and Rosy.'

'I'm making her a card,' announces Rosalind. 'I painted her a cat, a bit like her cat that died, the Siamese one. You can sign too if you want, Helena?'

Damn her and her ridiculous generosity. 'No, Rosy, I think if you're taking the trouble to make Nana a card then the least I can do is buy her one.'

'Why not nip into the newsagent's by the post office?' reasons Alicia. 'No need to go flogging all the way into town, and you could buy your grandmother some sweets from Beale's. She'd love that. Mint humbugs or Liquorice Allsorts, those are her favourites.'

'Actually, I was thinking bath salts,' Helena responds, 'and I can only get really nice ones from Boots in town.' Her mother looks doubtful. 'Oh,' blurts Helena, 'and I could nip into the optician's. One of the lenses keeps falling out of my glasses. I don't want it to smash. I think the frames need tightening.'

At last, her mother is convinced. 'Oh, OK, but make sure you come straight back. It's not the holidays quite yet.'

Helena inwardly celebrates. She might not be able to go to the party, but Liza can't stop her having a coffee in the Blue Monkey this afternoon. She doesn't own the place.

She pushes aside her toast. She needs to pack her make-up bag in with her school books; just her mascara, a bit of green eyeshadow and some blusher. Thank goodness she washed her hair last night and the spot that was threatening to erupt on her chin has been successfully witch-hazelled to death.

Helena is quite lucky with her skin. She is what her grandmother calls 'peaches and cream'.

At least my nose isn't home to a million blackheads, she tells herself smugly, glancing in the hall mirror as she goes upstairs to clean her teeth. She'll take a toothbrush too. No one likes a girl with bad breath. She's read that in loads of magazines. The words '*fresh breath, a nice smile and a friendly disposition*' roll around in her head. She'd read them last week in *Jackie* magazine, along with advice on the problem page to a girl who was jealous of her best friend's good looks. '*We're all different*,' the advice had read. '*Make the most of whatever assets you have and keep cheerful. Boys don't go for sulky girls.*'

Helena smiles a dazzling smile at her reflection. She scores herself an eight for her hair, which is blonde, thick and straight; seven for her eyes (they're a bit small); and five for her teeth. Maybe she should start smiling without showing them? Quickly she practises in the mirror, but it doesn't work and she rearranges her face before the wind changes and she is stuck looking peculiar for ever.

Glancing at her watch, Helena hurriedly secretes her quilted nylon make-up bag into her satchel. It contains all the tools she needs to elevate her looks and she tucks her toothbrush and toothpaste into a long, grubby tennis sock and shoves that into her bag too.

Her underwear drawer refuses to push back in. Everything in her bedroom is falling to pieces. It desperately needs an update. If they're truly not going on holiday this summer then the least her mum and dad can do is let her redecorate her room a bit. Maybe they can fork out for one of those mirrors with lights all around it, like Gwen's, and a big bean bag and some scatter cushions, or at least let her change the wallpaper.

Helena's parents had only recently broken the news about them not going away this summer; something about Rosalind and a specialist appointment, and not wanting to take any risks. Helena understands, but it's still bitterly disappointing. She vows to keep up the campaign to have a complete bedroom revamp over the summer. She can't wait until she's old enough to have her own flat. She wants a purple bathroom with an avocado-green bathroom suite, complete with a corner bath and bidet, ooh and really fluffy purple towels, not like the ones her mum insists on keeping, which are scratchy and thin.

'Make sure you're home by six thirty!' her mother yells as she leaves the house.

Helena hasn't any intention of being any later. She never intentionally wants to upset anyone. It's just that sometimes, stuff happens.

* * *

It's almost seven by the time she returns, and her mother's face is peering anxiously out of the kitchen window as Helena enters the back garden via the garage side door. Seconds later, Alicia is standing on the back step, her face furious, her voice shrill.

'What time do you call this? I said six thirty at the latest, Helena.'

Shit, thinks Helena. How does she explain what happened without telling her mother all her secrets? Potential excuses jostle for position – my bike got a puncture, I witnessed a car accident and had to give the police a statement, maybe she could even pretend to have lost her memory?

Helena's mind works overtime. Maybe playing the upset card will work on this occasion.

'I'm sorry,' she sobs. 'I'm so sorry, my watch stopped, and I just didn't realise what time it was!'

You bloody liar, her subconscious hisses at her as her mother draws her up into a big sniffing hug.

It's only after supper – fish cakes, oven chips and peas (one of Alicia's more reliable weekday numbers) – followed by a slightly sloppy egg custard and a placatory game of Operation with Rosalind that Helena manages to escape to the privacy of her own bedroom. Finally she is free to mull over what really happened in town that afternoon.

She takes her time, luxuriating as she picks up each piece of the jigsaw puzzle entitled 'The incident in the Blue Monkey coffee bar' and smiles to herself as she slots each piece into place.

Having first spent ten minutes in the school loos 'titivating' herself up as Nana Nancy would say, Helena had cycled into the town centre, her hair sticking to her thickly glossed lips, and chained her bike up behind a bus stop. She'd gone straight to Boots, and after treating herself to a bottle of 'Murky Mauve' Miners nail varnish, she had spent a great deal more than she'd intended on an extravagantly boxed 'Sea Jade' Yardley bath set for Nana Nancy.

Mission accomplished, Helena then decided to honour her own alibi by popping into the optician's and see if anyone could actually do anything about the looseness of her lenses. Only by the time she got there it was five o'clock, and the optician's sign had switched to closed. *Dammit*, she was a minute too late.

All was not lost, however. Next door in the Blue Monkey, Sally Winwood had spotted her through the café window. A moment later, she came out and hauled Helena inside for 'a word'.

It felt weird to hang out with Sally again so soon after yesterday's Liza embarrassment, and as she followed Sally into the tiny fuchsia-pink ladies' toilets at the back of the Blue Monkey, Helena wasn't sure where this conversation was going to go.

She'd been nervous until Sally admitted she thought Liza had been in the wrong and that it wasn't up to her who Helena fancied and which parties she went to.

'I've been treading on eggshells around her since I was seven,' Sally had confided. 'We went to the same primary, and she's been bossing me around ever since.'

Helena had felt a thrill at being confided in like this, and gamely laughed the Liza incident off. 'Honestly, Sally, it's not your fault,' and Sally had smiled and asked if she could borrow her eyeshadow, and just like that the whole thing was forgotten. In the mirror, Helena clocked Sally's lovebite again.

'It's a birthmark,' said Sally, noticing her look. 'I'm not that much of a floozy, not like *some* people we know!' and they both laughed.

When they were out of the loos, Sally had made everyone budge up for her. Some even smiled and said, 'Oh hi', and even though she was a little disappointed that Sticks wasn't around, it was still sort of thrilling just to be there. She'd ended up wedged between Sally and Gazza, who she realised was rather spotty close up, and his breath smelt like one of Nelson's doggie farts.

Helena wasn't sure if she could really fancy someone who didn't clean his teeth properly and it had been a relief when Sally had offered him a stick of Juicy Fruit gum.

No one really talked, but there had been a lot of mucking about. Someone threw a cold cheese toastie at their table and all the girls squealed, and then two boys in the booth opposite began arm-wrestling and everyone started egging them on.

Thinking about it now, she's not sure why it had been so exciting, it just was. There was a lot of shrieking and laughing, girls running to the toilets with other girls, boys slouching and smoking and hitting each other around the head with copies of *Melody Maker*, spilling their drinks and swearing. Helena had never heard so much swearing.

Occasionally 'Fat Ian', the owner of the Blue Monkey, or his wife 'Bitchy Sandra' would tell them to 'pipe down' and very occasionally Bitchy Sandra would come out from behind the counter and wipe down the tables with a filthy string cloth. At some point, a couple of middle-aged women came in, but once they saw what the place was actually like inside, one of them turned to the other and said, 'Oh no, Jean, I don't think so, do you?' and the other replied, 'Absolutely not, Pauline, not even if it was the last place on earth.' At which point they'd turned on their heels and marched out, to gales of raucous laughter. At that point Helena had suddenly found the nerve to impersonate the two women. 'Jesus Christ, Pauline,' she'd warbled in a posh falsetto, 'no wonder they call it the Monkey bar, the place is full of stinking, gibbering apes. Fuck me, that's not a café bar, it's a zoo!' And the whole café had roared its approval and everything had been perfect until she'd glanced at her watch.

Oh no, oh no, oh no. Her mum was going to kill her. She'd promised to be home by 6.30 and it was already quarter past. Shit.

She had grabbed her school bag from under the table and wormed her way out of the teenage knot of elbows and knees that had more or less hemmed her in. 'Got to go,' she managed to mouth at Sally, who was deep in conversation with Susie Jones and didn't seem to hear.

As soon as she'd walked around the corner, she started to run and by the time she remembered where she'd chained up her bike, she was sweating. As she'd fumbled over the padlock, Helena had dropped the tiny key, which bounced off the kerb and landed perilously close to the edge of an open drain, but before she could reach it, a figure waiting at the bus stop bent down and grabbed it for her, their heads almost colliding as they both straightened up at the same time.

Oh Lord, oh God, oh Jesus, it was Jimmy Simmonds. He passed her the key, his hand dry and warm, hers pink and damp with sweat.

He was taller than she'd imagined. She only came up to his chin and he had a huge Adam's apple that bobbed as he swallowed.

'Yours, I believe,' he said, and she had inevitably felt herself redden.

'Thank you,' she said. She had tried to keep her voice low and husky, but it came out as a growl.

A boy behind Jimmy suddenly peered over his shoulder. 'Are you Helena Treace?'

'Yeah,' she growled again. Oh God, she sounded like she was turning into a bear. How was that even possible?

'Ha, I thought so,' said the boy with a familiar ferrety expression. 'My sister's in your maths class.' Of course! He was the boy version of the equally ferret-featured Claire Chambers.

At that exact moment, the number 11 bus had pulled up and ferret face jumped on board.

Jimmy, she noticed, stood back to let an elderly woman on the bus before him, but as he stepped up behind the old dear, he had turned around and – yes, this actually happened – Jimmy Simmonds had winked at her.

In that instant, Helena had revised her list of most fanciable boys and Jimmy leapt up four places from number five to number one.

Oh God, it had been worth it . . . being late home, getting a bollocking, playing boring Operation with her little sister. Nothing mattered when she had that wink engraved on her brain. A wink and a smile, a divine lopsided grin of a smile, aimed straight at her, Helena Treace.

Lying on her bed, reliving every second of the afternoon, Helena decides that Liza can have Sticks. She is going to set her sights on Jimmy Simmonds. She doesn't know how, and she isn't sure when, but sometime soon she is going to snog him, Helena is quite sure of this. Shame it can't be this weekend. This weekend is a washout, what with her girlie night in and then Nana Nancy's birthday lunch. But there'll be other weekends, and there's the whole summer holidays ahead, just over a week to go.

Back in the present, reverie completed, Helena suddenly goes cold. Oh shit . . . She leaps off the bed and starts rifling in her school bag. Her make-up bag is in there, her schoolbooks are in there, but where the hell are Nana Nancy's bath salts? Helena tips her satchel upside down. Immediately the carpet is covered in chewing-gum wrappers, biscuit crumbs and pencil shavings. She can't have left it, seriously, she can't have done, only she knows she has; she has left the Boots bag in one of the red leatherette booths in the Blue Monkey. After going to all that trouble, not to mention spending her savings on one of the most expensive gift boxes in the shop, she's only gone and lost it.

There's no way it will still be there now. The Blue Monkey isn't the sort of place where people hand things in. Which means, since she has almost no money left, she's going to have to think of something else for Nana Nancy's birthday present, and considering this was her excuse for going into town in the first place, if she doesn't want to arouse her mum's suspicions, it'd better be something good.

She feels sick. Why does anything good immediately have to be spoiled by something really bad?

FRIDAY

Helena wakes up to sullen grey skies. If it hadn't been for that wink, she would be despairing right now. Not only has she lost her grandmother's birthday present, but the nail varnish is missing too. Dammit, her plan had been to take it to Elaine's house tomorrow night. Just last week the beauty editor of *Jackie* magazine (imagine having that kind of dream job!) had declared '*don't get stuck in a make-up rut*'.

Helena has decided it's time Elaine and Gwen made a bit more of an effort. Neither of them bother much with make-up, but both have features that would benefit from a little cosmetic help. Elaine has a very sallow complexion and could do with just a touch of blusher, while Gwen has rather piggy eyes that would no doubt benefit from some clever eyeshadow tricks.

As Helena takes her usual early morning cycle route down the back alley, the rain that has been spitting all morning decides to turn into a full-blown shower. Oh great, no doubt she will cycle past Jimmy Simmonds looking like a drowned rat.

Oh God, Jimmy winking Simmonds! She can't wait to tell her friends what happened yesterday. Helena shivers in the cold. Honestly, it's July; damn living in the north. Whenever Juliet rings home, it's always 'boiling in London'.

Sometimes when the weather turns ugly, Helena waits for Gwen and Elaine inside the newsagent's. This is definitely a day for taking cover and browsing through the magazines. Last time she was sheltering from a downpour, she managed to read an entire article about oral sex in *Cosmopolitan*.

Propping her bike up on its stand under the shop's canvas awning, Helena opens the newsagent's door and a bell chimes.

Old man Hawkins, the elder of Hawkins and Son newsagent's, comes out of the back room and grunts at her. 'I've just come in out of the rain,' she explains, and he grunts again and disappears back into where he came from. The son is much more of a laugh. Sometimes he shares his fags and lets her sit on the stool behind the counter while he busies himself in the shop.

Helena mooches around. What the hell is she going to do about Nana Nancy's birthday? Her mother had suggested sweets from Beale's, and it's true, Nana Nancy is a pushover for liquorice, but a paper bag of corner-shop sweets seems a bit mean, but that's all she can afford now. Helena eyes Hawkins's selection of chocolates, after-dinner mints and exotically packaged French fruit jellies, displayed at jaunty angles on glass shelves above the stationery section. Milk Tray, After Eights, Zingy Orange Matchmakers, and before she knows or can understand what she is doing, she has reached up and removed a slim box of Milk Tray chocolates from the shelf and slipped it into her school bag. Moving swiftly away from the scene of the crime, Helena knocks over a plastic drum of Bic biros, which scatter to the floor.

Alerted by the noise, old man Hawkins re-emerges from his lair at the back of the shop. He has a tea towel tucked into the neck of his shirt and he is obviously eating his breakfast. Brown sauce dribbles down his chin. Helena freezes.

'I'm sorry,' she stutters. 'That was my fault.'

He doesn't say anything, just looks at her and blinks, then shaking his head he turns his back and shuffles away again. Helena picks the biros up and puts them back into the drum, making sure every single pen is lid-side up and then leaves the shop.

She is sweating and she feels sick. What has she done? She has never stolen anything as big as a posh box of chocolates before. Up until now, it's been the odd sweetie from the Woolworths pic 'n' mix counter in town and once some change from her father's bedside table, but nothing serious. Now she is a proper thief.

Helena has never been more grateful to see Gwen and Elaine cycling towards her. 'Just go,' she mutters, but as she cycles off with her mates, Helena is suddenly exhilarated. She didn't get caught, old man Hawkins was clueless, and it was his fault anyway for leaving her alone in the shop. Imagine what else she could have nicked? Next time, she might reach out for a packet of fags, and she needn't restrict herself to the newsagent's either. Cosmetics would be a cinch, considering most items of make-up are small enough to fit into the palm of your hand. Thinking about it, she concludes that there is no real reason to go without anything. Fired up by the possibilities of future petty pilfering, Helena manages to reach the top of the hill before Gwen for once. She feels triumphant, she feels on top of the world, and she laughs like a hyena all the way down the other side.

'Helena Treace,' her form teacher yells. 'How many times?

'Yes, miss,' she finally answers.

'Oh, she deigns to respond,' her form teacher snipes. *Probably on her period*, thinks Helena. Miss Glenn gets very moody around the last week of the month.

Today's timetable is packed with all Helena's least favourite lessons, including double science in the morning and German and geography in the afternoon, but even this – plus her worst lunch, luncheon meat with disgusting Russian salad, followed by revolting synthetic strawberry blancmange – can't get her down.

Helena drifts through the day on a high, gleefully anticipating the prospect of the bike ride home, when she can tell her friends about her new love affair with Jimmy Simmonds. She hadn't managed to tell the girls about the wink this morning because it had been raining too hard, and then at lunchtime Gwen had a flute lesson and Elaine was in extra maths.

Sadly, due to an after-school dental appointment, Gwen would be missing out on this shiny nugget of gossip, but Helena decides she can't wait any longer. The incident is swelling inside her like a balloon and she will burst if she doesn't tell someone. So as soon as she and Elaine can safely cycle two abreast, she reveals all – the dropped keys, their hands touching, his lopsided smile, then – best of all – the wink.

Elaine looks bemused. 'So what does that mean? Maybe he had something in his eye?'

Helena is tempted to push her off her bike.

'No, that's not what it means, Elaine,' she snaps, and then races ahead on her bike, her face red with fury. Honestly, bloody Elaine, with her stupid fucking rabbits. She has all the sexual sophistication of a twelve-year-old.

Elaine catches her up. 'So basically, you fancy Jimmy Simmonds. You know he's my Saturday paperboy?'

Helena skids to a halt. 'What?'

'I think you mean *pardon*,' smirks Elaine. 'Yes, every Saturday he comes in by the side gate. I can hear him on the gravel path. He wears a bobble hat in winter,' she says, smirking again. 'Sometimes, if I'm out early giving Percy a run around the garden, he says hello. Once he said, "That's a big rabbit." I soon put him straight!'

'Why have you never told me this before?' squeals Helena, furious that Elaine has had an actual conversation with Jimmy before she has.

'I didn't think it was particularly interesting.'

Helena holds her hand up like a policeman as she interrupts her friend. 'Elaine, I need to ask you something. Do you actually fancy anyone, even if it's not in real life, even if it's someone on the telly, like the bloke off *Magpie* or the lead singer of Showaddywaddy?'

Elaine looks momentarily confused. 'Not really. I think I might be a late developer. I know Gwen likes Cliff Richard, and you fancy loads of people, but I'm just not –' she trails off – 'bothered. In fact, the idea of kissing a boy makes me feel a bit sick. It's the tongue thing. It's very germy, isn't it?'

Elaine looks so visibly distressed as she says this that Helena suddenly feels sorry for her. It's not her fault. Some girls are into boys and make-up and hair and fashion, and some girls like to train their Belgian hare to jump over sticks in the back garden. She feels a sudden rush of affection for her old friend.

'It doesn't matter,' she tells her. 'You don't have to kiss anyone if you don't want to.' And with that settled, Helena and Elaine brace themselves for the calf-achingly steep incline over the railway bridge, then freewheel all the way down the other side.

Helena yells, 'See you tomorrow!' over her shoulder as she veers off to the right and disappears into the back street, feeling much more cheerful than when she left the house this morning.

However, as soon as she steps foot in the kitchen, she can sense something is wrong.

Helena feels her stomach churn. Why is the house so quiet? Her mother only works a half day on Fridays and always picks Rosalind up from school herself. Oh God, is Rosy ill again?

'Helena,' her mother shouts. There is an edge to her voice.

Oh God, what if something's happened to Juliet? Juliet is a bossy cow, but Helena doesn't want her dead. Terrible things happen in London, the IRA, bombs . . . Oh God, what if her sister has been killed by a terrorist bomb? Helena follows the sound of her mother's voice to the sitting room.

Alicia sits in the straight-back chair beside the mahogany table in the bay of the sitting-room window.

A vase on the table contains pink roses from the garden.

Helena notices that some of their petals have fallen.

Her younger sister is nowhere to be seen. Usually on Friday afternoons Rosalind bakes biscuits with Alicia or has one of her friends to play, but the house is ominously quiet.

Her mother's face is set in stone. 'I had a telephone call this afternoon when I got back from school with Rosy.' Her mother always calls Rosalind 'Rosy'. Rosalind is her 'Rosy-Posy sweetheart-boo'. Helena is occasionally 'lamb chop', but not now.

Her mother continues. 'It was from Mr Hawkins, the man who owns the newsagent's where you sometimes wait for Gwen and Elaine. You know, when it's raining, like this morning.'

'He saw you, Helena,' Alicia continues. 'Apparently he has a mirror in the shop and this mirror is specifically angled so that Mr Hawkins can see what's going on out front when he's in the back room.' Alicia's eyes are narrow. 'And that's how he saw you steal the chocolates. I'm so embarrassed, Helena, and the worst thing is, he thinks you're a nice girl; he actually likes you. He said he was surprised because they've always made you welcome in the shop and he was shocked that a nice girl like you would do such a thing.'

Helena does the only thing she can think of doing – she collapses to the floor.

In books, when people get terrible news they faint. She wills herself to faint, but she can't. She manages the dropping down bit, but not the actual passing out. She is basically just lying on the carpet, fully conscious. The carpet is gold with swirly indentations. Maybe she can just lie here until this all blows over?

'Oh for heaven's sake, Helena, get up, you big lump,' her mother snaps. 'Don't you dare start feeling sorry for yourself. Your father is going to be so disappointed.' At this Helena genuinely manages to turn on the waterworks. She can cope with her mother being furious with her, but she cannot stand the idea of upsetting her father. She likes to believe deep down that maybe she is his favourite? After all, she is the one who makes him laugh the most. Oh God, this is terrible.

'Get up,' her mother repeats, 'because right now you are straight round to Hawkins and you are going to apologise to Mr Hawkins. Then you are going pay for those chocolates. What were you thinking of, Helena?'

'Nana,' she sobs back

'Oh yes,' her mother sneers, 'because obviously that's what every grandmother wants for her seventy-fifth birthday, a box of stolen chocolates from a criminal granddaughter. I don't think so, Helena. Go on then, what are you waiting for?'

Helena has no choice, of course. Hawkins supply her parents' newspapers. That'll be why the old man has their address and phone number.

Helena retrieves the chocolates from her school bag. She'd told herself she'd stolen them because she couldn't afford them, but counting up the change in her purse, she realises she could, she just preferred to spend her money on other things: bus fares into town, snacks at the Blue Monkey, records, nail varnish. The shame of this realisation makes her feel even worse as she walks down the back street, hoping against hope that the shop will be shut by the time she gets there.

It isn't, and as she pushes the door open, the bell clangs

alarmingly and both Mr Hawkins and Son look up from doing the football pools behind the counter. Helena feels herself blush. She waits for an elderly lady to buy a copy of *The People's Friend*, and then she starts talking, because the sooner she starts talking, the sooner all this will be over.

'I've come about the chocolates,' she gabbles. 'I'm so sorry, it was an awful accident. I didn't mean to do it and I don't know why I did? I can pay for them, or you can have them back? I haven't eaten any of them; they were for my nana's birthday.' She offers the box across the counter.

Old man Hawkins shakes his head. 'We don't want them after they've left the premises. Give me the money, then you can put them in the bin for all I care. I'll not have you in this shop again, you hear?'

She can feel her eyes watering. He can't mean it. How can you be expelled from a shop? The younger Mr Hawkins just shrugs and won't look her in the eye. 'Go on then, hop it,' growls the older man. 'No use standing round like cheese at fourpence. We don't need your type cluttering up the place.'

Helena puts the money on the counter and leaves the shop. The bell clangs and she feels like a defeated boxer exiting the ring. Burning with shame, Helena walks home and decides to plead with her mother not to tell her dad. She'll empty all the wastepaper baskets, de-slug the lupins, plait Rosalind's hair properly, *anything* as long as her mother doesn't tell Simon.

Alicia is in no mood to listen, though. When Helena returns through the back door, her mother is banging pans around and begins to speak before Helena can plead her case. 'And if you think you're going to Elaine's house tomorrow night, young lady, you've got another think coming. In fact, I've got a good mind to phone Mari Perks and tell her that she'd better watch her purse and the family silver when you come round, not that you're going round any time soon. You are going stay right here for at least a week, where I can keep an eye on you. I don't know what possessed you, Helena?'

Supper is awful. Not only has Alicia overcooked pork loins in an acidic tomato sauce, but her father doesn't even make his usual 'Ah, Shoe Leather Provençale' remark. They eat in silence, endlessly chewing the tough meat. Meanwhile, Rosalind had opted for a toast-topper tea in front of the television. *Lucky bloody Rosalind*.

Eventually her father puts his knife and fork down, clears his throat and wipes his mouth with his napkin. 'Your mother has told me about the incident in the newsagent's. I don't think you are aware, Helena, how serious this could have been, had Mr Hawkins decided to go to the police. You could have been looking at a criminal record.'

'But I'm not—'

He puts his hand up. 'We haven't brought you up to be duplicitous.'

Hold on, she knows this one. They did it in English. Miss Glenn used it to describe Iago. It means sneaky. Oh God, her father is calling her sneaky. He looks straight at her, and she can sense the disappointment seeping out of every pore.

'So, in terms of punishment, we've decided, no pocket money, no sleepover at Elaine's, no *Top of the Pops*, and you're to come straight home from school too. No bunking off into town. It's not the holidays yet. Do you hear me, Helena?'

She nods miserably. She can't ever recall her father speaking to either of her sisters like this. Honestly, why has she been lumbered with siblings who can do no wrong?

Pudding is gooseberry fool, which manages to be both sour and slightly hairy, as if a cat had peed then rolled around in it.

'We'll leave you to clear the table,' her mother snipes, when they have finally eaten enough not to appear rude, and Helena gathers up the dishes while her parents retreat to the sitting room.

Helena feels very sorry for herself and as she stacks the dishwasher, she eats some cooking chocolate from the cupboard above the bread bin. She's not even hungry. She just needs something to take the taste of hairy gooseberry pudding away.

She can't face phoning Elaine to tell her she can't come over tomorrow. Instead she takes the rest of the cooking chocolate up to her room and lies on the floor feeling sorry for herself and listening to 'I'm Not in Love' by 10cc over and over again on her record player.

Rosalind pokes her head around Helena's bedroom door before she goes to bed. 'I heard what happened,' she whispers. 'Helena, that's really bad of you. I don't know how you'd even dare?'

'Yeah, well, I'm not a snivelling coward like some people,' Helena attempts to joke back.

But her younger sister is not impressed. 'You made mum cry.'

Oh shit. Helena hates seeing her mother cry. She did it a lot a few months ago when Rosalind was ill and Helena never wants to witness it again. Parents shouldn't cry.

'But I still love you,' her sister admits cheerily, 'and I bought you this.'

73

It was a raspberry-flavoured chewy sweet in the shape of a shrimp. Rosy had obviously clutched it in her hand for quite a while and it was slightly grubby and misshapen, more like an ear now than a shrimp.

'Thanks,' says Helena, and for some reason she finds her eyes filling with tears. 'Now, bugger off and leave me alone.'

That night, before she goes to sleep, Helena seeks solace in her diary and finds herself writing a poem. She entitles it, 'The Middle Child'.

Who Am I?
A changeling child, swapped at birth,
The straight-haired girl,
Amongst the curls of better natures,
Squeezed between the two who can do no wrong.
I am the Marmite.

Which she thinks is quite good.

SATURDAY

On Saturday morning Helena is hoping that her parents will go out and that she will be free to sulk around the house and fry herself a nice full English.

The weather for once is glorious, warm enough to sunbathe. Maybe she shouldn't have the fry up? Her bikini was tight last year and twelve months on she's definitely bigger, certainly around the backside. Oh God, why is she such a classic pear shape? She's read about women's body shapes in one of her grandmother's magazines. Apparently, she must never wear horizontal stripes as they will accentuate her 'problem area'.

Venturing downstairs in her purple dressing gown, she discovers that her mother and Rosalind are indeed out. Of course, it's a Saturday morning and on Saturday mornings Rosy has a ballet class at Miss Rogers's Academy for Dance, which oddly enough is situated around the corner from the Blue Monkey café. For a moment she remembers sitting in that red leatherette booth again, the sound of everyone laughing when she did the impression of the posh woman, those fleeting seconds of sheer happiness, before everything went wrong. Sticks's eyes as she lit his cigarette that time, Jimmy's wink . . . Not that she fancies Sticks any more; Jimmy's her dream boy now. Oh, but Sticks's eyes . . .

Helena sighs, peels off three rashers of bacon and shoves a couple of pieces of bread in the toaster. Her father is in the back garden, mowing the lawn in precise vertical stripes. He is wearing his awful shorts, the ones Helena's mother threatens to burn every Bonfire Night. His legs are thin and grey with varicose veins. He inherited them from his mother, Nana Nancy. *Jesus, if I get them, I'll kill myself*, thinks Helena, laying the bacon in the pan and watching a tiny knob of lard melt into liquid. Once she's fried one side, she'll add the eggs. She likes her bacon crispy and her yolks runny. She likes Lurpak on her toast and a big blob of tomato ketchup on the side. She would never let a boy see her eat like this.

'Boys don't like to see girls stuff their faces,' says *Jackie* magazine, *'so keep it simple. If he takes you out for a meal, don't choose the greasy burger option. He'll have more respect for you if you choose a salad. But beware any hidden onions – boys don't like smelly onion breath!'*

There are so many rules, thinks Helena, breaking two eggs into the pan and fetching a plate and cutlery from the various cupboards and drawers.

The pans spits, the eggs are just how she likes them, and she piles her plate, turns the hob off and settles herself at the pine table, ketchup bottle in hand. She eats her breakfast so quickly, she would actually like to duplicate the meal and eat it all over again.

76

'Still not full? Why not take the hunger pangs away by crunching down on fresh celery sticks?'

Instead, she pays a visit to the larder and fills her pockets with slightly burnt flapjacks. On her way back upstairs, Helena decides to take advantage of the empty house and call Elaine. She needs to tell her that she won't be coming round tonight.

She takes the phone off the table and places it on the hall carpet. There is a space between the table and the front door where she likes to sit on the floor and have long chats. Helena dials a number that she has known off by heart for years. Elaine's father answers, 'Lytham 4218.'

'Hi, Mr Perks, it's Helena here. Can I speak to Elaine, please?'

'You *may*,' responds Gordon Perks, picking her up on the grammatically incorrect use of the word 'can', the old fart.

Mr Perks shouts 'Elaine!' up the stairs and Helena can hear her friend thundering downstairs to seize the phone from her father.

'Hang on, hang on,' she whispers to Helena, who is well acquainted with Gordon's freaky fuddy-duddiness, and the two girls wait until he is safely out of earshot, at which point Elaine squeals long and hard into the phone, 'Oh my God, Helena, something incredible happened this morning. Just listen . . .' For once, Helena lets Elaine speak first.

'I was out in the garden with Percy, who still has a poorly eye, and I was giving him a run around after his drops when loverboy, Jimmy Simmonds, came through the back gate with the papers. Anyway, he asked how the rabbit was, and I said he's a hare, and told him about his eye and demonstrated how Percy could jump over a bamboo cane and then I said – you'll never believe this, Helena, but it's true – I said, "Listen, me and Helena Treace and another mate are having a Chinese round here tonight around eight thirty, you know, if you fancied dropping by," and he said, "Yeah, maybe, can I bring a mate?" And I said, "Yes, but just one, we don't want an orgy," and I don't know why I said that, but he kind of laughed and then he gave me the paper and said, "Gotta go, maybe see you later. No promises, mind. Not sure what my plans are yet," and then, well, that was it.'

Helena chokes slightly. 'What, pardon, say that again?'

Elaine repeats her Jimmy Simmonds encounter and Helena struggles not to regurgitate her breakfast on the velvety moss-green hall carpet. Jimmy Simmonds is going to Elaine's tonight, for a Chinese, but he can't, he mustn't, because she won't be there.

There is a pause. Helena is literally lost for words. How on earth does she deal with this?

'I thought you'd be pleased?' queries Elaine, the excitement suddenly absent from her voice.

'Oh God, Elaine,' burbles Helena. 'It's the nicest thing you've done for me since you let me have the lucky gonk rubber in Mr Longdon's class, but the thing is I can't come tonight.'

'But why, you promised! Don't tell me you're going to that party?'

'God no,' Helena protests. 'Fact is something awful happened last night and now my parents have got me under house arrest.'

Elaine isn't daft, she knows Alicia and Simon Treace don't ground their daughter for nothing. 'Oh, Helena,' she asks, 'what on earth did you do?'

Helena tells her and Elaine is silent until, eventually, in a small strict voice, she says, 'I think that's quite shitty of you, Helena.'

Helena swiftly tries to change the subject. 'Yes, but that's beside the point. What are we going to do? Jimmy might turn up at your place tonight and I won't be there.'

'Well, that can't really be helped, can it? You should have thought about that before you decided to go on a shoplifting spree.'

'Can't you ring him up and tell him or something?'

'No, I can't. I haven't got his number. If he comes, I'll tell him you're ill.'

'But not diarrhoea,' Helena insists. 'Tell him I've got a migraine. Migraines are kind of sophisticated and sexy. Oh God, Elaine, I've really screwed things up. I'm not even allowed to watch *Top of the Pops*.'

'I'm not surprised,' snaps Elaine, and Helena suddenly can't bear to talk to her any more.

'I've got to go, Elaine. Call me if he comes round. Maybe I could talk to him on the phone.'

'I don't think so,' replies Elaine. 'You've got a migraine, remember; you should be lying down in a darkened room.' And without saying another word, she puts the phone down.

Helena phones Gwen. Mrs Sanderson answers, 'Hello, St Anne's 2376, to whom am I speaking?'

'Hello, Mrs Sanderson, it's Helena.'

'Helena! I presume you'd like to speak with Gwendoline?'

Jesus Christ. 'Yes, please.'

'Well, she's having a piano lesson in the sun lounge until

79

eleven. May I pass on a message?'

'Could she call me back, please?'

'Certainly. Give my regards to your parents, Helena. Tell them we'll be having the usual open garden in aid of the Rotary Club in the summer holidays. Plenty of tickets available.'

I'll bet, thinks Helena, replacing the telephone and disconsolately dragging herself back upstairs, while mentally composing a letter to *Jackie* magazine's agony aunts Cathy and Claire.

Dear Cathy and Claire

I'm in the most terrible situation. My parents hate me because I accidentally stole some chocolates and now they're keeping me under lock and key when I was about to get off with the cutest boy in the neighbourhood . . . What shall I do?

Yours, sad n freckly of St Anne's

Dear Sad n Freckly

Have you ever paused to think that your criminal actions must have broken your parents' hearts? Imagine what it must be like for them, bringing an innocent child into the world only to watch her turn into a confectionery thief. Spare a thought for their feelings before you start begging us for sympathy. As for the cutest boy in the neighbourhood, why should he want to go out with someone as untrustworthy as you? Remember, boys don't like girls who steal. It's not clever and it's not cute.

Blimey, even her subconscious is giving her a hard time.

* * *

Gwen doesn't call her back until after lunch, and from the tone of her voice Helena guesses that she still isn't aware of the situation. She sounds upbeat, whispering conspiratorially, 'I've got six mini bottles of Babycham from the stash in the garage hidden in my pyjama case!'

Of course Gwen has a pyjama case. Her mother is obsessed with disguising things. Ordinary cardboard tissue boxes crouch under velvet rickrack-braided covers, the spare lavatory roll on the cistern is tucked under the crocheted skirts of some weird kind of doll, and even their *Radio Times* has a tooled leather jacket.

Helena hates to burst Gwen's bubble, but when her friend finally pauses, she slips in a subdued but firm, 'I can't be there tonight, Gwen, I'm really sorry. Elaine will explain everything.'

And then she puts the phone down.

Suddenly the thought of Jimmy Simmonds turning up at Elaine's house later makes her stomach roil. What if her old friends come across as weirdos? I mean, they are weirdos. Elaine is happiest in the company of a Belgian hare and Gwen is infatuated with a has-been Christian pop singer and will no doubt take his latest hideous album over to Elaine's and play it over and over again. Not that Elaine has any better taste; she likes The Rubettes.

'Madness,' sighs Helena. If she hadn't known them since she was five, there'd be no reason to be friends with them.

As soon as she's had this thought, she knows it's mean; after all, Elaine invited Jimmy round on her behalf. She blushes, half embarrassed by her own nastiness, but mostly at the thought of Jimmy turning up at Elaine's and realising that two of the girls she hangs out with are complete freaks. Whatever happens, he mustn't go round to Elaine's when she isn't there.

Suddenly she has a brainwave. She grabs the phone book from the hall table, tucks it under one arm and then carries the phone into the barely used dining room. Fortunately, there is just enough cable to accomplish this manoeuvre and she closes the door behind her. She needs to be quick; she needs to warn Jimmy off, tell him Elaine's parents have decided not to go out and that the Chinese is off.

Rifling through the Yellow Pages, she finds five Simmondses locally, and starts dialling. Her first attempt goes unanswered, the second is picked up by an elderly lady who sounds confused, while the third, which has an accompanying address in Fairhaven, yields results.

A woman who sounds about her mum's age answers and Helena very politely asks if Jimmy's home.

'No,' the women responds. 'Is that Lucy?'

Helena is momentarily derailed. Who the hell is Lucy? 'Er no,' she responds. 'It's, er, Desdemona.' It's the only girl's name she can think of. Blast her English homework. Mind you, considering her mother's penchant for naming her daughters after Shakespearian characters, it's not surprising.

'Desdemona,' snorts Jimmy's mum. 'Sorry, love, Jimmy's gone out, but I think he was talking about some big party tonight if that helps. He doesn't tell me much; boys don't, you know. I always wished I'd had girls, but you can't pick and choose.'

'Thank you very much, Mrs Simmonds.'

'That's all right, Desdemona, I'll tell him you called.'

82

Desdemona! What on earth had she been thinking? Helena spends the rest of the afternoon on a towel sunbathing in the back garden. She falls asleep while lying face down on the lawn and wakes up at 6 p.m. having burnt the backs of her legs.

Supper is a very greasy pork fried rice eaten in silence at the breakfast-room table with her furious parents, neither of whom will even look at her.

The evening stretches out in front of her. She can't even hang out with Rosalind, who has a pal round for a sleepover. The pair of them can be heard shrieking and giggling in her little sister's bedroom.

Helena suddenly feels incredibly sorry for herself, alone and bored on a Saturday night, 'when I'm in my prime,' she seethes. Honestly, what a waste, and all because Nana loves Milk Tray.

Somehow the evening melts into the night. Rosy and her annoying screechy mate eventually go to bed and her parents sit in front of the television, her father nursing a glass of beer and her mother having her usual Saturday night tipple, a gin and tonic. Helena tiptoes into the kitchen for a snack and manages a quick swig from the neck of the gin bottle, before her mother shouts, 'What are you doing, Helena?' Honestly, her mother has the ears of a bat.

'Nothing,' Helena lies, grabbing a crust from the bread bin before opening the fridge and seizing a handful of Dairylea triangles.

Once under the covers, Helena spreads the cheese on the slightly stale crust using her comb instead of a knife. It's a bit messy and she wishes she had some crisps. If only she hadn't been such an idiot, she could have been sharing pork balls with Jimmy Simmonds.

With nothing better to do, she delves into her mother's copy of *The Carpetbaggers* by Harold Robbins and riffles through it for a while, trying unsuccessfully to find the dirty bits.

Helena looks at her clock. It's only nine but she feels oddly sleepy. Boredom is exhausting. For a second, she imagines the party Liza forbade her from attending. Things will be jumping by now, people will be snogging all over the place, Liza Branwell will no doubt have her tongue down Sticks's throat. Oh God, it's not fair. She wonders if Sally will have got off with anyone and what they're all dancing to. Then she makes herself cry by playing her David Bowie *Young Americans* LP, lifting the stylus so that she can play 'Young Americans' over and over again, until she is bored of crying and she closes the lid of her record player, turns the light off and curls up under the covers. The last thing that crosses her mind before sleep takes her hostage for the night is that at least tomorrow is Nana's birthday and with any luck her mother will have bought a shop-made cake.

SUNDAY

Helena is charged with setting the table. 'Properly, mind,' her mother instructs, meaning Helena should dig out the melamine place mats and neatly fold the green linen napkins, both of which are kept in the left-hand drawer of the large wooden dresser.

Once upon a time, this big piece of mahogany furniture belonged to Alicia's mother, Grandma Olive; all the good stuff did. There's jewellery too, which Alicia keeps hidden in a big burgundy leather box behind her collection of terrible hats on a shelf in her wardrobe.

Helena moves around the table, placing everything as neatly as her mother would wish; no point making matters even worse and after all it is her nana's birthday.

By some sixth sense, she hears the phone almost before it starts ringing and darts into the hall to snatch up the receiver before her mother can ask who's calling. It's got to be Elaine.

The timing of the call is perfect. From the sound of it, her mother is busy with the food mixer in the kitchen and her father

85

has gone to fetch her grandmother. As for Rosalind, she is in the garden picking flowers to present to her grandmother, the creep.

'It's me,' says Elaine, and suddenly Helena feels a bit sick.

'Well . . .'

'Well, he came, with his peculiar friend, Greg Fellowes. Do you know him? They turned up on their bikes around eight thirty.'

'Oh God, what was he wearing?' She needs to see a picture of him in her head.

'Oh, jeans and this striped cheesecloth shirt, I think. Anyway, we were having the Chinese in the sitting room with Percy, and that Greg bloke started sneezing like he was allergic. Couldn't have any Chinese either because he said it didn't agree with him. It was like having an old woman in the house.'

'So they came in?'

'Yes, Jimmy had a pork ball, then he noticed you weren't there, and I said you weren't well.'

'What did you say I'd got?'

'A migraine, like you asked, and the Greg bloke said poor thing, I get them sometimes, and Jimmy just rolled his eyes and said, "Come on, Greg, let's go to that party" and they left.'

That was it, he just left; he didn't even ask for her number. Helena sits on the hall chair in shocked silence, as Elaine witters on.

'I suppose he can always find your number in the book,' says Elaine, reading her mind. 'I don't think there are many Treaces.'

But that's beside the point. The point is, he just wasn't fussed enough to ask. Helena can't speak, but Elaine keeps yacking.

'Percy's eye is much better. I think he can see well enough to do the new circuit of jumps I've put up for him. Anyway, I have to do his cage now. See you tomorrow, Helena, and I wouldn't worry, there's plenty more fish.'

But she doesn't want a fish, she wants Jimmy Simmonds. He'd obviously been keen enough to turn up at Elaine's, but not interested enough to write down her number. She could always call his number again, but Helena knows that she won't. He has to phone her, that's the way things work – boys phone girls. Girls only phone boys:

a)   if they're going out with them,
b)   if they knew them when they were babies/are related,

or, as Helena has experienced for herself,

c)   if they are pretending to be someone else.

Suddenly she is aware of a commotion at the front door. Her grandmother has arrived. Nana Nancy is a noisy kind of person. She can't just walk into a room. There is always an air of drama around her. She trails scarves, carries too many bags and is always insisting that she has lost something along the way.

Helena allows herself to be enveloped in her grandmother's embrace. ''Ere she is, my favourite,' Nana Nancy squawks. She says this to everyone, but Helena secretly thinks she does like her the best. Juliet finds her grandmother common, so keeps her at arm's length, while Rosalind is slightly scared of her because she's so loud.

Her grandmother whiffs of the brown scent she keeps in a bottle on the dressing table. It smells as if it's slightly gone off. There is also a hint of liquorice about her. Come to think of it, chocolate trails way behind liquorice when it comes to her grandmother's confectionary preferences. Why hadn't she remembered that before she'd nicked the Milk Tray? She could so easily have avoided all this grief.

Helena's father goes to hang his mother's coat up. It's summer but she has come equipped with mac and brolly because she doesn't trust the weather not to 'play silly buggers'.

Behind Simon's back, Nana Nancy mutters conspiratorially into Helena's face, 'Your father says you're in disgrace, but we're not talking about it.' Her upper lip is hairy and her breath faintly fishy. 'Happy families and all that.'

And then she taps her nose in a 'nudge-nudge wink-wink, say no more' kind of way, and all of a sudden Helena feels better than she has done in days.

She hugs Nana Nancy gratefully, noticing that she is wearing red plastic dangly earrings that most people would think were far too young for a seventy-five-year-old woman. Nana Nancy has a tendency towards 'mutton dressed as lamb', as Alicia puts it.

Helena eyes her grandmother's make-up; maybe she subscribes to *Jackie* too? Today she has experimented with a pale-blue shimmery eyeshadow. Unfortunately her blending leaves a lot to be desired. As for her lipstick, Nana Nancy has completely ignored her natural lip shape and, like a five-year-old with a bright-orange crayon, has very much gone 'outside of the line'.

Before lunch, there is present-giving in the sitting room. Nana Nancy accepts a glass of sherry and sits on the sofa with a granddaughter on either side. Helena has wrapped the wretched chocolates in some of the recycled wrapping paper Alicia keeps under the stairs, having carefully removed a 'to Juliet' birthday tag, before taping up her grandmother's gift.

Nana Nancy opens Rosalind's card first and raves about what a promising artist she is, then Rosy gives her the flowers she collected from the garden and receives a big hug and a kiss in return. Helena notices Nana Nancy's eyes are very shiny. She isn't crying, is she?

Next, she opens her present from Simon, which is a chiffon scarf in tasteful muted pastels, obviously chosen by Alicia, and an Engelbert Humperdinck Greatest Hits album, which Nancy insists is put on the record player at full blast while she opens everything else. When 'Please Release Me' starts, Nana Nancy puts her presents to one side and bellows along to the chorus with Rosalind, Simon and Helena joining in, while her daughter-in-law goes to see how the potatoes are doing.

By the time Alicia gets back to the sitting room, surreptitiously turning the record player down en route, Nancy has opened her daughter-in-law's gift. It's a lovely beige cardigan from Marks. 'Very nice, dear,' says Nancy. 'Do you have the receipt, only I might swap it for something with a bit more oomph?'

Alicia has also bought Nancy a very smart set of bath salts, but as she goes to put lunch on the hostess trolley, Nancy presses the gift box on to Helena. 'Don't tell your mother, but anything scented makes my noo sting, 'ere, you can have these.'

On the other hand, she is delighted by her chocolates. 'You

shouldn't have,' she tells Helena, and her father mumbles, 'No, she shouldn't,' but Nancy doesn't notice because Engelbert is singing 'Quando Quando' and it's her favourite. 'Quando, Quando, Quando,' she trills.

Seconds later, Alicia yells that 'everyone needs to sit down at the table NOW, please' and they all troop through to the dining room.

As Alicia bumps the hostess trolley from the kitchen down the hallway, Nana Nancy asks, 'Has someone burnt the potatoes?'

'No,' Alicia snaps. 'They're fine.' She has cooked a chicken, with slightly watery cauliflower, peas and some baby new Jersey Royals, some of which are very black around the bottom.

Nana Nancy has the nose of a bloodhound and she smirks at the sight of the scorched potatoes. 'What, no gravy?' she asks, making a big fuss about getting comfortable and bringing her handbag to the table.

'I've made some mayonnaise,' Alicia responds.

'Oh dear,' says Nana Nancy, turning to Rosalind. 'Be a good girl for your nana, fetch me some salad cream from that la-di-da pantry of your mother's.'

Helena could swear at this point she can hear her mother mutter 'give me strength' under her breath, and despite being utterly miserable and having had the worst weekend on record, Helena can't help but smile.

MONDAY

Helena checks her watch again. The girls are late, but at least it's not raining. There's no way she will ever set foot in Hawkins again. She leans against the postbox, ready to pedal off as soon as she sees Elaine and Gwen approach. Even from a distance, it's obvious Elaine's been crying. Helena might be short-sighted but she doesn't need glasses to see that her friend's face is one big red blotch.

'It's Percy,' Gwen mutters as a tearful Elaine cycles blindly ahead. 'Apparently he started fitting last night. Her mother's taken him to the vet. He might not be there when she gets home.'

Helena is slow to catch on. 'Are they going to operate?'

Gwen looks at her. 'They might put him down, Helena.'

Bloody hell, obviously Elaine is in no mood to discuss Jimmy Simmonds, but considering Helena hasn't heard Gwen's verdict yet, she jumps right in while Elaine is out of earshot. 'So what did you think?'

'Of what?'

'Jimmy!'

'Oh, the boy who came round to Elaine's on Saturday night with his peculiar friend Greg?'

'I don't know Greg,' Helena protests. 'It's Jimmy that I—'

'Yes,' interrupts Gwen, 'I know. Well, I can't see anything in him myself. I mean, he wasn't exactly scintillating company, and he was very rude when I asked if he'd heard Cliff's latest album.'

Helena's heart sinks. What if Jimmy thinks she's the kind of square that listens to Cliff too?

'Anyway, Helena, they barely stayed five minutes and then I believe they went to a party.'

'Do you know which party?'

Oh God, I hope he didn't get off with anyone else, thinks Helena.

Suddenly Helena is aware that Elaine is back with them. She has overheard the conversation and has braked sharply. 'Honestly, Helena Treace,' she yells. 'You are a selfish cow. Who cares about bloody Jimmy Simmonds when Percy might die?'

And with that Elaine pedals off even more furiously, with Gwen in hot pursuit.

Arriving at school Helena is locking her bike when she spots Sally strolling across the courtyard. 'Hey, Sall,' she yells, but Sally ignores her, in fact she seems to start walking faster and Helena wonders if she is trying to avoid her?

It's not until the mid-morning break that Helena manages to track Sally down to the girls' loos next to the library. Helena bounds over to where Sally is washing her hands at the sink and watches her turn pink in the mirror as she sees Helena approach. Has she contracted scarlet fever over the weekend, or is she blushing?

'Hey,' Helena starts. 'I've been trying to catch you all morning.' Sally looks panic-stricken. She stands back, wiping her hands on her school skirt, and there is an uncomfortable pause before both girls start speaking at the same time.

'How was your weekend?' they chorus.

'Mine was shit,' states Helena, and she is about to tell her about being grounded when Sally comes out with one long word that sounds roughly like, 'HelenaIgottotellyousomething andyourenotgoingtolikeit.'

Helena waits and Sally goes on. 'Thing is, I, er, went to that party on Saturday night and, er, I got off with this guy and . . .' Helena is grinning but Sally isn't; what's wrong with her? Helena would be chuffed to bits if she'd got off with someone at the weekend. Sally continues, 'He told me his name was Jimmy, but seriously, Helena, I didn't know until yesterday that he was your Jimmy Simmonds and now I feel awful, but I really like him and, well, I'm seeing him again.'

Helena feels like she does when the teacher says 'turn over your papers' at the beginning of an exam and for the first thirty seconds she cannot make head nor tail of the questions.

'Hold on a minute,' she says. 'So have I got this right? You went to that party, got off with a Jimmy but you didn't know he was my Jimmy and now you're going out with him?'

'In a nutshell, yeah, sorry and that, but you know, all's fair in thingy and thing.'

'Love and war,' responds Helena, faking an insincere and

terrifying smile, at which Sally spins on her heel and exits the toilets.

So, not just a shit weekend, thinks Helena, *but a shit Monday too*.

By the time Helena gets to her maths class, Sally is sharing a double desk with Claire Chambers and Helena is forced to take the spare place next to warty Angela Harris.

Mr Matthews isn't at his desk. Suddenly a small, vole-like woman bustles through the door and informs them that she will be taking the class as Mr Matthews is unwell and unlikely to be back before the end of term.

'But not to worry,' she smirks. 'He has already written your reports.'

Shit, thinks Helena.

Helena braces herself for an awkward cycle home with Gwen and Elaine after school, but she's unprepared for quite how awkward, as they squeal to a halt at the first set of traffic lights on The Drive. With the green man illuminated, two people begin to cross the road from the pavement on the opposite side, a boy and a girl. The boy has blonde hair and the girl is laughing. It's Jimmy and Sally. Of course it is.

'Oh, hi, Jimmy,' says Elaine.

'Um, yeah, hi,' responds Jimmy, looking unsure as to who Elaine is. Helena keeps her head down, praying for the lights to change so that she can cycle off at speed and feel some breeze against her burning cheeks.

By the time Elaine and Gwen catch up with her, she has blinked back the tears and informs them with as much dignity as she can muster, 'Jimmy Simmonds has decided he won't be requiring my services for girlfriend duties and has decided to employ Sally Winwood instead. Possibly because she knows how to give blow jobs,' she adds spitefully, which makes Gwen blink a lot.

'Honestly,' says Elaine, 'I think he's a fucking fool.' She doesn't swear very often so Helena appreciates the effort.

'Hear hear,' echoes Gwen. 'What a pranny.' And suddenly Helena feels moved to tears not only by the depth of affection she has for these two girls but also by their utter uselessness at really being able to help.

Before she peels off down the usual back street, she wishes Elaine luck with Percy, then she goes home to have a proper good cry in front of her bedroom mirror.

When Helena appears for supper with a swollen face and refuses pudding (tinned peaches with Carnation milk), her mother asks if she's coming down with something.

'I'm fine,' mumbles Helena, leaving the table and taking sanctuary once more in her bedroom where she starts making a list of 'Sad songs to play when you're heartbroken'. She has just added Eddie Holman's 'Hey There Lonely Girl' when there is a knock on her bedroom door and her mother slips in and sits on her bed.

'Listen, Helena, I know why you're upset and I know it's disappointing, but sometimes life isn't very fair and we have to deal with it.'

Helena is confused. How the hell does her mother know about Jimmy Simmonds?

'Fact is, I bumped into Lorraine Sanderson when I was out shopping and she told me.'

95

Now Helena is really puzzled. Never mind her mother, how the hell does Mrs Sanderson know about Jimmy?

For once in her life, Helena cannot think of anything to say, but her mother fills the silence. 'I know this summer is going to be hard for you, and that at times you might feel a bit lonely . . .'

Hold on, thinks Helena, *OK, I'm upset, but it's not as if we were going out with each other* . . . She opens her mouth to say this, but Alicia holds up her hand.

'I know you're going to feel left out, but as Mrs Sanderson said, they can't take everyone. There's only one extra space in the car and . . . well, it's just one of those things. I know it must be disappointing that Gwen has chosen Elaine, especially as we're not going away anywhere this summer, but we can't take any risks with Rosy.'

Finally the penny drops. Those bloody bitches! They're going on holiday without her and neither of them had the guts to tell her. Well, bugger them to hell, who wants to spend the summer holidays with those two idiots anyway?

Tears are splashing off her knees now and her mother is stroking her hair, which is something she only does when Helena's ill, or, as it turns out, when she has been betrayed by her supposed best friends. Small choking noises accompany her tears and her heart really hurts. Never mind Rosalind, what if she's the one with a life-threatening illness? That would teach them, if she died tonight; then they'd all be sorry – Jimmy, Sally, Gwen and Elaine, especially Gwen and Elaine.

Helena dries her eyes and lets her mother give her a cuddle. Alicia whispers, 'No more tears, lamb-chop. You're not a bad girl, Helena, and we all love you very much,' which makes her gulp some more and then the phone rings and her little sister yells, 'It's Juliet!' and her mother hurries downstairs. *Of course she does*, thinks Helena, wallowing in self-pity and a growing sense of fury.

TUESDAY

Helena cycles into school by herself, she's not waiting for those two bitches, but halfway down Kingsway, Gwen catches up with her. 'It's Percy,' she gasps breathlessly. 'He died last night and Elaine is too upset to get out of bed. Mrs Perks doesn't know what to do with her.'

'Well, I'm sure a nice holiday will cheer her up,' snaps Helena. For a split second Gwen looks shocked, but then she says, 'Please, Helena, can we get off our bikes and discuss this properly?' and Helena duly dismounts, her face thunderous.

She is still utterly livid. Last night she'd been up till midnight writing poems about the treachery of female friendships. 'Foes and woes' had rhymed nicely.

Neither of them can look at each other. 'My mum said she saw your mum out shopping,' Gwen eventually blurts.

'Yeah,' sneers Helena. 'Seems like you didn't have the guts to tell me to my face.'

'It wasn't easy,' admits Gwen. 'I could only choose one person, and, well, I chose Elaine because she and I have been spending more time together recently because, well, you've been hanging out with other people, and in any case, my mum thought she might be a bit easier.'

Whoa. Helena stops in her tracks. 'Your mum thinks Elaine's easier than I am? Has she got any idea how bonkers Elaine is? What with her animals and the way she won't eat anything that's green and wet, like cucumber, but suddenly *I'm* the difficult one?'

'You got pissed and threw up in her cheese plant.'

'We were all pissed,' protests Helena

'Yes, but you were the only one who was actually sick. My mum says sometimes you just don't know when to stop and then there's the boy thing.'

'What?'

Gwen continues, 'My mum said you behaved like a common tart when Nigel's friend Ralph came to stay, and where we're going, there's a beach which loads of teenagers go to and . . .'

No, no, this can't be happening, thinks Helena. Not only is she missing out on a foreign holiday and a tan, but it seems like she's missing out on a foreign holiday, a tan and a beach full of fit, French teenage boys.

Gwen says in a very matter-of-fact manner, 'It was a bit embarrassing actually, Helena. I mean, boys are just people too, I don't know why you get so hysterical around them?'

She doesn't get it, thinks Helena. She just doesn't understand. Maybe she's frigid?

There was an article about being frigid in *Cosmopolitan* once. Helena can still remember the phrase, '*Frigid women are unable to respond sexually, they can be emotionally cold and are often averse to the very idea of intercourse.'*

Yup, that was Gwen, the frigid weirdo, and Elaine is just as bad. Helena suddenly feels utterly outraged that a beach full of hunky French boys in skimpy swimming trunks are about to be completely wasted on the wrong holidaymakers. But rather than say anything more, she opts for a hurt, dignified silence, which works brilliantly, considering by the time they reach school, Gwen is weepy and apologetic and Helena, despite still feeling furious about missing out on the holiday, enjoys the rare sensation of having claimed the moral high ground.

As Helena struggles with the rudiments of photosynthesis in biology, she writes a 'SUMMER PLAN' in the back of her science exercise book:

1. Buy Tanfastic fake tan
2. Spend the summer holidays hanging out in St Anne's
3. Make some new friends and get a boyfriend

As lists go, it's quite modest. It's not like when she was small and genuinely believed in Father Christmas and for years never really got over the crushing disappointment that the man in red hadn't managed to smuggle a pony down the chimney.

Helena laughs, a cynical bitter laugh, like a woman in an Agatha Christie film, and Mrs Cram, the science teacher, shoots her a warning look.

Nipping into the girls' loos to change her tampon before

geography, Helena once more comes face to face with Liza Branwell's pouting reflection in the mirror. Liza eyes her warily, then blurts out, 'Yeah, well, that party was great and yeah, I did get off with Sticks, and as you know, Sally's going out with Jimmy, so you know . . . ?' Then she shrugs her shoulders in a 'what can you do kind of way', before banging out of the toilets, leaving a miserable Helena in a cloud of her dry shampoo.

WEDNESDAY

By the time Helena cycles out of the back street the next morning and on to the main road, she sees that Gwen is already waiting for her by the postbox. She's very much on her own.

Having avoided each other on the bike ride home from school the previous day, neither of them really knows what to say to each other. Gwen breaks the silence by explaining Elaine's absence. 'She's still far too upset to face school,' she says in a serious tone. 'I popped round just now. She looks awful and her mum says, considering we're breaking up on Friday, she may as well stay at home.'

Immediately Helena wonders whether Elaine might be too upset to go to France.

'Listen, Helena,' Gwen begins as they cycle two abreast down Kingsway. 'I don't know how you're going to feel about this . . .'

Here we go, thinks Helena. Already she can conjure up the taste of her continental breakfast, smell the intoxicating aroma of Ambre Solaire slathered on the glistening limbs of tanned French teens.

'Well, um,' Gwen continues, 'the thing is, Elaine really wants you to come too?'

It's on the tip of Helena's tongue to say, 'Well, yes, obviously this would be the best solution,' but her subconscious intervenes and stops her. Something doesn't add up. Surely they can't all go? Even Helena understands there's only so much room in the back of the Sanderson's car.

Gwen keeps talking. 'She says it won't be the same without you and that she knows deep down you loved him too.'

What on earth is Gwen talking about?

Helena brakes and Gwen follows suit. 'Sorry, Gwen, I'm confused. What are you talking about?'

'Percy's funeral. It's going to be on Friday evening. Elaine's burying him in the back garden. There'll be a ceremony, some sandwiches, crisps, sausage rolls, and a toast to Percy. I've still got some Babycham left over from when you couldn't come last weekend. Then obviously Elaine and I will need an early night because we're off to France at the crack of dawn on Saturday.'

Helena doesn't know whether to laugh or cry. Seriously, so this is what her end-of-term Friday night has been reduced to: a funeral for a dead Belgian hare.

But even as the words 'you must be joking' are forming on her lips, she instinctively knows that she will be at the graveside. She swallows back her disappointment, and mutters, 'OK then, straight after school?'

But Gwen shakes her head. 'No, remember we break up on Friday, so we finish early. Elaine would like us to go home and change into something more suitable and she says if there's a special song you'd like to bring to play, or a reading, in memory of Percy then that would be nice.'

Fucking hell, thinks Helena privately, but she nods and cycles on.

Helena has never been to a funeral. She'd been too young to attend her Grandmother Olive's funeral, while Grandfather Lionel and Nana Nancy's husband, Poppa Hubert, had died before she was born.

When Helena goes to visit Nana Nancy in her bungalow in Poulton-le-Fylde, Nana Nancy sometimes gets out her memory box and shows Helena Hubert's mouth organ, and his pipe and his shirt studs and signet ring. 'He was a very funny man,' she always says. 'He could have been on stage, he could sing, he could dance, he could tell jokes, he was very popular down the pub and he went every night, Helena, every night.' At this point her mother always rolls her eyes. 'Oh, ignore your mother,' Nana Nancy whispers. 'Her dad was a miserable old git. We used to have to spend Christmas day with the pair of them, Olive and Lionel; faces like a wet weekend. Never trust anyone who won't wear a paper hat out of a cracker on Christmas Day, Helena, trust me.' And Helena does.

With just two and a half days of school left before the holidays, Helena wishes Queen Anne's employed the same end-of-term traditions as her old primary school. This morning Rosalind had set off for Greendale's with both Kerplunk and Operation. Sadly, at the grammar, some teachers liked to operate their classes as if the summer holiday didn't really exist.

There are, however, some exceptions. Some weeks ago Miss Glenn the English teacher announced she would be getting married in August, and now in their last class of the year she informs them that 'in light of my own forthcoming nuptials and because your reports are already written, I've decided we're going to have a quiz instead of a lesson today. Just something fun,' she says, waving her hand around, her little diamond engagement ring winking on her finger, 'about marriage and romance in literature, art, politics and . . . well anything,' she trills.

She's like the rest of us, thinks Helena. *She can't wait to break up.* Miss Glenn has a glow about her and Helena wonders if she's already shagged her husband-to-be and if she'll be wearing white or 'ivory' (which everyone knows is a sign of having 'done it').

Forty minutes later, Helena has scored nine out of twenty, having correctly answered:

Romeo and Juliet
Anthony and Cleopatra
The Lady of Shalott
Fred and Wilma Flintstone
Jane Eyre and Mr Rochester
Cathy and Heathcliff
John Lennon and Yoko Ono
Queen Victoria and Prince Albert
Popeye and Olive Oyl
John F. Kennedy and Jacqueline Onassis

And that's that. The last English lesson of the year. Just this afternoon and tomorrow's classes to go, then on Friday morning it's the end-of-term assembly when the new head girl and deputy are announced and all the sixth formers cry. Once assembly is over, desks are cleared, reports are handed out and the girls are finally set free for six whole weeks.

Helena can't wait. *I'm going to have the time of my life*, she promises herself. I might not be going abroad, but that doesn't mean to say I'm not going to have fun, even if I am kicking off the holidays with a funeral for a dead rabbit – hare, she corrects herself.

With poor Percy in mind, Helena decides she can do without food for once and sneaks into the art room at lunchtime. In any case she doesn't feel up to facing Liza and Sally in the dinner hall today. Quietly she helps herself to the materials she needs and spends the next forty-five minutes carefully painting a Belgian hare in a field of grass studded all over with buttercups and daisies – a kind of bunny heaven for poor old dead Percy.

Making the card is oddly therapeutic. It gives her time to really think about her friendship with Elaine and Gwen and how much the relationship between the three of them just isn't the same. They've each changed so much – correction, *she's* changed. It's OK, she tries to persuade herself, you can still be friends, it's just never going to be what it used to be, and this realisation makes her breathless with loneliness.

She needs a best friend. Her sister Juliet's had the same one for years. Juliet's best friend is called Elizabeth Rittle. They met on their first day of primary school when they discovered their coat pegs were next to each other in the cloakroom. Elizabeth Rittle will be Juliet's chief bridesmaid, and vice versa. How typical of her older sister to have sorted out her 'best friend for life' so efficiently and easily.

As for Rosalind, she has a gang of adoring school mates, including Colin and Roger, AKA the Kray Twins of

Greendale's, who, despite being younger than Rosalind, would defend her to the death. Rosalind instils that kind of loyalty in people – that desire to protect her.

'Gwen,' Helena asks, breaking the slightly awkward silence as the two of them cycle home together later that afternoon.

'Have you ever thought of having your hair permed?'

Gwen rolls her eyes, 'Honestly, Helena, weird as it might seem, some of us are quite happy with what God gave us.'

Oh oh, thinks Helena, *I might have known God would be at the bottom of all this*.

'You're as bad as my mum,' Gwen continues. 'She gets annoyed because she'd like me to be more vain. She compares me to her friend's daughters and I fall short of her expectations, because the fact is, I'm a bit dumpy, I've got rubbish hair and I wear glasses but the thing is, I'm not fussed.'

Yes, but why not? screams Helena's subconscious. Gwen's parents are rich and her mother is always beautifully turned out, so much so that Helena's mum Alicia once said, 'Lorraine Sanderson looks like she's about to board the QE 2 even when she's in the supermarket buying mince.'

Helena can't help feeling that the Sandersons' money is wasted on Gwen. If her parents were anywhere near as loaded, she'd have a wardrobe bulging with cool stuff from Miss Selfridge and Chelsea Girl. Honestly, it's really not fair. Even Elaine gets more stuff bought for her, not because her parents are well off but because she's an only child. *Trust my luck to be one of three*, despairs Helena, as she waves goodbye to Gwen on the usual corner. 'See you tomorrow.'

THURSDAY

There is a vaguely carnival air about Queen Anne's the next day. The corridors reverberate with girls laughing and chatting and for once the teachers don't bother to tell them to be quiet. All the wooden cubbyholes along the staff corridor, normally full of deposited exercise books waiting to be marked, are empty, and even more cigarette smoke than usual seems to emanate from under the door of the staffroom.

I wonder if they're having a party behind that door, thinks Helena as she walks by on her way to the last geography lesson of the year, and momentarily she imagines brimming ashtrays, Twiglets and overflowing paper cups of Mateus Rosé.

The summer term, despite all its trials, has flown by. This time next year she will have completed her O levels and the school holidays will be overshadowed by the dreaded results day. She's seen her own sister go through this, though in Juliet's case it ended with tears of relief and triumph, rather than the sobs of regret that might befall Helena.

I might have to actually start trying a bit harder, she thinks, before spending the next forty minutes nodding off during a slide show of rock formations and ammonites, which the geography teacher mistakenly thought they might 'enjoy as an end-of-term treat', like it was *The Rocky Horror Picture Show* or something.

As is tradition at the end of the school summer term, the weather so far this week has been perfect. It usually is, right until they break up, at which point the skies cloud over and the rains blow in from the Irish Sea.

Refreshed from her 'ammonite nap', Helena strolls to the dinner hall with Gwen and some of her other classmates. All the corridor windows on to the internal garden quads are open and as she catches a whiff of pale-yellow roses, Helena suddenly senses something that feels a little bit like nostalgia. She is dizzy for a couple of seconds. Life already seems to be going quite fast.

Despite it being the hottest day of the year, today's school dinner consists of 'savoury mince and mashed potatoes'. It's basically shepherd's pie but without anyone bothering to put the potato on top of the meat. Pudding is pink blancmange. Helena sits with Gwen and her swotty maths chums. One of them asks Gwen if she wants to go over to her house to listen to records after they break up tomorrow. Helena feels peculiarly left out.

'I can't,' answers Gwen. 'Even though it's a lovely offer, Dee, but Helena and I have a funeral to go to.'

That shuts everyone up and while Gwen explains that the recent tragic death is pet-related, Helena decides to forgo the blancmange and spend the rest of the lunch break sunbathing instead. As she clears her plate and heads outside, she realises that no one seemed to notice her leave, not even Gwen.

Soon she is sitting on her own, back against the sun-warmed brick wall of the sports hall when Sally Winwood comes and sits down next to her. Helena can't be sure, but she suspects Sally has checked to see whether Alex or Liza are in the vicinity before she arranges herself on the ground next to her.

'My mum lays out on tin foil in our back garden, covers herself in olive oil like a great big salmon, then burns herself to a frazzle,' she says, before adding, 'I'm lucky, I've got my dad's colouring. I just go brown.'

Well, another point to you, thinks Helena, suddenly feeling very self-conscious about her doughy white thighs compared to Sally's slender caramel-coloured pins.

Helena closes her eyes against the sun and listens as Sally continues to talk. 'I'm sorry things got so messy, Helena. If it's any consolation, I might be going out with Jimmy but Liza hasn't heard from Sticks since the party. She's a bit pissed off to be honest, plus her grandma died last night, so she and her family are going down to Birmingham to sort a load of family stuff out. They're going to be stuck down there for a couple of weeks, so, you know . . . basically I just wanted to tell you that . . . well, the coast is clear, if you . . . not that I'm . . .'

Helena slowly takes in what she's saying. 'No, of course not!' she says, a little flicker of hope igniting inside her. 'But it would be nice to pop into the Monkey now and again and see you and the gang without Liza giving me daggers.'

'Yeah,' mutters Sally. 'I'm going to miss it, and Jimmy, of course, but I'm going on holiday for two weeks from tomorrow.'

Helena's heart sinks again. So that's everyone, literally

everyone going away apart from her. 'Where are you off to?' she asks, trying not to sound bitter.

She expects Sally will be going somewhere like Torremolinos, to one of those big white hotels with a pool and night-time entertainment, the kind of place Helena's parents would hate, especially her mother. Alicia can be very snobby. She once said that bingo was gambling by any other name and that Nana Nancy was an addict because she goes twice a week with her friend Madge.

No doubt Sally will get a really brilliant tan and even more cute freckles on her button nose and all the Spanish waiters will flirt with her.

'We're going on a Christian youth hostelling holiday,' Sally confides. 'But don't tell anyone. My parents are very religious, so we're going to spend the next two weeks singing "Kumbaya" round a campfire with a lot of men called Brian with beards and guitars.'

For once Helena doesn't know what to say. Maybe there is something worse than not going on holiday at all? She tries to work out the appropriate expression to rearrange her face into.

'Gosh,' she manages to stutter, before Sally bursts into shrieks of laughter.

'Ha!' she snorts. 'Got you! Of course we're not going on a Christian youth hostelling holiday. We're going to Torremolinos! Honestly, Helena, you really fell for that one.'

That afternoon, after her final lesson of the year, Helena cycles home alone. Gwen is in choir rehearsal, of course she is, *I'm lonely*, Helena admits silently to herself.

FRIDAY

The final-day assembly is held in the wood-panelled main hall with its vaulted ceiling. On the stage sit the teachers and the school prefects, while the rest of the upper and lower sixth have chairs on the balcony. Girls in the lower years are forced to sit cross-legged on the floor below, only standing when instructed for prayers and hymns. The hall is packed with girls of every shape, size and hairstyle, a mass of ponytails and pigtails, bobs and perms, fat girls, thin girls, brainy girls and girls who 'may have to consider secretarial courses'.

Inevitably during the two-hour ceremony there is a great deal of fidgeting and yawning, and once a girl in the lower fourth spewed up right in the middle of the head girl's departing speech.

This year Sara Brent, the outgoing head girl, is reading a poem. She begins her reading in a calm and measured tone, but as she gets to the second line she is audibly choked up and by the end she is sobbing uncontrollably. Helena feels like she might start laughing, the kind of out-of-control laughing that happens when someone makes a fart noise in class, even if it's not actually a fart but a squeaky desk lid that just sounds like a fart.

This always happens; the type of Queen Anne's girl who makes it to head girl or prefect always gets horrifically emotional about leaving school while the rest can't wait for the interminable service to be over so they can get on with their holidays. The head girl's speech, half drowned in tears, finally ends and a hysterical Sara is helped back to her chair while the head thanks her and 'her splendid team for all their hard work this past year'.

On it goes, prayers and hymns, speeches and special mentions, and goodbyes to parting teachers. A golden carriage clock is presented to a retiring geography master, and good-luck wishes bestowed upon Miss Glenn for her forthcoming nuptials. At this point there is a smattering of applause and someone on the sixth-form balcony dares to wolf-whistle long and hard, which makes Miss Glenn blush and the head look furious. The thanks and goodbyes are followed by a complicated madrigal by the choir and a violin solo by a girl Helena can't recall ever seeing before and then everyone stands for the school song and at last, as the huge clock above the stage nudges midday, it's all over and it's time for the girls to return to their form rooms, pick up their report books and leave the building. But not before the head reminds them that 'we don't want any silly nonsense on the way home, girls. Let's remember that you may be on holiday, but while you are wearing the Queen Anne's uniform, we expect decorum at all times. Don't let yourselves down, girls, and don't besmirch the reputation of the school,' but nobody is listening.

Hundreds of girls stream from the assembly hall, filling the corridors with chatter and laughter. In just an hour's time, the place will be deserted, save for a few stragglers and the caretakers in their brown overalls. Over the next six weeks, the school will be cleaned, painted and polished, broken furniture will be mended, outdated equipment replaced and a brand-new state-of-the-art audio language lab finally installed. It is 1975 after all, and technology is the future.

Helena finds her feet dragging slightly as she approaches her form room. Finishing school would be great if it wasn't for the downer of her report. If only she'd tried a bit harder and mucked around a bit less. Too late now. The brown manila envelopes are piled high on the form teacher's desk, and as Miss Glenn calls the girls' names out in alphabetical order, both Helena Treace and Gwen Sanderson are among the last to be called. In fact, by the time they are handed their reports, only Sharon Vincent is left waiting at her desk.

Free, thinks Helena. *Free at last.*

The toilets are crammed with sixth-form girls changing out of their uniforms and into something more suitable for the end-of-school piss-up at the nearest pub. Meanwhile, outside, a tide of brown uniforms flows out of the gates, as girls fill coaches, jump on buses and gradually melt away.

Usually, when they break up, Gwen, Elaine and Helena cycle halfway home before stopping at a Toni's café on the bridge for 'brown cows'. Helena isn't sure Gwen will want to stick to this tradition without Elaine, but as they cycle down the drive, Gwen shouts, 'Usual? My treat,' over her shoulder and Helena feels oddly grateful. There's nothing that says 'end of term' better than a great ball of vanilla ice cream floating in a special tall sundae glass brimming with Coca-Cola.

Having ordered at the counter, Gwen and Helena slide into a slightly sticky, cream vinyl booth next to the jukebox. Fortunately for Helena, Gwen can't play a Cliff Richard number on the Wurlitzer because none are available. The machine plays Motown records only, and at the moment Martha and The Vandellas are belting out 'Jimmy Mack'.

As the waitress brings over their order, Gwen tells Helena that even though it might be quite hot, she's going to wear the black velvet dress she wears for her piano exams to Percy's funeral, 'to show my respect'.

'Mad really,' chuckles Helena. 'Showing respect to a rabbit.'

'Belgian hare,' Gwen corrects her, but then she smiles and they chuckle together until Helena starts trying to pick open the flap of her school report envelope and Gwen stops laughing and looks at her in a disapproving manner. *Like a Sunday school teacher*, thinks Helena.

'Won't your parents go mad?' ventures Gwen. She has a big, frothy ice cream and Coca-Cola moustache.

'They won't know,' insists Helena, even though she has already torn the envelope. She'll swap it for a fresh one from her parents' stationery stash.

Seconds later Helena wishes she hadn't bothered. Her report is awful. Her eyes scan an uncomfortable number of C's and even a dismal D for PE. She's never had a D before. Her heart sinks as she skims the comments. *Helena could do better if she tried harder, Helena is an able but unenthusiastic member of the class, Helena could contribute more to class discussions*

115

but often seems to be half asleep.

The positive comments are few and far between. Her art teacher is nice – *Helena has flair and ability and when motivated produces some excellent pieces of work.* And English starts well, with *Helena has a vivid imagination and an engaging writing style*, but then Miss Glenn has added, *but her essays often lack detail and her spelling and punctuation are poor.* Helena glances to the left of the comments in the column where the grades are written and sees Miss Glenn has given her a B minus, the bitch. English is her best subject. *Surely* she deserves more than a measly B minus.

'I hope her groom stands her up at the altar,' Helena seethes, and, snatching a blue biro from the counter beside the till, she deftly changes the minus to a plus.

Gwen is horrified and blushes hard as she pays for the brown cows in silence.

Oh, here we go, thinks Helena. Miss Prissy Knickers is about to give me a lecture on being not only a thief but a cheat too.

But in fact they barely speak for the remainder of their journey, the uncomfortable silence only being broken by a half-hearted 'See you later' from Helena as she cycles off the main road and into the back alley.

Neither of her parents are in when Helena gets home, which is a relief. She switches the torn envelope for a fresh one from the drawer in her father's desk and leaves the report on the kitchen table. The inevitable post-mortem can wait. Right now she needs to find something black for Percy's funeral service. It's a five o'clock ceremony apparently, with a light buffet supper to follow. What a way to spend her last Friday night of term. Helena sighs as she burrows in her wardrobe for the black skirt she wore as the maid in *Le Bourgeois Gentilhomme*. It's a bit tight and the button's come off the waistband, but she can pin it with her little yellow smiley badge.

After a good rummage in Juliet's bedroom, she manages to find a slightly smelly Pink Floyd *Dark Side of the Moon* T-shirt. If she turns it inside out, you can barely see the pattern. It'll have to do.

Percy's funeral is a subdued event. Gwen has brought an LP of Mozart's classical chamber music from her parents' terrible record collection and Elaine plays it on repeat in the sitting room with the windows open so that they can hear it in the garden.

Helena hadn't been able to find anything suitably rabbit-related among her record collection, so she'd scribbled a short poem for Percy instead.

The three girls stand around Percy's grave. Elaine dug it herself. It's lovely spot, just under a weeping willow, which has always looked slightly out of place in the Perkses' small, suburban back garden. Alicia has often commented on it. 'I don't envy Mari Perks much, but I envy her that tree.'

Helena is finding it hard to concentrate. Elaine is in deep mourning. Even her hairband is black. Her mother hovers in the kitchen arranging the buffet; her dad, mercifully, is at work. If anyone could make this situation even more uncomfortable it's Gordon Perks.

Gwen has decided to go down on her knees with her hands in prayer position. The running order of the ceremony has been pinned to the tree beneath Helena's painting of Percy in heaven.

Elaine will begin with a eulogy to her much-loved pet, followed by Helena reciting 'Ode to Percy' and then, while Gwen says a prayer, Elaine will put Percy to rest in what is obviously a cardboard box that once upon a time contained a pair of size six knee-length brown leather boots from Russell & Bromley. Finally, once the coffin is in the earth and covered, the girls will join hands for a minute's silence, at which point Mrs Perks has been primed to turn off the record player and stand with her head bowed.

What a palaver, thinks Helena, desperately trying to keep a straight face, as Elaine rambles on about a girl's best friend being a Belgian hare and how when he first arrived as a gift for her eleventh birthday, Percy had been just a tiny defenceless bundle of soft grey fur, but that it soon became obvious that Percy's emotional intelligence put him above other mortal animals, elevating their relationship to a spiritually different level, and that she will think of Percy every day for the rest of her life. On and on she goes about Percy's favourite food and the welcoming noises he used to make when he heard her footsteps in the garage, his jumping prowess and his bravery over the eye infection that distracted her from the heart condition that caused his terrible, premature death.

At this point Elaine starts weeping and Gwen gets up to comfort her, shooting Helena a look of urgency and nodding at the tree. Helena finally takes the hint and launches into 'Ode to Percy', wishing instantly that she had given this poem a lot more attention than she had.

'Oh, Percy,
How we shall miss thee,
Hairy bundle
Warm upon our knee,
Percy, what a pal you were
Bright of eye and soft of fur'

There is a massive wail from Elaine at this point but Helena soldiers on.

'Loyal friend with a mighty hop
Who would ever think your heart would stop.'

Elaine sinks to her knees, shoulders heaving, sobbing harder than Sara Brent during final assembly, and as she lays Percy in his final resting place, Mozart booms through the open window and Gwen, shutting her eyes tightly, starts to pray.

'Father of all, we pray to you for Percy, and for all those we love, but no longer see. Grant to them eternal rest, let light perpetual shine upon them. May his soul and the souls of all the departed, through the mercy of God, Amen.'

Elaine and Helena join in with the 'Amen' as they all hold hands. Mrs Perks stops the music and the three girls stand with heads bowed for the required minute's silence.

Helena desperately wants to stop her mind racing. Why can't she just be still and think about Percy? But she can't. Her thoughts ricochet around like ball bearings in a pinball machine. She sees herself walking into the Blue Monkey where Sticks just so happens to be sitting alone, envisages her parents' faces when they open her report, imagines what Jimmy Simmonds would think if he happened to walk past the house now? And finally she wonders if there's money to be made writing poems for dead pets and tries her very hardest not to laugh.

SATURDAY

Helena lies in bed on the first day of her summer holiday wondering if she can be bothered to locate her clitoris. A few weeks ago, she'd looked the word up in an anatomy book in the school library.

Clitoris, she read: *A small erectile body situated at the anterior portion of the vulva and projecting between the branched extremities of the labia minora forming its prepuce and frenulum.*

Hmm . . . so what *is* the difference between the vagina and the vulva and why are sex education classes so hopelessly vague? Suddenly the hunt for her clitoris reminds her of 'hunt the thimble', the parlour game that Nana Nancy used to insist on playing.

Helena sighs, remembering how her nana liked to hide the thimble under the tea cosy in the kitchen. At least she's not likely to find her clitoris there. *It's not fair*, she thinks. Everyone in the whole wide world is off doing something more exciting than her and for the umpteenth time she thinks bitterly of her 'best friends' Gwen and Elaine, who are right this minute in

Gwen's dad's swish Ford Granada, heading for Dover to catch the ferry to France.

No doubt Elaine will still be blubbing her eyes out. Honestly, how could anyone cry so much over a dead rabbit?

Helena lies back, her hand still vaguely foraging around her front bottom and recalls sitting in the Perkses' front room after the 'service' with Elaine hiccupping through her tears and Mrs Perks turning in circles on the carpet like a performing poodle, offering everyone squares of brightly coloured Battenburg cake.

In the end, she'd got home a little after eight and tried to tiptoe through the kitchen and up the stairs without alerting her parents. Never mind burying a dead rabbit, the last thing she wanted was a post-mortem on her distinctly below-average school report. But the third stair had betrayed her with its tittle-tattle creak, and she'd been called into the sitting room.

Her parents had looked visibly upset. Simon rubbed his face while her mother twisted a handkerchief, the report perched visibly on the arm of the faded green velvet sofa.

Her parents turned the television off, which was always an ominous sign, even more so considering they were watching *The Likely Lads*, which was one of their favourite programmes. Helena had braced herself; this was going to get ugly.

'Shut the door,' Simon said.

Helena's heart sank as she waited for the inevitable.

'Obviously we're disappointed,' her father went on. 'You're a girl with so much potential, Helena, and that's just not reflected in this report.'

'*However*,' her mother had interrupted, 'your father and I feel that you've had a very tricky year and that we haven't given you our full support. We've been distracted what with Rosy being so poorly and Juliet starting at university. We've kind of left you to your own devices and I think, well, you may have felt a bit neglected.'

For some reason, at this point, Helena had burst into tears, and even now, she can't quite remember if it was relief or guilt than made her cry, or maybe it was a combination of both? Lying here now, still lounging in bed at 9 a.m., one hand inside her pyjama bottoms, Helena can't help feeling she's been let off the hook and makes a vague mental promise that next term she really will try harder. Who knows, one day in the future she might even decide to apply for university in London like Juliet?

Hmm, that was another thing, *bloody Juliet*. Helena feels a bit sick when she recalls her older sister's news. Apparently her parents had been waiting for the right time to tell her that, after spending a couple of weeks working on the posh scarves counter in Liberty's to earn some money, Juliet and her 'uni friends' would be flying off to Italy. Apparently one of them has a place there.

What sort of friends have a place in Italy? ponders Helena, instantly livid and now completely forgetting her quest. *Juliet really is a jammy cow.* Trust her to get a holiday job in a fancy department store, rather than changing sheets and cleaning toilets in a crummy hotel, which will no doubt be Helena's fate this summer.

However, Alicia's admission that Juliet won't be coming home for the summer seems to have played into Helena's hands for once.

'And that's why,' her mother had said, 'we've decided that you can redecorate your bedroom this summer. You can start stripping the wallpaper tomorrow and I'll fetch some samples from Curtis's in the morning while Rosy is at ballet, if she's well enough to go.'

A shadow had passed over her mother's face at that point, as it always does when she suspects Rosalind might be sickening again. Helena pushes the thought out of her head; she's sure her little sister is fine and her mum is just worrying unduly, but she decides to get up and pads down the landing to Rosy's room to check.

Outside her sister's bright-yellow bedroom, Helena surprises herself by momentarily closing her eyes and muttering, 'Dear God, please keep her safe', but to her relief as she nudges the door open, she sees that Rosalind isn't in her bed and her nightie is neatly folded on her pillow, which means she's up and dressed and as right as rain, which typically it is doing – raining that is; of course it is, it's the first day of the summer holidays.

Driven downstairs by hunger, Helena hopes to have the kitchen and breakfast room to herself. If Rosalind and her mum have already set off for ballet and the coast is clear, she will cook one of her mega breakfasts, complete with a pot of tea all to herself and loads of toast. But her dad is in the kitchen wearing his denim DIY apron and fiddling around making one of his complicated cups of coffee. Helena notices a tatty old washing-up bowl containing a grubby sponge and wallpaper scrapers sitting on top of the washing machine.

'I brought these in from the shed,' Simon explains. 'I thought you might want to crack on with getting that old wallpaper off.'

To be honest, the only thing Helena wants to crack is a few eggs: three at least, scrambled, with bacon and mushrooms, yum. But her father keeps banging on. 'You need to fill that bowl with hot soapy water, give the walls a good soaking and *then* start scraping. It's best to find a seam in the paper and slide the blade in from there.'

Knowing her father won't be satisfied until she makes a start, Helena gulps down some Frosties, before squirting Fairy Liquid into the bowl, filling it with hot water and carrying everything she needs upstairs on a wooden tray. By the time she reaches the top of the stairs, her pyjamas are soaking, so she uses her mum's hair dryer on them for a couple of minutes.

The wallpaper in Helena's room is woodchip. It has a texture like lumpy porridge. When they first moved here, her parents were going to 'do something about it', but what with one thing and another, they hadn't got round to it and the deal has always been that in the meantime, to cover it up Helena can stick whatever she likes on her ugly, lumpy walls.

Only now it's all got to come down, which is weirdly painful, like peeling plasters off a semi-healed scab. Down comes the *Diamond Dogs* poster, her *Jackie* magazine pin-ups of David Essex and Steve Harley, the slightly cross-eyed lead singer of Cockney Rebel. Down comes her Mark Bolan shrine and the fashion spreads from the rare copies of *Vogue* her mother let her disembowel. She moves around her bedroom ruthlessly. All of it has to come down, every Blu Tacked photo and postcard, even the review of the school play that refers to Helena's performance in *Le Bourgeois Gentilhomme* as 'impishly comedic'. She unhooks the picture of two ponies that Nana Nancy's friend Madge painted for her when she was going through her pony phase, and her swimming medal certificates, which her parents had framed, and peels away the grainy black and white photo of herself and Juliet cut out from the local newspaper featuring the two of them carrying a goldfish home from the local fair, captioned, 'Sisters Strike Gold (fish) at Fair'. Gilbert lived for less than a day.

An hour or so later, with her room stripped bare and all her pictures, posters and paper memorabilia in a pile under her desk, Helena begins to soak the walls, sloshing soapy water around until the woodchip is well and truly drenched, and then, taking the scraper her father had given her, she worries the blade under a sodden seam of wallpaper, and as she pushes the tool upwards, a rewardingly large strip of the paper comes clean away.

At around midday her dad appears, offering to 'chip in' and laughing uproariously at his own feeble joke. Together the two of them scrape away, eating garibaldi biscuits and listening to Radio 1. Simon delights in telling her which bands are rubbish and which are worth listening to. Helena mostly ignores him. Just because he's a music teacher doesn't rule out the fact that he is also an old fart who knows nothing about 70s pop.

After lunch (calorie-counted cheese on Ryvita and an apple), Alicia and Rosalind join in, though Rosy soon gets bored and disappears to do whatever eleven-year-old girls do. But Helena, Simon and Alicia plough on and by late afternoon the floor is littered with reams of soggy woodchip strips.

The school report isn't mentioned and instead Helena grills her mother about Juliet's trip to Italy.

'Where in Italy?'

'Tuscany, apparently.'

'Is that by the sea?'

'No, but the villa has a pool.'

'Bloody Nora.'

'No need to swear, Helena.'

Oh, but there is. 'And is Mr Magoo going?'

'If by Mr Magoo you mean Juliet's boyfriend Gareth, no, he's staying on in his uni digs in Birmingham. I think he's got some work in an orchestra.'

'Hmmm.'

'What's that supposed to mean?'

'Nothing, only I know he's meant to be a pianist but I bet he's doing some fiddling on the side.'

Helena's mother throws the damp sponge at her.

By six o'clock, all three of them have had enough and Helena, adding one of Alicia's rose-scented birthday bath cubes to Rosalind's old bath water, luxuriates in the scented, slightly grey water. Reaching for a discarded copy of *Woman's Own*, she reads an article about 'dealing with a prolapsed womb'. No wonder her mother had put the magazine in the bin. It's terrifying.

At seven, Simon returns with fish and chips, and Alicia lets them eat with their newspaper parcels on their knees in front of the television. They watch *The Good Life* with Rosalind, who pretends to get the jokes by looking around and laughing when anyone else does. Helena is *almost* enjoying herself, until she remembers that watching telly with your parents and kid sister is a really crap way to spend your Saturday night, and she grabs the book of wallpaper patterns her mother lugged home from Curtis's that morning and stomps upstairs.

For the next hour or so she plays her favourite records and experiments with putting her hair into lots of skinny little plaits, just to see what it looks like in the morning. Of the three Treace girls, Helena has the straightest hair. They are all blonde, but Rosalind and Juliet's tresses are more pre-Raphaelite, their hair ripples, while Helena's, although satisfyingly thick and shiny, refuses to curl.

She spends the rest of the evening trawling through the wallpaper patterns book. It's bewildering. There are so many patterns, colours and textures. There are designs featuring trees and birds, geometric shapes, concentric circles, vivid stripes, random splodges. Helena is confused. *Who is she and what does she want?* Which wallpaper screams, 'I am Helena Treace!' Or rather, Lenni Treace? Her new nickname for herself hasn't really stuck yet. She imagines herself saying to a complete stranger, 'Hi, I'm Lenni,' and wonders how it would sound.

Eventually she sees the pattern she wants – it's a kind of pink and purple swirling floral design. Bold and bright, like her, like her new life is going to be.

It's gone ten now and raining heavily. Helena switches her bedside light on, noticing how different the shadows look on the bare walls.

The wall beside her bed looks so empty, like a blank page.

Without thinking, she picks up a biro from her desk and starts to write on the freshly revealed pale-pink plaster.

Hi, I'm Helena Treace. I am fifteen years old.

I have blonde hair and two sisters, I want to be famous and I want a boyfriend, I luv David Bowie, Marc Bolan, Roxy Music and spaghetti bolognaise, which isn't a band by the way.

I'm a Pisces, which means I'm indecisive, romantic, imaginative and pleasure seeking – oooer Mrs! At school my best subjects are English and art, but I think I might want to be an actress, yeah right, in my dreams. Anyway, here I am . . .

Helena draws herself in a cartoon *Jackie*-magazine style. She makes her face more heart-shaped than it actually is, her eyes bigger, her hair wavier, she puts herself in a skinny-rib V-neck T-shirt with a pair of really wide flared jeans, striped socks and the denim wedges from Dolcis that her mum refused to buy her. She looks cooler than she really is, but that's fine, because this is the Helena she's going to grow into this summer. Her life is going to change, she can feel it. Underneath the message she writes the date, 26th July 1975.

PART TWO

2021

HERMIONE

SATURDAY

I run my finger over the blue-biro message.

The girl who wrote it has drawn a picture of herself too, all legs and hair, wearing massive flared jeans and ridiculous platform shoes.

The writing, which is old-school italic, is dated 26th July 1975, which means this Helena Treace was sleeping in my bedroom when she was the same age as me, almost half a century ago.

I quickly work out how old she would be now and google 'Helena Treace actress' to see if she's in a film or a soap or something, but nothing comes up. Course, she could have changed her name; showbiz types often do. My dad had an actor mate called Bobby Stardust, whose real name was Robert Smellie.

As I sit on the bed rereading Helena's message on the wall, the room suddenly feels different, darker and colder, and I swear I can smell fish and chips. Suddenly I'm so tired I feel like getting back into bed so I lie down and listen for a minute to what sounds like rain on my window. Only how can it be raining, when my mother is stretched out on a deckchair on the back lawn catching rays in her undies?

Suddenly I feel overwhelmed by it all, the move, missing my friends, the unfamiliarity of everything, this house, the relentless loneliness and uncertainly of it all and before I know it, I'm fast asleep.

It's early evening by the time I wake up. Even my mum has given up on the sunbathing and has come indoors reeking of coconut and clanking around in the kitchen with bottles of gin and tonic and an ice bucket; she's even put crisps into little bowls. 'We're having a take away,' she grins. 'Pizza. I'll order your usual, with extra salami and pineapple,' and she snorts with laughter, because this is her idea of a joke.

I've slept for hours but even so, I feel weirdly groggy. Back in my room, I google Marc Bolan on Spotify and let a song called 'Ride a White Swan' pulse through me and the next thing I know I'm dancing. I'm dancing and I'm wondering, if Helena was here with me, whether she'd be dancing too.

1975

HELENA

SUNDAY

Sadly the hair experiment backfired. Once I took all the plaits out, I was left with this hideous frizzy mess and I had to wash it out using a saucepan over the bath, because our rubber shower hose attachment has got a great big hole in it. Dad told me I could mend it with a puncture repair kit, but seriously, I mean, why haven't we got a decent shower like at Gwen's house?

Dammit, I was trying not to think about Gwen, because when I think of Gwen I think of Elaine too, and the pair of them not even noticing how many cute boys there are on the beach, playing volleyball and running into the sea.

I remind myself that I live by the sea too, but let's face it, it's not the same kind of sea. For starters our sea is so full of sewage it's basically brown, and our beaches aren't exactly full of sexy tanned teenagers; it's mostly pensioners with blankets on their knees, false teeth chattering in the breeze.

It's raining, of course it is; that's the summer holiday tradition. I wish I had the guts to go into town by myself but everything will be shut, apart from the Blue Monkey and I don't think I'm ready to just waltz in on my own. So I waste the day finishing off the wallpaper scraping, listening to the radio and eating snacks from the pantry because Simon and Alicia have taken Rosy to visit some friends who moved to the Trough of Bowland. 'You're welcome to come with us,' Mum said, like I didn't have better things to do, though to be honest I was glad when they got back, because sometimes I get a bit scared when I'm in the house by myself. Honestly, sometimes I have to remind myself that I'm fifteen years old and this cannot be how I spend my summer holidays, eating biscuits and playing Kerplunk with my eleven-year-old sister. Tomorrow, I promise myself; things will start to happen tomorrow.

HERMIONE

MONDAY

Apparently, Paul has taken this week off work. He came downstairs this morning bulging out of a bright-pink Aertex T-shirt stuffed into the waistband of a pair of blue shorts which pulled tight over his lady bum. Everything looked three sizes too small. He looked like he'd been blown up with a bicycle pump and I swear I saw Mum push her breakfast away. This doesn't bode well. I've seen her go off men before. It doesn't take much. They eat a boiled egg badly or wear grey slip-on shoes. One got dumped for having a stupid middle name and sounding a bit Welsh, even though he was from Basingstoke. Thing is, she can't afford to go off Paul. If she wants to live in this nice big house with the posh sun-loungers, she's going to have to put up with him wearing long socks with trainers and having calves that remind me of going on a school trip to Barcelona once and seeing tapas bars with windows full of massive hams.

Remembering my old school makes me feel a bit sick. I mean, it was crap, because all schools are, but sometimes the crap you know is better than the crap you don't know, and I miss my mates, and social media only makes it worse. Typing messages isn't the same as sitting in Rhiannon's bedroom with Millie and Amisha trying to get high on tin of hairspray which turns out to be empty, and sniffing a Pritt Stick instead, which I can tell you right now is no class A. In any case, they don't seem to have even noticed I've gone. They're all getting on with their summer, which is boiling hot, obviously – because London is nearer the equator than the bloody north – and they're hanging out in the park with boys from The Charter School and queuing to get into Brockwell Lido.

Paul says there used to be a lido in St Anne's, and he goes misty-eyed and repeats 'fun times' until I want to vomit. Apparently, it closed down in 1989, which is like over ten years before I was even born, so totally of no use to me whatsoever. He says he's going to potter around the house today, maybe do a spot of gardening, tidy up the garage. My mother looks faintly horrified, as if having him around the house wasn't really part of the deal. I think they're still a bit surprised to see each other during daylight hours. I get the impression that before Paul invited my mother to share his home and the rest of his life (presumably), they conducted a relationship that was a great deal more nocturnal. They met when my mum worked in the bar of a wannabe four-star hotel in Waterloo which Paul frequented while on 'business'. Basically they were bonking every other week for about six months before Paul switched jobs and the prospect of never seeing my mum again forced him into a drunken offer of sharing a future together. My mum jumped at the chance. I'm not sure at this point he even knew I existed. Sometimes I feel a bit sorry for him. I know my mum's professional barmaid persona and she's ever so much fun, but in reality she's quite hard work, and she comes with a load of baggage (including me) that most men would run a mile from.

I can't really stay around the house while the two of them are acting out this terrible happy-family sitcom, especially when the actors are so badly cast – my mum, pretending that she wouldn't rather still be in bed with a black coffee and a fag, and Paul, wandering around looking dazed as if he can't understand why on earth he's sharing his house with a couple of complete strangers? No wonder his bowels are playing up.

Before I slip out of the house, I take the precaution of nicking a fiver out of my mum's purse. It's not like it's hard earned any more. Paul is giving her an allowance until she finds 'some kind of gainful employment' (he'll be lucky). I add a fistful of ten-pence pieces from the big glass jar that sits under Paul's desk and head for the door.

1975

HELENA

MONDAY

Wonders will never cease, it's actually not raining. I lie in bed eating Alpen and rereading what *Jackie* magazine says this week about how interesting things happen to interesting people. They say that if you look like you're having fun then fun will usually follow, that basically fun is contagious; a bit like a verruca then.

I snigger at my own joke, leap out of bed, get dressed, stuff the magazine in my bag and head downstairs.

I refuse to mope about this house a minute longer. I'm never going to get a boyfriend/tan hanging round here.

I spur myself on by belting out the chorus from mum's favourite song on her Helen Reddy album, 'I am strong, I am invincible, I am WOMANNNNN.' Then I ferret around in all the coat pockets in the cloakroom for any loose change and find fifty pence in my dad's winter overcoat; result. That's my coffee and bus fare sorted. I'm not cycling, it's naff. I'm heading into town for a mooch. With any luck I'll bump into someone I know and if not, maybe it's time to make some new friends?

HERMIONE

It's warm enough for denim shorts, but I nabbed one of Paul's cashmere sweaters on the way out to be on the safe side; you just can't trust those northern isobars. The jumper is baby blue and I notice it's been darned on the elbow and wonder whether his dead wife mended it.

I can't find my headphones, which is driving me crazy, but I've got everything else I might need for the day shoved into my knock-off Prada shoulder bag. Seriously, you can't tell the difference. Amisha's dad had a stall in Camden. Honest to God, I never realised how cool my life was until I ended up here.

No one sees me leave, so no one can ask me where I'm going or what I'm going to do when I get there, which is a relief because I haven't got a clue. But there's bound to be a Costa round here somewhere, and if the worst comes to the worst, I'll do what me and the gang usually do in London – I'll use my fake ID, buy a bottle of Smirnoff Ice and go and sit in a park. Though the prospect of doing this on my own is a bit weird.

When I was little and I used to go on holiday with my mum and dad, or with my mum and one of her mates, or my mum and her latest bloke, Mum used to push me into making friends. When I said I was shy, she'd say shy people aren't really shy, it's just an excuse for being boring. She used to choose a spot on the beach as close to a family that had kids around my age as possible – the more kids the better – then she'd hiss 'go on, they won't notice an extra one'. And sometimes they didn't. Sometimes I'd end up hanging out with proper families, families with big picnic hampers, complete with sandwiches and cold cooked sausages wrapped in tin foil. My mum didn't really bother with lunch on holidays, not when it was hot and there was a beach bar, so I used to sit on the edge of other people's towels and help myself to their crisps.

I discovered that I wasn't really shy, though because some people used to laugh at my name and say stuff like, *Oh, Hermione, is it, so where's your wand?* I'd call myself something easier, like Alice, Katy or Hannah.

I turn left out of the house. There's a big recreation ground opposite and behind the boundary fence sits an estate of small red-brick houses with woodland at either end. On the corner up ahead is a dark-yellow stone church, all stained black like it's been burnt, but I think it's just rain and dirt. There's a battered 'Jesus Loves You' poster on a wooden hoarding outside. Across the main road, on the opposite side, I can see a pub called The Blossoms with a massive car park. I decide to make a detour through the churchyard, I don't know why; my feet just instinctively walk that way. The path is shaded with overhanging trees and gravestones on either side. My spine tingles and I think about my mate Millie, who's a fiend for a graveyard. She once dragged us all up to Nunhead Cemetery. I think we were trying to have a séance and Millie kept pointing out all these gravestones of dead babies and kids and then it started pissing it down so we caught a bus to Peckham for tacos.

But it's different being in a graveyard by yourself. Suddenly I feel this odd heaviness in my heart and a cold shiver runs up my spine. I'm glad I borrowed Paul's jumper.

I leave the churchyard through a wooden gate and cross over the road to the bus stop. There's no shelter and nowhere to sit, so I lean against the nearest garden wall and wait for the stupid bus.

Paul said I'd want the number 11, and as luck would have it, five minutes later one turns up, a funny-looking thing, the same kind of shape as those old-fashioned London Routemaster buses people sometimes hire for weddings and stuff. As I step up to pay my fare, a blur of blonde hair streaks in front of the bus's windscreen, causing a squeal of brakes from a car travelling too fast in the opposite direction. The driver blasts his horn and a girl jumps up behind me, breathless and laughing.

HELENA

I manage to catch the bus by the skin of my teeth, almost trampling over this girl who is just hovering at the front of the bus and blocking the way.

'Well, go on then,' I grin, moving past her. She really does look a bit gormless. Pretty but gormless.

HERMIONE

I'm confused for a moment as there doesn't seem to be anywhere to swipe for contactless payments, but I move along the bus behind the blonde girl, and follow her up the stairs to the top deck. Upstairs smells shockingly of cigarettes, as if the smoking ban doesn't exist in the North. The blonde girl takes the front seat on the right above the driver, which is my favourite seat, but considering she got there first, I sit across the aisle on the left. She glances at me and smiles, pulls out a battered packet of cigarettes and asks me for a light. To be honest, I don't smoke cigarettes, but I do carry a lighter in case anyone has a cheeky spliff on the go, so I dig the pink disposable lighter out of my bag and as I stand up and hold the flame to her slightly bent cigarette, the bus jolts and I almost fall on top of her. She laughs, patting the seat next to her, so I sit down and she offers me a cigarette. I smile and say no thanks. There's no way I'm going to be the one who gets fined for smoking on this bus if an inspector gets on.

Figuring I've got nothing to lose, I ask the blonde girl her name.

145

HELENA

This is the opportunity I've been waiting for! I take a puff of my cigarette, have a tiny choking fit, and then I say it out loud for the first time.

'I'm Lenni.'

It feels weird, like I'm wearing a false nose or something.

I look at her to see if she suspects anything, but she doesn't seem to. I notice she's done her make-up really well. She's wearing eyeliner and mascara, sort of sixties style with a little cat-like flick at the corner of each eye. I'm wearing a new blue mascara. It's an experiment and to be honest, it's a bit claggy.

'What's your name?' I ask.

HERMIONE

'Hermione,' I tell her. She looks puzzled, as if she's never heard the name before, which is a first. 'Like in Harry Potter?' I add, figuring I might as well get it in before she does, but before she can react, a woman comes up behind us with a large metal contraption around her neck and says, 'Fares, please.'

I can't believe Lenni hasn't put her cigarette out! I guess either there's no smoking ban here or they're just very relaxed about the rules. It's crazy; we haven't been able to smoke on buses for years in London. I didn't know the north had different laws.

She says to the lady, 'Half to St Anne's, please,' and she gives the woman some copper coins, which the woman slips into this leather money belt around her waist. She then makes some adjustments to the metal contraption, turns a handle and it prints out a ticket. I don't know what to do, so I copy Helena and say, 'Half to St Anne's, please,' and I hand over a fifty-pence piece, which the woman inspects closely for a minute. Then she shrugs and exchanges it for a ticket and a handful of loose change. The coins are all strange though, and when I add them up they come to 41 pence. So that's 9 pence for a bus ride? That can't be right.

Helena grins at my confusion. 'You're not from round here, are you?' She's Northern, but not full-on *Coronation Street*. I say, 'No, I'm from London,' and I imitate the *EastEnders* theme tune, which seems to confuse her, so I quickly add, 'But I'm living up here now, just round the corner.'

'Ooh, me too,' she says. 'Arundel Road, number 49.'

I blink. 'Hold on,' I say. 'That's where I live, number 49, opposite the housing estate?'

But she just shakes her head, and says, 'No, there's no housing estate, just sports fields. Do you mean Arundel Close? We sometimes get their post.' I must look confused, because she adds, 'Listen, don't worry, if you're new round here, you can hang around with me. I'll look after you.' She grins again, and for a moment I almost relax because it seems like I've just made a new friend, only there's something strange about her, about all of this.

She stubs out her fag and gets a weird vintage magazine out of her bag. She opens it up, like it's completely normal, and immediately begins drooling over a pair of denim hessian wedges retailing at a crazily cheap £6.99 from a shop called Freeman, Hardy and Willis, then starts flicking through the pages again, pausing only to drop a quick kiss on a full-colour photo of a very young Marc Bolan, who I know for a fact, because I looked him up on Wikipedia, died in 1977.

I peer round her so I can see the date on the front cover.

I blink. It reads 24th July 1975.

148

HELENA

The girl keeps blinking. Maybe she's got a nervous tic? There's a girl in my school who jerks her head like a pony. She can't help it, it's just one of those things. I flick to the back of the magazine.

'Right, what star sign are you?' I ask, adding, 'I'm a Pisces, which apparently means I'm indecisive, romantic, imaginative and pleasure-seeking.'

HERMIONE

Hold on, I've heard that description before.

The bus stops at some lights and, glancing out of the window, I notice there seems to be some sort of old-fashioned car rally going on.

I try to shake off the creeping feeling that something is very wrong. My brain starts working overtime. 'What did you say your name was?' I ask.

'Lenni,' she replies, then she adds after a moment, 'But my real name's Helena.'

Suddenly there is a roaring noise in my ears and my head swims as suddenly all the pieces click into place – the strange coins, the smoking, the old-fashioned cars, the date on the magazine, the girl looking quizzically at me – and even though I know that logically this can't be happening, I also know that somehow it is. It is 1975 and I am sitting next to Helena Treace, the girl who wrote her name on my bedroom wall.

HELENA

For a moment, I'm freaked out because it looks like she might faint. Not that I haven't seen people faint before. Girls are always fainting at my school, like when we dissected a frog in biology and Claire Chambers went down like a sack of spuds, or when the girl in the lower sixth who everyone says has got an eating disorder passed out in the dinner queue.

In the end, Hermione just goes really pale and then seems to get herself together again. She keeps just staring at me with these big wide eyes though, so I tell her to put her head between her knees and breathe, only she says she can't breathe with her head between her knees and she feels a bit claustrophobic and can I take my hand off the back of her neck? So I do and then I open a window and she gets some colour back in her face. Not that she's got much in the first place. She's really pale. I think her legs are even whiter than mine, though they're loads thinner.

Maybe she's travel sick, I muse. Some people are like that. Whenever we go on school trips, there's always someone puking up. I offer her a Fox's Glacier Mint from the bottom of my bag and rub her back like I've seen Mum do with Rosy when she's not well, and she gradually starts breathing normally again, though she's still muttering 'fucking hell' over and over again.

I wonder if she's got delayed concussion, because Sandra Casey once got hit on the head with a hockey ball and was absolutely fine until she collapsed halfway through a biology lesson, but eventually this Hermione seems to give herself a little shake and a moment later, as if nothing strange had just happened at all, she says she's a Taurus.

Which is cool, I tell her, because that means we'll get on, as long as she doesn't get all bossy, to which she smiles and says she'll try not to.

Because she's new to the area, once she's sitting upright again, I point out some landmarks, like the local comprehensive, which it turns out she's due to start at in September.

I tell her the girls from the comp call the girls from my school 'the brown virgins' and she laughs loudly. It's the first time I've heard her laugh and as soon as I hear it, I want to make her laugh again.

By the time we get off at the square, I've found out that she likes David Bowie, but she looks a bit blank when I mention Suzi Quatro. She asks me what gigs I've been to and I tell her me and my mates went to see Gary Glitter in Preston last year and even got asked backstage but my friend's dad was waiting in the car across the road from the venue, so we couldn't go. 'Good job too,' she said, looking weirdly shocked, which didn't really make much sense to me, because who wouldn't want to go backstage with a pop star and hang out in his dressing room?

I decide to take her to the Blue Monkey. It's a bit like having an exotic pet on a lead. Maybe it's because she comes from London, but she's got this kind of weird, cool vibe about her. On the way I point out where the cinema is and the theatre and the park and I tell her that when it's properly hot everyone goes to the lido and her eyes light up. Maybe they don't have those in London?

The Blue Monkey is pretty empty, and so we sit in a booth and Hermione looks at the menu and laughs at the prices and I say, I suppose it's cheaper than London? And she says, you could say that, and she offers to pay for anything I fancy. So I order a Fanta and a teacake and she asks Bitchy Sandra for a cappuccino and Sandra snaps, 'What's that when it's at home?' So Hermione says never mind and gets a Fanta instead like me, and laughs some more when Sandra gives her the change. I tell her to bung some of it in the jukebox, liven the place up a bit, and as she walks towards it, I feel a thrill of excitement at sitting in the Blue Monkey with my new, cool friend – then suddenly I get anxious in case she picks something really crap on the jukebox and I can't ever talk to her again.

HERMIONE

Oh God, I can't believe any of this is happening. I'm in 1975 trying to select a cool 70s song on an actual 1970s jukebox! I don't even know how to work this thing. It's not like Spotify. I can't just type 'cool music from the 70s' into the browser. I have to put the right money in the slot for starters, and then use a dial thing to choose a track. Seriously, I feel like my mum must do when she has to do anything new and complicated on her phone. I drop a weirdly large 5p coin from my bus change into the slot and the machine lights up. As I lean in to take a closer look at the choices, I spot a Marc Bolan track. I already know Helena loves Marc Bolan – she kissed his face in the magazine and wrote his name on her bedroom wall – so I press the corresponding numbers and hope for the best.

Beats start reverberating around the café. It's . . .

HELENA

It's 'Hot Love!' Hermione's a Bolan fan too! This is turning into the best day ever. I grin and she grins and we do a thumbs-up at each other at EXACTLY the same time, then she sits back down again.

I ask her lots of questions:

Where did you live before?
In a flat in South London with my mum
Where's your dad, sorry, he's not dead is he?
No, he's not dead, he lives in London but somewhere else, he's well, he used to be in bands, but um, they're separated, in fact they might be divorced, but I doubt they ever got round to doing the paperwork.
Have you got any brothers and sisters?
No, no pets and no brothers and sisters
God, you're so lucky, I've got two sisters and I'm the middle one, so I get ignored most of the time, have you got a boyfriend?
No, but I identify as straight, so you know . . .

(No, I don't know.) So how come you're living here now?

Basically my mum, Tess, hooked up with this bloke called Paul who was staying in the hotel where she was working in London, but it turns out he lives up here. He asked us to move in as they've decided to make a go of it together, so . . . here I am, she finishes.

My eyes grow wide as she tells me this. She's smiling, but I feel a bit sorry for her. It must be really hard to leave your home and all your friends in London and come to a little town like St Anne's.

'What's he like, this Paul bloke?' I ask.

'Complete plonker,' she says, and we both laugh. 'Only he's letting me redecorate my bedroom, in bright-orange paint, which is nice of him, I guess.'

'I'm redecorating my room too!' I tell her, 'in a kind of psychedelic purple floral pattern,' and she gives a massive smile and says it sounds great.

Just then the door clangs open and three lads roll in, and one of them goes, 'Budge up, girls,' and the next thing I know, OH MY GOD Sticks is sitting right next to me! Dog-breath Gazza has sidled in next to Hermione and the other lad, who I don't actually know, is at the counter buying a pot of tea for three and juggling sugar cubes. Hermione is telling Gazza what her name is and holding out her hand to shake, which is weird. She doesn't seem fazed by the arrival of three strange boys. She doesn't blush or touch her hair or start chain-smoking, though she does kind of flinch when Gazza breathes out and I don't blame her because even I can smell his breath from the other side of the table, like a burned egg. Sticks must realise this too, because he gets a packet of Polos out of his pocket and offers them around and when Gazza reaches out his hand, Sticks says 'take two, mate'.

'So what are your names?' asks Hermione, cool as anything, to which Gazza says, 'I'm Gazza, he's Bazzer and this one here –' he jerks his thumb at Sticks – 'is a Steven, but we call him Sticks on account of the drums.'

Oh, be still my beating heart, why did no one tell me that he's a drummer? So that's where his name comes from. Nothing to do with the fact he looks like a skeleton. And as if to prove it, Bazz puts Cozy Powell's 'Dance with the Devil' drum solo on the jukebox and Sticks drums along on the table with a broken biro and a dirty fork and he's like *brilliant* and even Hermione, who I am realising doesn't do impressed, looks impressed, and I can feel his leg next to mine, which is fine because Liza Branwell is at her nan's house so hahaha.

His eyes are pale grey and his hair is what my mum calls dishwater blonde and I don't think he tans very easily either because his forearms look a bit pink and raw, like he caught them in the sun, but that's fine because it means we can both burn together and then I can lend him my aftersun.

Gazza asks Hermione about what it's like to live in London and does she know Pinner because he's got an aunty that lives there called Gwen Barlowe and does Hermione know her? And Hermione explains very patiently that London's a really big place but she'll look out for her when she next goes back.

She catches my eye and we smile and I don't want her to ever go back.

Suddenly Bazzer checks his watch and says, 'Ladies, we

must leave you, gotta see a man about a van,' and they all get up and leave.

What's weird is that even when Sticks has gone, I can still feel the heat of his leg next to mine, see the little round cigarette burn on the thigh of his jeans, and just as they're about to disappear round the corner from the café, he turns and gives me a wave through the window.

'That boy fancies you,' says Hermione, and I can feel my scalp prickle as I blush from my chest to my roots.

'How can you tell?' I ask.

'Just can,' she says, adding, 'He's quite cute, if you like the freshly dug-up corpse look,' which makes me laugh Fanta out of my nose.

Later on, after we've mooched around Boots and she's bought some lip gloss and a load of pic 'n' mix from Woolworths, we go and sit on the grass in Ashton Gardens. The sun is getting lower in the sky but it's still warm as we stretch out on our backs eating sweets and talking about boys and music and life and I do an impression of Bitchy Sandra's face when Hermione asked for a fancy coffee and Hermione laughs and says, 'You crack me up, Helena.'

Eventually the sun dips down behind the trees and it's time to go home and I wonder if I should ask her for her phone number but I feel a bit shy, so instead as we're sat on the bus home, I write my number on the back of an old envelope which I find at the bottom of my bag. It's got a shopping list on it that my mum sent me to the Co-op for a few weeks ago, and I pass it to her and say, 'Just call if you want to hang out. A lot of my friends are away at the moment,' and she takes

158

it from me and smiles and puts it in her bag, though as I hand it over I notice the shopping list includes Dr White's night-time pads, which is kind of embarrassing.

I want to say, come for tea, meet my little sister, we can play records in my room and eat my mum's famous watery lasagne, but I don't, and instead we sit on the top deck of the bus doing a 'How loyal are you?' quiz in my *Jackie* magazine. We both score mainly B's, which is good because it means we're loyal and caring but not scared of dobbing on our mates if we think they could be in danger. Then we get off the bus and I reluctantly wave goodbye as I cut down the back street and she goes round the other way by the church and by the time I get home, I already miss her.

HERMIONE

I'm still pinching myself as I wave goodbye to Helena, before slipping through the gate into the graveyard.

I can't believe what has just happened. Helena is great. She's really funny and really kind and just ... different. She feels younger than me, even though she's a couple of months older. It's like she's got this sweetness, a sugar coating, that makes me want to protect her.

The weirdest thing about all of this is that I can't tell anyone about it. For starters, it would sound mental, and in any case, I'm still not sure if any of it is actually true?

Maybe I hit my head or accidentally took a load of hallucinogenic drugs like Amisha's sister did just before her French A level. She still got a D, which wasn't bad considering she was off her head on mushrooms.

But I didn't hit my head and I don't eat mushrooms, which drives my mum mad because I pick them out of everything with my fingers. So I guess it must be real.

As I exit the graveyard on to my road, I wonder if it's going to be Paul's house or Helena's that I arrive at, but I can see the estate opposite as I approach, so I guess it must be Paul's.

The house is quiet when I get in, so I go and lie down on my bed and consider the facts.

I got on a bus in July 2021 and spent the entire day in another millennium, hanging out with a girl who lived in the same house as me almost fifty years ago.

I know I haven't made Helena up because I check in my bag and I've still got the envelope she wrote her name and number on, and the writing matches the message on the wall. Helena Treace is real, and right now I feel closer to her than any of my old friends who are 250 miles away, even though right now in 2021 Helena must be sixty-odd, and probably married with kids or even grandkids of her own.

I can't quite get my head around this scenario. All I know for certain is that life was loads cheaper in the 70s and Boots used to have a record department at the back of the shop! Who knew . . .

I must have dozed off, because the next thing I know it's seven o'clock and Mum is standing over me telling me to get my skates on because we're going out for dinner. She's all glammed up; tight white jeans, big hair and strappy heels. She is rosy from the sun and her lips are a sticky coral colour.

'Where are we going?' I ask.

'La Dolce Vita,' she says. 'It's a pizza place in town; hurry up.'

I'm still in a daze, but I do what I'm told. I slip into a floral playsuit and my pride and joys, a pair of vintage red studded cowboy boots which I found in a charity shop last year, and head downstairs.

Paul blinks rather hard when he sees us. The stink of his aftershave almost knocks me off my feet and he's wearing one of those awful shirts with contrasting cuffs and collar.

Sometimes I feel sorry for Paul, because he's so determined to have a nice time. He lets the top down on his tragic convertible and refers to us as 'his lovely ladies' before putting on his Raybans and whacking the stereo up as high as he can. Inevitably Bruce Springsteen blasts out of the speakers and I sit in the back wanting to die.

Paul is musically possibly the uncoolest man I have ever met, and I think about my dad with his massive collection of weird old vinyl and foreign bootlegs and I wonder when I'll see him again? He still hasn't replied to my message. It's been ages since he even texted.

It's weird being back in the same town I last visited in 1975/just a few hours ago. The only shop that's still in exactly the same place is Boots. All the other shops have changed, some are boarded up, and the big posh department store on the corner is empty and for sale.

Suddenly Paul veers off the main drag, parks up and turns off the ignition. 'Here we are, girls,' he announces, pointing to a restaurant across the road. 'La Dolce Vita!'

My world seems to tilt as I get out of the car, because I'm one hundred per cent positive La Dolce Vita used to be the Blue Monkey, although inside it's much bigger than it used to be, with brand-new red leather booths, black and white floor tiles and massive monochrome stills from old films hung on the walls.

My reflection in a big silver-framed mirror is ghostly

white and Paul asks if I'm feeling OK.

'She just needs some food,' my mother butts in. 'Low blood sugar. Get her some olives and few breadsticks and she'll be as right as rain,' then she shoots me a look as if to say, *buck the fuck up*.

So I try. I say 'this is nice' and Paul looks grateful before puffing out his ridiculous chest and stating it's 'as good as anything you'll find in London'. I wish he wouldn't do this, because it just makes me want to snipe back, 'Oh really, have you been to Quaglino's?' which would just be bitchy. In any case I only ever went to Quaglino's once, and even then my dad's credit card was refused and he had to phone a mate to come and pay the bill.

La Dolce Vita is basically a pizza joint, but because it hasn't got a salad trough, it thinks it's posh. It's got those big movie-set-style lights, massive, laminated menus and giant, phallic pepper mills.

We order. Paul attempts the correct Italian pronunciation for his *quattro formaggi*, which sounds fucking ridiculous, my mother just wants a *tricolore* salad and I go for the *penne arrabiata*, because I need something simple that I can eat off a fork while my mind adjusts to living in two different time zones.

My mother, who has ordered a bottle of Pinot even though she's the only one drinking, asks, 'Has this place has been here long?'

'Oh, once upon a time it used to be a very different establishment, believe you me,' says Paul, and he laughs at his own non-joke, like he always does.

Seriously, it's bizarre. He makes these really inane comments but reacts like he's listening to a brilliant comedian in his head. 'I think you'll find that once upon a time, back in the annals of history (chortle, chortle), this place was a coffee bar for the young reprobates about town (chuckle, chuckle). I even used to come down here myself now and again.'

'Oh, you rebel, you!' says Mum.

'It was called the Blue Monkey,' reminisces Paul. 'There was this sign outside the door, a painted blue monkey holding a cup of coffee with his tail! It was a bit of a dive, to be honest. When the new owners bought it, they knocked through to the optician's next door and tarted the place up.'

So I didn't dream it, I have been here before. And now I know there's no way I could have imagined it, because how would I have known the name?

I came here forty-five years ago with a girl called Helena Treace, a girl with blonde hair who once upon a time slept in my bedroom and wrote about herself on my bedroom wall.

If all this was happening in a film, I'd probably enjoy it. I loved *Back to the Future* when I was a kid, but when it happens to you in real life, it's different. I excuse myself from the table and nip to the ladies', my head buzzing with questions.

1. What if it happens again?
2. What if it *doesn't* happen again?
3. What if it happens and I get stuck there, in a world of shit coffee and no mobile phones?
4. What if Helena realises that there's something not right about me and, I dunno, they burn me as some kind of futuristic witch?

But somehow I can't see that happening. In any case, if I don't see Helena, it's going to be a long, lonely summer until I start my new school in the autumn. And besides, I really like her.

By the time I get back downstairs, my mother has drunk two thirds of the bottle of wine and is letting Paul feed her his pizza crusts. This is typical of my mother. Her self-discipline dissolves in alcohol and before I know it, she has ordered three tiramisus, even though I don't want a pudding and I'm desperate to go home.

When we finally leave forty minutes later, my mother is swaying slightly. Paul hands a cloakroom ticket to an old woman perched on a stool behind a flip-up counter. As she passes me my denim jacket, I realise with absolute certainty that it's Bitchy Sandra from the Blue Monkey.

HELENA

I was hoping she might call tonight. I even checked to see if the phone had been put down properly – sometimes it gets knocked off the hook – but it was working fine. She just didn't call. Maybe I won't ever see her again? I really hope I do though, and in case I do, I go to bed thinking of all the fun things that we can do together around town. Like, I can take her to the lido if it's sunny, then I remember I've got an interview for that chambermaid job at the Cravendale Hotel tomorrow morning, so if I get that I'll have some money too, and maybe we can go clothes shopping together. I bet she's got great taste. I honestly can't think of anything better than spending a summer with my new friend. I mean, it would be nice to have a boyfriend, but even if Sticks did ask me out, I'd still want to see Hermione. Then I stop thinking about Hermione and think about Sticks for a bit before I fall asleep.

HERMIONE

TUESDAY

The next day, my mum is hung over and pretending that Paul's offer of a trip to the local garden centre is a dream come true. Ha! I know for a fact that Mum's 'dream come true' would be a snog with Daniel Craig and front-row tickets to see Robbie Williams in concert. They offer me a lift into town and I have a job persuading them that I'd rather take the bus.

'I need to get my bearings,' I insist as I usher them out the door, 'so I can find my way around.'

Soon as they're gone, I turn left out of the house again and walk down to the end of the road, then left again, past the church on the corner, and over the road to the bus stop.

A bus comes almost immediately, only this time when I get on, it doesn't stink of fags and there's a contactless payment facility, so I get off, pretending I've forgotten something.

I'm panicking slightly, trying to think what I did differently. It can't be my shoes, because I was wearing the same sneakers, and anyway this isn't *The Wizard of Oz*.

I decide to retrace my original footsteps and finally, it clicks:

I walked through the graveyard last time, and even though the place gives me the creeps, it's got to be worth a go.

As I step through the gate I have to admit, there *is* something magical about the place. Fat bees buzz and the air is heavy with the scent of roses, and there's something else . . . a sensation around the back of my neck, a fizzing in my veins, a feeling that someone is trying to tell me something. Even though I'm a bit freaked out, I'm tempted to hang around and explore a bit more, but I also want to get back to 1975. I want to see Helena.

This time as I walk through the gate on the other side and back out on to the main road, I can feel the difference in the air, and sure enough, a moment later a stinking 1970s double-decker rounds the corner. I bound straight up the stairs, hoping that Helena might be on board already, but she isn't, so I sit by myself on the top deck.

Behind me, two young pregnant women spend the entire journey whispering about their varicose veins and sharing a cigarette, which I have to remind myself was completely normal in the 1970s even for pregnant women, besides, as one of them says, 'they're only menthol so they don't really count.'

It feels weird to be back in the 1970s without Helena and there's a voice that nags at the back of my head, *Yeah, great idea, Hermione, catch the magic bus and get stuck back in the dark ages* . . . But I figure if I got back safely before, then surely I can do it again, especially now I know that the graveyard is the key to it.

The bus drops me in the square and the differences between time zones are even more noticeable now that I haven't got

Helena to distract me. Everyone on the street seems to be wearing 1970s fancy dress, but really casually, as if for a low-key party. Lots of flares and puffed-sleeve blouses, some hilarious patchwork shirts, a few fringed suede waistcoats and loads of denim. There's more wood and less plastic and metal around, like the bus shelters and the bins, but the biggest difference is that not a single soul is looking at a phone. In fact, modern technology doesn't seem to exist yet at all. A shop advertising 'the latest in electronic goods and home entertainment' has a window full of fat-backed TVs, record players with smoked Perspex lids and huge radio-cassette players. My dad always told me that romance died when cassette tapes went out of fashion but I'd rather have my Spotify playlists any day, thanks. Instinctively I feel for the iPhone in my pocket and slide it into my bag. Some things are best kept hidden, especially when they haven't been invented yet.

So far, Helena has excused anything weird about me as being 'a London thing', which suits me just fine as a cover, but I'd still better be careful, as who knows how she'd react if she found out the truth.

It's quite warm when the sun comes out from behind the clouds, but I've learned from teeth-chattering experience not to trust the weather in the north, even in July. Today I'm wearing my trusty denim jacket over a vintage Hawaiian shirt that I bought for a laugh at Camden Lock, my black jeans and a filthy pair of red Converse trainers. I had a quick look at 70s fashions online and realised that some of my clothes might give the game away. Thankfully, I've always been a bit of a charity-shop kind of girl, so I've got enough vintage stuff to keep me under

169

the radar. Money is something else I have to watch out for. Back in the twentieth century, pound coins didn't exist, which gave me a shock when I passed Sandra a fiver in the Blue Monkey yesterday and she handed me back a pile of pound notes and some loose change. Fortunately Sandra isn't the type to check the dates on bank notes, and with all the change I got back, and given how cheap everything is in 1975, that should keep me going for a while.

However, I've also clocked a pawnbroker's in the square, in case I need a load of readies in the future. I'm sure I've got something I could flog if I needed to.

I walk up the high street and round the corner to the Blue Monkey, hoping that I'll see Helena in there. A bell rings as I push through the door. Today the air inside the café is thick and blue. Basically, the place stinks, but it only takes a few breaths to get used to it – chips and fags with a top note of BO and a tang of something sweet and citrusy, a perfume perhaps, or maybe an air freshener, fighting hard to do its job.

The seats by the window are full of people I don't recognise, so I hover at the counter, about to order a peppermint tea, before deciding to leave the 'peppermint' out of the order. 'Just a tea, please,' I tell Bitchy Sandra, who is back to being in her late twenties, rather than pushing seventy, as she was when she handed us our coats in the pizza restaurant last night.

I check out the back of the café, looking for a place to sit. There are people sprawled everywhere. Most are teenagers with a few twenty-somethings sprinkled into the mix. Some of the older lads wear leather jackets covered in studs. I'd noticed a couple of massive motorbikes parked up outside on my way in, and quickly put two and two together. They must be bikers, or maybe even Hell's Angels?

I take a seat at one of the tables by the toilet, wondering how I'm going to swallow the hideous milky dishwater that Sandra has poured into a thick white china cup for me. Without Helena here, this is all a bit weird. Suddenly I notice Sticks and I wave, but he pretends not to see me. He's in one of the booths and a girl is sitting more or less on top of him. She's wearing a low-cut, cheesecloth gypsy-style top, and her boobs are spectacular, but her face is mean and covered in a thick, orange-coloured foundation. Instinctively she senses me looking in their direction and throws me a dirty look before whispering into Sticks's ear and then convulsing into fits of giggles. She laughs so hard her boobs nearly fall out of her top.

'Not many of them to the pound,' comments one of the Hell's Angels loudly, passing her as he walks back from the gents', and as he says it, he mimes weighing the girl's boobs in his hands and for some reason she laughs at this too, along with everyone else in the café, rather than telling him to fuck off.

I decide to drink my tea and head for the park, but just as I'm forcing down another mouthful, the sky darkens, thunder rumbles in the distance, and everyone goes 'oooooh' as the lights flicker and rain splatters across the windows. Seconds later, the door clangs open and Helena comes running in. I watch her as she scans the room, the expression on her face changing from relief to be out of the rain to confusion and embarrassment when she sees Sticks with the girl. Her cheeks flush and she looks so mortified that I immediately stand up and without thinking, shout, 'Hey, Helena!' and the way her face lights up when she sees me makes me feel properly happy for the first time in ages.

HELENA

What the hell is Liza doing back? Soon as I finish my job interview, I head to the Blue Monkey, hoping to find Hermione there, but the first thing I see is Liza and Sticks. I'm about to turn around and scarper, rain or no rain, when I hear someone shout my name from the back of the café and when I realise it's Hermione, a massive smile breaks across my face.

I don't want to walk past Liza, but knowing I've got an ally and that Hermione is on my side, I decide to take a deep breath and kind of propel myself forward towards her. I can feel people are watching us, A) because Hermione just shouted really loudly, B) because she's a new face in town and C) because she is pretty damn drop-dead gorgeous.

As I brush past Liza Branwell, who is openly scowling at me, I pretend to have clocked her for the first time, and I say straight to her face, 'Hi, Liza, I'm so sorry to hear about your nan. I heard you had to go to Birmingham.'

'Yeah,' she pouts, 'but I'm back now,' and she wriggles closer to Sticks, who looks down at his Fanta. I can't see his face, but

I notice that the tips of his ears are very red.

'But you have to go back for the funeral,' he mutters, giving me a sideways glance, which I completely and utterly ignore. The cheek! I notice he's wearing the jeans with the hole in the thigh again.

'Yeah,' grimaces Liza. 'The bloody funeral. Thought I might wear this top, give the vicar a heart attack. What d'you reckon, Sticks?'

And she pushes her tits out at him. I don't hang around to hear what Sticks thinks, instead I make a beeline for Hermione, who for some reason decides to hug me in the middle of the Blue Monkey! Maybe it's something people down south do? It's definitely not something we do up north though, and as I disentangle myself from her, there's a jeering wolf whistle from some older bloke in a leather jacket sitting in a booth at the back. He licks his lips and says, 'Don't let us stop you! Come on, girls, we could all do with a floor show.'

At this point I could quite literally die of shame, but Hermione turns around, eyeballs the man in the leather jacket, gives him the finger and simply says, 'Oh fuck off, you weirdo letch,' at which point, to my utter amazement, Bitchy Sandra starts whooping and clapping from behind the counter and yells, 'You tell him, darling!' and the next thing I know, everyone's laughing and the bad atmosphere breaks and suddenly the sun comes out and I promise you and this is no word of a lie, at that precise moment a bloody great rainbow sticks its neck out of the clouds and everyone gawps like it's a magic trick.

'Let's get out of here,' mutters Hermione, wincing as she

finishes her tea, and together we walk out of the door.

Out on the street she links her arm through mine like it's the most natural thing in the world, and the sun shines so hard we can almost see the pavements drying in front of our eyes as we make for Ashton Gardens. 'So what's the deal with that Liza girl?' she asks, squinting across at me as we stroll through the square. And it all comes tumbling out, all the trouble of the last few weeks, the shoplifting and being grounded and not being able to go to the party and Liza getting off with Sticks and Sally getting off with Jimmy and how in one night I lost my chance with the two boys that I fancy most in the whole world. Honestly, I tell her, I'm going to die a virgin.

'How old are you?' she asks, squinting at me again.

'Fifteen,' I say.

'Well then,' she says. 'It's illegal till you're sixteen anyway.'

'Have you ever done it?' I ask.

She shakes her head. 'But I have done other stuff.'

'Like what?' I ask, leaning forwards.

She smiles. 'You know, the usual.'

'Like what? Snogging?' I ask.

'Yes, I've snogged,' she says, laughing.

'Well, that's more than I've done!' I say.

Her eyes go wide and I tell her about my one and only kissing experience at the Radio 1 Roadshow, hoping to make her laugh, but she doesn't find it very funny.

'Well, in that case,' she says, 'this summer we should get you well and truly snogged.'

'I agree!' I say, and we both fall about laughing.

After a bit more prodding, Hermione finally admits she's

done most things, 'but not penetration' as she calls it.

I can't really think of anything to say to that, so I just say 'gosh', and then we both sit there laughing and saying 'gosh' in increasingly shocked tones like maiden aunts until I have to nip behind the bushes for a pee because I'm not paying a penny to use the public convenience, which makes Hermione laugh even more and she goes for a pee behind a bush too and as I stand guard for her I think to myself, it's like we've been best friends for years.

When we've calmed down a bit, she asks, 'So where were you this morning anyway?' and I tell her about the interview for the hotel chambermaid job, and that I start tomorrow, and she frowns and says, 'But you're only fifteen. I thought you had to be sixteen to have that kind of job?'

London really does seem to have a completely different set of rules to up here in Lancashire.

'I'm only making beds,' I tell her, 'and I'll be finished by lunchtime, so it's perfect really. My sister used to do it.'

And after that I let rip about Juliet and how jammy she is, what with her holiday in Italy with her uni mates and then I find myself telling her about Rosalind and how ill she was and I have to try very hard not to cry. Hermione just listens while I blurt out all this stuff about ambulances and blood transfusions and vigils through the night.

When I tell her all this she doesn't try and change the subject like Elaine would do or tell me to have faith in the Lord like Gwen. She just listens, she listens until even I'm bored of me, and then she tells me a bit more about her dad, how she sees him less now than when he was in prison.

Prison! I have to try very hard not to look shocked, even though this is by far the most exciting thing that has ever happened to a friend's parent. I realise as soon as she tells me that I'm going to have to keep this one quiet, because if I ever told my parents, they'd jump to conclusions about Hermione and how she must be really rough, and she's not, she's lovely.

'OK, that's enough serious stuff!' says Hermione suddenly, wiping tears off her cheek, and she pulls both of us up on to our feet and we run over to where she's spotted an ice-cream van and Hermione treats us to two 99s with flakes and strawberry sauce. As we sit on a slightly damp bench eating them, I see two boys walking towards us, one of them, the short one, has a dog on a lead. There's something familiar about them, but I can't see without my glasses – damn being short-sighted. As they draw close, I realise the taller one is Jimmy Simmonds

'Oh cute!' says Hermione to the shorter one, who's holding the dog. 'My nan had a Westie, but it had to be put down because it got doggie dementia and started weeing in the wardrobe. Unless it was my nan who was weeing in the wardrobe and she was blaming it on the dog!'

The boys laugh and I realise that this is what Hermione does, she talks to boys as if they're normal, as if she is just talking to girls. She doesn't seem to differentiate between the two species, which is great until she goes on to tell them, 'To be fair, we just wee'd behind the bushes.' To which Greg responds with a mock bow, saying, 'I applaud you, ladies, considering the female anatomy is not designed for al fresco urination,' which makes all four of us laugh even more. He's obviously a bit of a strange one, but he does make me laugh and it suddenly crosses my mind that maybe he and Elaine would make a nice couple? Which reminds me that just about everyone I know is away on holiday, and out of politeness – and to prove I'm no longer under the spell of his wink – I ask Jimmy when Sally's back and he says sometime next week and both of us blush.

Suddenly Greg looks up at the gun-metal grey sky and, like an old man, says, 'Looks like rain. Come on, Jim, I'd better get Buster home,' and the two of them disappear through the gates.

'Are they a couple?' Hermione asks.

I'm confused for a minute. 'Who, Jimmy and Sally?'

'No, those two . . . Oh wait, was that *Jimmy*? The winker?' Hermione asks.

'Yes,' I say wistfully.

'Hmm, guess not then,' she mutters to herself, then seeing the look on my face, she rubs my arm sympathetically.

The wind has got up and I realise my cords are damp from sitting on the bench and I'm shivering slightly, so we decide to go for a little walk to warm up.

As we stroll back through the square, we see a crowd from the Blue Monkey hanging around outside the phone box on the corner by Woolworths and it turns out there's a couple of lads prank-calling random people from the phone book and everyone's donating two-pence pieces to keep them going. Hermione and I hang around on the edge of the group and I get the feeling she thinks it's all a bit naff but I'm not ready to go home yet, and in any case being on the edge of something feels better than being left out completely.

I see Alex leaning up against the wall and wave at her, then when I turn around, I notice Hermione is sitting on one of the benches near the bus stop and she's talking to Susie Jones, who I used to know from Brownies. Susie and I have quite a tricky relationship because she thinks I'm a snobby bitch and my sister Juliet was her sixer in the elfs at Brownies and apparently was a bossy cow, which I can well believe. My heart sinks when I see the two of them talking to each other, but I brace myself to join them because I can't have Susie spreading all sorts of malicious lies about me to Hermione.

Hermione grins as I wander over. 'Susie's been telling me about a party tonight,' says Hermione.

Susie looks vaguely annoyed. 'I didn't say *everyone* could come,' she snaps.

'Where did you say it was again?' nudges Hermione.

'It's at Liza Branwell's. Her mum's away because of her nana so her older sister is having this party tonight from around eight o'clock, only you've got to bring a bottle – 17 Renton Road.'

Hermione looks at me, her eyes glinting with mischief.

Renton Road isn't far from my house, in fact it's just round the corner from my old primary school.

Susie Jones and I were in the same class at Greendale Primary and to be quite honest, I never liked her. In fact I was relieved when she failed the eleven-plus and we ended up going to different secondary schools, but right now I could kiss her.

HERMIONE

Helena is so thrilled about the prospect of a party that she talks about it non-stop on the bus home: what she's going to wear, what kind of booze she's going to try and lift from her parents' stash, how she's going to have something light for tea, so she doesn't feel too full, and then back to what she's going to wear again. I can't help smiling at how excited she is, and I feel myself getting excited too. Her enthusiasm is infectious.

We part ways again at the entrance to the alleyway that leads to the back gate of the house we both live in, forty-five years apart, and Helena makes me promise to meet her at this exact same spot at eight o'clock, which is in three hours' time.

'You could always come round to mine first?' she offers, but I make some vague noises about needing to check with my mum first and have something to eat and in the end she just shrugs and says, 'OK, maybe next time,' and for a moment, seeing the disappointment on her face, I feel like saying *OK! I'll come* . . . In truth, there's nothing I'd like better than to get ready for a night out with Helena – I bet she's got some killer 70s clothes I could try on – but I have no idea what's actually possible at this point. Is it only town I can go to? Can I go into people's houses? Can I go into MY house, which is also HER house? What would happen? I just don't know where the lines are yet, the ones that I can't cross, so until I do, I decide it's better to play it safe and meet her on the corner instead.

'You can always ring me if you change your mind,' Helena shouts as I walk away from her. 'You've got my number, right?' and I say, 'Yes, I've got it. OK cool, see you at eight!' and carry on walking until I'm back at Paul's house.

If Helena and I existed in the same time frame, she would have walked through the back door just a couple of minutes earlier and we would bump into each other in the hall, but obviously we don't. The only trace of Helena in this house is her handwriting on my bedroom wall.

However, someone else is obviously visiting, judging by the buggy parked inside the what Paul calls 'the vestibule' and I bend down to pick up a red knitted elephant that's been dropped on the floor.

'Thanks, that's William's,' comes a voice from the living-room doorway and I look up to see a rather fat, bad-tempered-looking woman standing there with her hand out. She has exactly the same jawline as Paul's dead wife Melanie. Very quickly I put two and two together. I hand over the elephant.

'You must be Sally?' I say, smiling.

'Lucy, actually,' she replies.

Dammit, that's what I meant to say, but before I can apologise something starts screaming in the sitting room and she instantly disappears. I put my head around the door and there's this horrific scene of domesticity spread out all over the sitting-room floor. A brightly coloured knitted blanket has been laid out on the carpet and sitting in the middle of it, surrounded by a billion toys, is a screaming purple-faced toddler. Seriously, the kid is the colour of a plum. Perched right on the very edge of this scene is my mother. Mum looks like she might be heading for a migraine. Her face is kind of screwed up and one eye is tightly shut. Paul, on the other hand, is on his hands and knees on the blanket pretending to be a dog. 'Woof-woof!' he barks, and the baby screams, 'Woof-woof!'

'That's enough, Dad,' says Lucy, and she scoops the kid up and plonks him on her knee.

My mother spots me at the door. 'Oh goodie,' she says over-brightly, 'Hermione's here. Let's make a fresh pot of tea and you two girls can get to know each other.'

Lucy and I exchange dubious looks and she fakes a smile. Jesus, the woman has the gums of a donkey.

My mother pushes me through to the kitchen. 'It's a bloody invasion,' she hisses. 'The invasion of the hideous toddler, and of course Paul is besotted.'

Apparently, they are staying the night. My mother looks stricken. 'I have to cook supper and everything.'

I'm wondering if now is the right time to ask her if I can go out tonight, but I decide it's not the moment. I'm going to have to just slip out later, say I'm going for a walk. With any luck, I can still meet Helena on the corner at eight.

HELENA

I knew this summer holiday was going to be great, I just knew it! OK, maybe I didn't, but now I've met Hermione and we've got a party to go to and everything is just brilliant.

I wish she'd give me her phone number and I wish I knew where she lived, but she's a bit cagey about all that and I have this horrible feeling that maybe she's really embarrassed about her 'unfortunate circumstances', as my mum would put it. Maybe this Paul chap doesn't really live in a nice big house? Maybe they live in a grotty flat somewhere, maybe they don't even have a phone? It would explain why she hasn't called.

Anyway, I don't have Hermione's number and I don't have her address, so I just have to hope that she's waiting for me on the corner at eight, although I've already decided that if she doesn't turn up by ten past, I'm going by myself.

I'll tell Mum the girl having the party is someone I used to go to Brownies with and it's mostly for girls who went to Brownies, like a sort of Brownie reunion, and that I'll be home by eleven.

The house is empty when I get in but a roll of wrapping paper on the breakfast-room table reminds me that Rosalind was invited to the twins' birthday party today and that Mum has probably gone to pick her up. As for Dad, he could be anywhere. I take advantage of the house being empty by helping myself to biscuits and eating cereal out of a mug, a habit my mum can't stand. I add a banana and a glass of Ribena to my mini feast and make my way upstairs to get ready, even though I'm not a hundred per cent sure I'm going to be allowed to go yet.

The state of my bedroom shocks even me. It looks like a bomb's hit it. The walls are mostly stripped now, which adds to the air of dereliction, plus my clothes are all over the floor and I forgot to make my bed before I went out this morning.

I decide to give my hair a Charlie's Angels makeover by borrowing my mum's electric curlers, so I creep into my parents' bedroom to fetch them from her wardrobe. Their big double bed with the pink candlewick bedspread is neatly made and I wonder what it must be like to sleep with the same man for over twenty years? Then I wonder what it would be like to sleep with any man, or rather boy, full stop. Obviously I'm not really thinking about *sleeping*, I'm thinking about shagging, which is what people call it, even though my mum says the word is common and demeans the act of lovemaking. Then I wonder if my sister ever got round to doing the deed with Gareth Morley or if she's in Italy right now shagging someone else?

I plug the electric rollers in and decide to paint my nails while I wait for them to heat up. I go for a bright-blue colour, even though it's gone a bit sticky because I've nearly finished the bottle. Dammit, I wish my birthday was in the summer and then I'd have a whole new stash of clothes and make-up to play around with. I'm so bored of the stuff in my wardrobe and I can't help wondering if Hermione has some cool clothes I might borrow one day? She always looks great, even when she's just wearing jeans and a top. There's something about the way she wears clothes that just looks a bit different, and I can tell that other people think so too. She's what Nana Nancy would call a 'head turner'.

Hanging out with Hermione is great because we get on so well, but I also have to admit, I like the extra attention I get when I'm with her, and when it's the two of us getting attention together, it gives me the confidence to deal with it. I know I'm OK because Hermione's OK, she can handle it, like she handled that idiot in the Blue Monkey. I honestly feel like she might be the friend I've been waiting for. She might be my Elizabeth Rittle! Only an interesting version. Because to be brutally honest, Juliet's best mate Elizabeth Rittle has the personality of dishwater. But that's beside the point, I suppose, because what people really want from a friendship is someone who sticks with them through thick and thin, and really understands how their brain works and how their heart works, and if they can make you laugh on the side, well then, that's a massive bonus too. It's like my mum has this friend she met at art school and even though Angie lives in Australia and they only ever phone each other on their birthdays because it's so expensive, my mum truly loves Angie, and if an airmail letter arrives from Melbourne she gets really overexcited. Whenever Mum talks about Angie, you can see what she would have been like when she was twenty. My dad has a mate from his college days too, a guy called Tom that he was in a skiffle group with, once upon a time. Sometimes Tom will arrange to meet Dad in Blackpool and the next day my dad can't get out of bed. Tom doesn't come to the house because my mum doesn't approve of him. Apparently he's a 'reprobate', which I had to look up in the dictionary (it means rascal).

I hear Mum and Rosalind coming through the back door. Rosalind is shouting my name and I go down even though I haven't yet painted the nails on my right hand. She is pink-cheeked and is clutching firmly with both hands a paper plate containing a great wodge of chocolate cake. It's for me, from the twins' party. I'm about to say I don't want it, but I do; it looks really chocolaty. While my mum is distracted in the kitchen putting on the kettle, I casually inform her that 'I've been invited to a little party tonight, some girls from my school, just a gathering really, mostly girls I went to Brownies with.'

Immediately my mother rounds on me.

'Whose party exactly?'

'Liza Branwell.'

'Do I know her parents?'

'Um, I don't know. Do you know a Mr and Mrs Branwell?'

'All right, smarty-pants, where?'

'Just around the corner from Greendale's, so walking distance.'

She pauses. 'Who are you going with?'

I decide to tell her. 'A girl called Hermione. She's just moved here from London. She's really nice and I thought it would be a good way for her to get to know some new people.'

'Hermione,' repeats my mother dreamily. 'From Shakespeare's *The Winters Tale*, of course. The virtuous queen . . .'

I can feel her softening. My mother's logic is a mystery

to everyone except herself, but at this very moment, it's working in my favour. My mother is more inclined to trust a girl she has never met because she is called Hermione, which is a Shakespearian name and therefore respectable, hence Hermione must be a nice girl. I thank my lucky stars that my new best pal wasn't lumbered with a name that would rouse Mum's suspicions. In the past she has taken exception to girls called Tina, Bev and, in particular, Lacey, an American girl who was in my sister's class for a short time. In Lacey's case, my mum was right, she was appalling.

'I'll be home by eleven,' I promise. 'I've got work in the morning.'

This is my trump card.

It's the first Mum has heard of my chambermaid job, and she's so delighted that I've actually got up off my backside and got myself employed that she suddenly caves in.

'OK, fine,' she says. 'I suppose if you're old enough to have a job, then you're old enough to go to a party, but eleven at the latest, Helena. And by the way, feel free to invite Hermione round for supper; I'd like to meet her.'

'I will,' I promise, bounding back up the stairs with my cake, yes, yes, Yes!

I start putting my hair in the rollers before realising that the varnish on my left hand is still a bit tacky and the smudging is so bad, I have to take it all off and start again. This puts me behind time-wise, but fortunately Mum lets me get away with just crackers and cheese for my tea. I think she's grateful not to have to cook anything for once. She and Rosalind clearly stuffed themselves at the twins' birthday tea and Dad's out 'with bloody

Tom' and won't be back till late.

I'm tempted to ask why she can't stand him, but I don't want to get embroiled in a long and complicated story when I need to steam my face and squeeze out any blackheads, so I take my supper upstairs on a tray along with a bowl of boiling water and fetch a towel to put over my head. I steam my face until I'm too hot and bored to cope any longer, at which point I prod around my nose with my thumbnails and manage to extricate a couple of long-tailed beauties before wiping around my face with a cotton-wool pad soaked in Anne French cleansing milk.

While my pores are still open, I pluck my eyebrows.

'Grooming is about respecting yourself. Spending time on how you look is never time wasted.'

That's what *Jackie* magazine says anyway, and I experiment with two shades of blue eyeshadow, applying a light blue first and then a darker blue in the socket, which seems to work pretty well. I don't want to make too much effort though. Hermione only really wears eyeliner and mascara, so I just sweep a tiny bit of Helena Rubenstein blusher stick over my cheeks and leave it at that. As *Jackie* magazine says, *'You don't want to look like an overpainted doll, you just want to enhance your natural features.'*

Once I've done my face and taken out the electric rollers, I can't put off deciding what to wear any longer. It's already 7.30 so I need to set off in twenty minutes.

I clean my teeth before I get dressed (I've made the toothpaste-dribble down my top mistake before), then I gargle with Dad's Listerine, regretting the action as soon as I've put the lid back on. Everyone knows that Listerine is for bad breath, therefore if my breath stinks of Listerine, I must have bad breath. So I clean my teeth again, before deciding that I'm going to wear a dress.

It's not a great dress, but it does fit nicely. It's a pale-blue gingham-check seersucker number, with a sweetheart neckline, quite tight to the waist with a flared skirt and matching flared short sleeves. I wish my legs were browner, but tights look stupid in summer, so I brave bare legs and buckle my wedges, wishing they were new. That's the first thing I'm going to do when I've saved enough money from my job. I'm going to take a bus to Blackpool and have a splurge. I hope Hermione will come with me. I mean, I know it's not London, but there is a Chelsea Girl and a Miss Selfridge.

I loop several strands of tiny love beads around my neck and pick my denim jacket up off the floor in case it gets cold later. Downstairs, Rosy and Mum are curled up together on the sofa. Rosy is reading *Bunty* and my mum is reading *The Valley of the Dolls*, or 'that dirty book of your mother's' as my dad refers to it. Which reminds me to sneak it off her bedside table when she's busy and check out the rude bits.

'Eleven!' my mother reminds me and then, 'You look lovely, darling,' which I wasn't expecting. 'For a pig!' adds Rosalind, sticking her tongue out at me, which makes my mum laugh. Honestly, Rosalind gets away with murder. Ever since she was ill she can do what she likes.

I'm worried about turning up at the party without any booze, so I decide to swipe a bottle of my dad's homemade cider on the way out. Beggars can't be choosers, and while I can pass for sixteen with a face full of make-up, eighteen is pushing it, and the idea of being turned away at the offie makes me die a bit inside.

The evening is warmer than I expected, and suddenly I get this feeling. It's hard to describe, especially as it only lasts a couple of seconds, like a soap bubble, but I think it's a feeling of utter happiness. I think that for once I'm really happy with what I'm wearing and how I look and that this is the very best time to be young and alive and going to a party with my new best friend. It's one of those moments you could imagine yourself bursting into song, like in a musical, but I can't sing, so I don't. I just feel really good about everything and as the back street winds around the corner on to the main road, I glance at my watch. It's not quite five to eight and everything is possible.

HERMIONE

Thanks to the feeding, bathing and putting to bed of the giant potato baby, we don't sit down to eat until almost quarter to eight.

At this point I have to accept there's no way I'm going to make it to the corner by eight, so while everyone is seating themselves, I run quickly up to my room to get my bag and the envelope with Helena's number on it. I have no idea if my mobile will connect with it, considering the number is fifty years old, but I've got to give it a try. Only I cant find it; it's not in my bag. I empty the whole bag on to the floor, but it's nowhere to be seen, and it's not in any of my pockets, or around the room. I can't have thrown it away? I check my wastepaper basket, but that's empty too. Dammit, it's gone.

Mum is screaming up the stairs at me, so I give up and join the others at the table. My mother has tried her best with some chicken breasts and a jar of pesto, but something has gone a bit wrong and the chicken swims tastelessly and slightly undercooked in a lake of fetid green oil.

Mum serves this with new potatoes and frozen peas. Everything is green and white. We are eating in the dining room and when I glance at the photograph of Melanie, she seems to be smirking. Lucy, on the other hand, can barely disguise her horror. 'I'm still getting used to the oven,' my mother bleats, and while we all push food around our plates for the next twenty minutes, the conversation stops and starts like Mum's friend Marcie's shitty old car.

Lucy obviously hasn't taken to Mum, Mum obviously hasn't taken to Lucy, and Paul is oblivious and just smiles at everything, chewing his way through this terrible meal and only pausing to say, 'He's such a great little chap, Lucy.'

'Who is?' asks my mother, and I kick her under the table.

'Ow,' she yelps. 'What did you do that for?'

I look at my watch. It's just gone eight. I haven't got time to get changed or tart myself up, but if I go right now, I might just catch her.

'I think I'll go for a walk,' I blurt. 'It's such a nice night and I still haven't made it round that lake.'

My mother looks at me pleadingly, but weirdly it's Lucy that comes to her rescue. 'That sounds nice,' she says, and then comes the zinger. 'Why don't you take your mother with you and then Dad and I can clear everything and have a proper catch-up?'

Shit.

My mother leaps up from the table.

'Brilliant idea, Lucy. Come on then, Hermione, what are you waiting for?'

I can't get rid of her. My mum is like chewing gum stuck to

the bottom of my shoe. My mind is spinning. Will Helena still be waiting on the corner? Normally I'd go via the churchyard, but my mum manoeuvres me through the kitchen, out of the back door, down the garden path and into the back alley.

Several awful thoughts are simultaneously flitting through my brain.

1. What if my mum gets transported back to 1975 with me?
2. If that happens, is it possible that she will automatically revert to the age she was back then?

My brain suddenly freezes. 1975, that's the year my mother was born. She'd be a baby. Don't tell me I'm going to end up in 1975 carrying my mum as a baby. That would be too much to bear.

3. On the other hand, she could remain the age she is now, which is possibly even worse?

Helena and I could be lumbered with taking my middle-aged mum to the party. For a horrible moment, I can see her tagging along with us, and I get this horrific image of my forty-five-year-old mum, swigging a bottle of lager and boogying down to whatever is on the record player. Mum loves to dance (unfortunately) and she always insists that the music from the 70s is the best. Come to think of it, this is probably why I recognise most of the tunes on the Blue Monkey jukebox. They're songs I've grown up with: Bowie, T-Rex, Abba and a whole load of Tamla Motown.

'I get the feeling Lucy doesn't like me very much,' Mum mutters as we walk down the street together.

'I'm sure she thinks you're fine,' I lie.

'Hmm,' mutters Mum. 'Let's face it, she more or less ordered me out of the house, and to be honest with you, Hermione, I couldn't wait to get out of there. I mean, it must be weird coming home and finding complete strangers living with your dad,' she says. She looks stricken.

Suddenly I realise that my mum is feeling really vulnerable and I feel torn between wanting to help her and wanting to be back in 1975 with Helena. I let my mum ramble on, but I'm not really listening. I find myself holding my breath as we exit the back alley, bracing myself for the moment of truth – will she be there? For a second I imagine I can smell the fresh sherbet lemony scent of her, see her grinning at me, pink-cheeked and impatient to get to the party.

My heart is in my throat, but she's not on the corner. My heart plummets; Helena is nowhere to be seen.

HELENA

She isn't here. Hermione isn't waiting for me, and she's not walking up the street either. I try to tell myself it's fine, it's only just turned eight, that people are often late and I don't know Hermione well enough to know whether she's that type or not.

Mum thinks lateness is the height of bad manners. Mind you, according to her, so is being too early. Manners are a minefield with my mum.

Other things my mum considers 'rude' are talking with your mouth full, staring, chewing gum, looking bored, saying 'what' not 'pardon', shovelling your peas, slurping your soup, milk bottles on the table, elbows on the table and whispering, to name a few.

I decide to go and sit on the low wall outside the post office opposite the entrance to the alley. From here I can see in all directions. Maybe she set off early and went to the off licence? I think Hermione might be able to get served, not because she looks eighteen, it's more that she could *seem* eighteen. I think it's a London thing. She seems a bit more sophisticated or worldly-wise than . . . well, than me for starters. There's something about Hermione that makes you think she could roll a cigarette, give a lovebite and buy a decent bottle of cider from the offie rather than turning up to a party with a bottle of something that looks like a urine sample.

Maybe she's just too cool to want to go to a party with me.

By ten past eight, I have to choose between going home and going on my own. I decide to toss a coin for it and flip a two-pence piece a bit too hard, drop it and watch it roll off the kerb, into the gutter and down the drain. For a moment I wonder whether this is an omen, and then I remember that my horoscope in this week's *Jackie* said, '*Now is the time to dive into a more exciting social life.*'

I decide to take the plunge. I'm a good swimmer, so why not? But as I walk down Common Edge, I keep looking back over my shoulder, hoping to see her, hoping to hear her shout my name.

Walking this way reminds me of walking to primary school, Juliet striding ahead as fast as she could, not wanting anyone to know we were sisters.

When Juliet left for Queen Anne's, I walked to Greendale's by myself, which I liked. I used to pretend I was being filmed for a documentary about 'Extraordinary Children Around the World', though I could never decide on why I was extraordinary. When Rosalind first joined the infants, I had to hold her hand all the way to the school gates. Now she just waltzes off down the back street with Tania and the twins.

It's only a short walk to 17 Renton Road, but I don't think I've ever been there before. Let's face it, Liza Branwell and I aren't exactly on 'going round for tea' terms, and suddenly I feel really shy. I don't know what I was expecting, but it turns out Liza lives in a brown pebble-dashed semi. I try not to notice that the garden is a mess because I'm only fifteen and I don't want to turn into my mother just yet, but even so I can't help noticing that the window frames could do with repainting and the whole place looks a bit depressing.

There are two big motorbikes parked up on the driveway and another three on the road outside the house. A couple in black leather jackets are standing by one of the bikes arguing. They're older and suddenly my dress feels like something you'd wear to a children's birthday party and I'm furious not to be wearing my jeans.

I can see that the door on the side of the bungalow is open and leads directly into the kitchen, so I make my way in, wondering how long I should stay before I can leave. The kitchen table is crowded with bottles and cans, there's no food, not even a bowl of crisps, and I have to remind myself that there probably won't be pass the parcel either and that this is what parties will be like from now on. Suddenly I have an utter craving for a cheesy football and some jelly and ice cream.

For want of anything better to do, I try to unscrew the lid of the cider bottle. It's tight and I'm struggling when someone who looks like he's come to the party dressed as a Hell's Angel reaches for the bottle, unscrews it, swigs it and says, 'Fucking hell.'

He then hands me back the bottle and says, 'Crikey, that'll put hairs on your chest.' I feel rude wiping his saliva off the neck of the bottle so I don't, I just grin a thank you and take a slug of the murky liquid, which I immediately spit out into the sink. For a second I worry that I might have picked up a dangerous chemical from the garage which is going to eat through all my vital organs and make me go blind, but there's a label on the front of the bottle written in my dad's handwriting which clearly states, *Windfall cider, autumn 1974*. I leave the bottle on the table and fill a paper cup with some kind of beer instead, then I light a cigarette and venture further into the house, deciding to leave my denim jacket on the newel post at the bottom of the stairs.

The Eagles are blaring out from a stereo in the sitting room and the entire downstairs seems to be carpeted in the same orange and brown swirled carpet. A couple of blokes are sitting on the sofa, going through a pile of albums, a girl perched on either side of them looking bored, while a couple are snogging on an easy chair in the corner, his hand creeping like a big white spider up the inside of her thigh. I think the girl snogger might be Susie Jones, but I'm not exactly going to go up and ask.

French doors lead from the rear of the sitting room into the garden and as I squeeze past the dining-room table, I notice a framed photo of Liza and her sister on the sideboard, the two of them flat-chested in ribboned bunches, smiling sweetly.

There are around seven people in the garden, which is small and paved, with a washing line that droops across it at an awkward neck-garrotting height. It's not the kind of garden you can wander around pointing at flowers and saying things like, 'The roses are marvellous this year,' because there aren't any roses, or anything else for that matter.

So far no one has said hello to me, and I haven't seen Liza or her sister Tina. I duck under the washing line and sit on an upturned bucket, looking 'approachable and interesting' as they suggest in *Jackie*. I also arrange my arms so that I manage to give myself a bit more cleavage and I promise myself that if no one speaks to me in the next twenty minutes, I will walk home via the chippie and eat chips with curry sauce to cheer myself up.

HERMIONE

I'm so disappointed I could cry. It's Saturday night and rather than being magically transported back to a party in 1975, I am going for a walk with my mum.

Mum is still mumbling about trying her best and not expecting things to be so difficult.

'There's the lake,' I offer, not knowing what else to suggest. 'We could walk around that?'

I must sound as desperate as I feel, because my mother suddenly stops in her tracks.

'Oh God,' she says. 'Hermione, what have I done? I've dragged you all the way from London to this strange place and now look at you. You shouldn't be keeping me company on a Saturday night, you should be out having fun with your own friends like I did when I was your age.'

In that split second, I almost come clean and say, 'It's OK, I've made a new friend, she's called Helena and I was going to go to a party with her tonight, so if you don't mind . . .' But I suddenly realise I can't even remember the address. I've blown it.

To stop myself from crying, I march my mother over the railway bridge and down the other side towards the lake. The whole time she keeps up a running commentary about how she has made a mess of everything and how sorry she is and how everyone always said she'd come to nothing and now look at her. Mum has gone into full self-pity mode. I've seen her do this before; it usually ends in vodka and tears.

I tell her that everything's going to be OK and that Lucy's bound to be a bit protective of her dad and no wonder she's suspicious of us and that we're all going to have to compromise and find some way of making things work. I'm not really convincing myself, but it seems to be working for Mum. I sound like a terrible American afternoon-TV chat-show host, but then Mum has always been gullible. She's a sucker for an inspirational quote and she truly believes in astrology and fortune tellers and tarot readings.

'I'm such an Aries,' she sighs, and looks wistful. 'You never think when you're young that you still won't have a clue when you're older,' she says.

'You think that everything will be sorted and all the paperwork will be kept in a safe place so that if you ever need to find anything, it'll be where you put it. But I'm forty-five now and I still don't know what I'm doing and I don't know if this was just another stupid thing in a whole long list of stupid things I've done in my life.'

Oh God, this is getting a bit deep. I don't think I'm ready to be my mum's counsellor, so I just say, 'It's going to be OK, Mum, we'll work it out.'

We start walking around the lake for the second time and with every step I'm wondering what Helena's up to.

HELENA

I think I'm quite drunk, which at least makes time go faster. I should just leave, but I refuse to give in just yet. I want this party to be something I can tell Hermione about, and the disappointment of her not being here gives me the kind of tummy ache I used to get when I was little.

'Oh, hi, Helena,' says a voice behind me. 'I wasn't expecting to see you here.' I look round. It's Alex King looking like a *Jackie* cover girl. She's wearing a bright-yellow wrap-around knee-length skirt and a denim waistcoat with NOTHING on underneath. Alex has obviously just washed her hair, which ripples over her bare, tanned shoulders, shining bronze and golden in the light. She's with her boyfriend, who is wearing a pair of sunglasses on top of his head, a pair of cream high-waisted trousers with an open-necked purple shirt, and some kind of cravat thing. He is very obviously holding a pair of car keys, and looking really out of place.

I'm so relieved to have someone to talk to, I start blathering on immediately. 'Oh, you must be Paul, really nice to meet you.

I'm Helena.' Paul doesn't say much, he just keeps turning his keys around in his hand and staring into the distance until Alex tells him to find some chairs, at which point he goes inside and fetches two dining-room chairs which he and Alex sit on, leaving me on the upturned bucket.

Paul Thursby must be about twenty. He's got a gold signet ring and a silver hip flask from which he pours amber-coloured liquid into my beer. I think it must be brandy because all of a sudden it smells like I'm drinking Christmas cake.

When the hipflask is empty, Alex goes to find more drink and comes back with a bottle of sangria. I'm sure you're meant to mix it with lemonade, but we just drink it neat and by now there are loads more people in the garden. I don't know anyone, but Alex does and for a while she chats with some lad called Stevo until Paul tells her he needs a word, in the car, 'NOW'.

As soon as they leave, two other people sit down on the chairs and for some reason I find myself shouting, 'What this party needs right now is a game of musical chairs,' and a tall girl in a long purple skirt and a Hawkwind T-shirt starts whooping, and suddenly piles of chairs are being lined up on the patio, plus a Moroccan leather pouffe from the sitting room. The tall girl's very short friend Fiona, who has a feather cut and a tattoo on her neck, takes control of the record player and somehow a shambolic, very pissed game of musical chairs ensues. Every time the music stops, I seem to end up on the upturned bucket, and everyone is laughing and screaming and the bloke from next door shouts out of his bedroom window to 'keep it down' because he's trying to get his kids to sleep, and someone starts throwing wooden clothes pegs at the open window, which strikes me as hilarious. Status Quo blasts at full volume from the stereo. Fiona has obviously cranked it up as far as it will go, because it's deafening, and the garden is crammed now. Some people are just dancing, but when Fiona lifts the stylus again, I run for my bucket, only someone has got there before me and I end up sitting on this bloke's lap. He grabs me round the middle and squeezes me like I'm some kind of toy. He smells of dope and beer and I suddenly realise it's the Hell's Angel who opened the cider for me and the next thing I know, we're rolling off the upturned bucket on to the grass and he's landed on top of me and we're both laughing, but somehow he's got me pinned underneath him and I can feel the weight of what I instinctively know is his cock against the front of my dress and he seems to be grinding into me and his breathing has changed but I'm still laughing, only I'm not sure why any more.

I'm starting to feel panicky when someone reaches out a hand and says, 'Albie, mate, I think Tina's looking for you,' and the biker bloke kind of springs away from me like he's been electrocuted. I grab hold of the hand, and as I get back on my feet, I realise the sky has turned the colour of spilt ink and Tina's at the French window going mental about the dining chairs being outside and the pouffe being ruined. She is very pissed indeed; everyone is. It takes me a second or two to realise that the hand holding mine is Sticks's. Time seems to stand still until he offers me a cigarette and as he holds a lighter to my lips, I can see his beautiful eyes behind the thatch of his fringe and he's looking at me and I'm looking at him and just as he leans in, Alex comes storming over shouting that Liza is being sick upstairs and she's asking for him.

HERMIONE

Just when I'm contemplating accidentally on purpose hurling myself into the lake to put an end to this awful evening, a poodle comes running up and starts dancing around our ankles.

Mum is immediately distracted. I swear she's like a goldfish. 'Oh, look at it!' she coos. 'I wonder if Paul would let me have a puppy!'

The dog, we're told, is called Ginger. 'As in Ginger Rogers,' says a small thin man wearing thick black-rimmed glasses. 'She's a marvellous dancer, aren't you, poppet?' The poodle immediately obliges her master and proves his point by standing on her hind legs and quick-stepping backwards. 'The only thing she hasn't mastered yet is the high heels,' the man adds.

I must have looked a bit blank, because my mother butts in with, 'Excuse my daughter, she's a complete philistine. She's not big on musicals.' She takes a seat on the bench next to the man and the dog jumps up on her lap.

I'll say this for my mum, she's better with dogs than she is with small children.

The man winks at me. 'Ginger Rogers and Fred Astaire, fabulous Hollywood dancers, made some great movies, and of course, as the quote goes, Ginger Rogers was famous for doing everything Fred Astaire did, but backwards and in high heels.'

'Who's a clever girl?' my mother gushes.

The man suddenly offers Mum his hand. 'My name's Greg,' he says, and for a moment my head swims, because I realise with complete certainty that this is Greg, of Jimmy and Greg, the boy that I met in the park this afternoon. And though I can't say for sure, it seems my gaydar was working even back in 1975, before such a thing existed.

'Nice to meet you, Greg. This is Hermione and I'm Tess,' says my mother.

For an uncomfortable second or two, I half expect him to recognise me, and then I realise that while it's only been a few hours since we last met for me, for Greg it's been forty-five years, and I calm down.

Greg asks my mum if she'd like a drink in the pub opposite the lake. 'We can sit outside with the dog and I'll tell you all about myself,' he offers.

Greg is good company. He buys my mum a double vodka and tonic and makes her laugh. I have a Diet Coke and listen to the two of them yak on.

It turns out he's a choreographer for a gay club in Blackpool called Funny Girls, does a bit of local panto directing and has family nearby.

'There are worse places to grow up,' he tells us. 'Coming out in the early eighties was tough, but things are easier now,' he grins.

He and my mother exchange phone numbers. 'You must

come and see a show,' he suggests. 'I'll make sure you and your partner have the best seats in the house.'

Mum and I share a look. Somehow I can't see Paul being comfortable in a bar full of big-wigged queens lip-synching and dancing, but we both say thanks, it's a lovely offer and it is. I love a bit of drag.

When I was really small, my mum had a part-time cleaning job at the infamous Vauxhall Tavern in South London. I used to go with her and colour in at the bar while she mopped the floor and cleaned out the ashtrays. Sometimes we'd still be there when the drag queens came in to rehearse for the evening show and so from an early age, I didn't find anything odd about the sight of a man in a frock.

It's almost ten by the time we get home and Paul greets us in the hall with a finger over his lips. Apparently, we must be completely silent because the baby has just gone to sleep and poor Lucy is exhausted. So the two of us tiptoe upstairs in total silence until my mother accidentally steps on a rubber dinosaur, which shrieks with such force that it might as well be a real dinosaur.

'Waaaaagh, waaaaagh!' comes the cry from upstairs, and the next thing we know, Lucy flings open her bedroom door and yells, 'Well, thank you very much. Have you any idea how hard it is to get a teething baby to sleep? I don't even know what either of you are doing in this house?' My mother and I just freeze, too scared to move, like we're playing a terrible game of musical statues on the stairs, while Lucy bursts into tears, returns to the bedroom and slams the door.

'Waaaaggh,' wails William, even louder now.

HELENA

Mayhem has broken out in the garden. The bloke from next door whose kids 'can't fucking sleep' has climbed over the wall and is yelling his head off and threatening to call the police. Someone throws a dining-room chair at him and another bloke grabs the wooden clothes prop and starts waving it around his head, then girls start screaming and clutching each other, and one of the big bikes gets pushed over on the drive and Tina is crying and dustbins are being kicked over and when I look at my watch I see it's 10.45 p.m. and I have fifteen minutes to get home so I start walking like those people who do speed walking for the Olympics, and once I'm back on Common Edge, I take my shoes off and run. I know I should go round the long way because it's pitch black down the alley and the long way round is safer, but I don't have time. Instead, I head into the darkness.

I've got two minutes to get home, only before I can reach the safety of my back gate there is a man, facing the alley wall and having a wee. I freeze. I don't want to stop, but I don't want to pass him either, he's really unsteady on his feet, and I dither

208

about for a second, deciding whether to head back out and go round the other way or press on through. In the end I decide to make a run for it down the alley and as I dash past the man I realise . . . it's my dad.

He is drunk, I mean *really* drunk, and by the time I get him through the gate, my mother is standing on the back step in her nightie looking absolutely furious.

I help him stumble up the path with my arm around his waist, while he trips up over his own feet and my mother turns to go back inside and put the kettle on. As I help him navigate the back steps, it dawns on me that the great thing about my dad being so pissed is that my mother hasn't noticed that I myself am three minutes late and, like my dad, completely and utterly off my tits.

HERMIONE

In bed at last, I lie under the covers wondering what I've missed out on, both in London and in 1975.

Digging my phone out of my bag, I discover a string of messages from Amisha and Millie. They've just seen a gig by some brilliant new band in a pub in Balham and now they're queuing for chicken in KFC.

Another message pings up from Millie.

And now we're on the night bus

With a bucket of wiiiings

adds Amisha.

I throw my phone back in my bag and switch the bedside light off. Helena's blue-biro message on the wall by my bed is the last thing I see before the room goes dark.

Eventually I fall asleep and I dream about being on a bus with all my friends, until one by one they all get off the bus and there's only me and Helena left.

HELENA

WEDNESDAY

My alarm wakes me at seven thirty. The two brass bells on the top of the clock vibrate madly and the noise is terrible. I feel sick, the roof of my mouth is dry and it's hard to swallow. I wonder for a second if I'm about to come down with tonsillitis (or my 'nemesis' as Mum calls it), and then I remember – Liza's party, the upturned bucket, Albie's weight on top of me, his hot, sour breath in my face, Sticks's hand in mine, the toxic cider, the beer, brandy and Sangria . . . and the penny drops. I think I've got a hangover! It's my first and I wonder if I've got time to write a quick note in my diary to mark this momentous occasion, maybe even a short poem?

<u>Ode to Liza's party</u>
Head bangs, guts churn and there is a taste in my mouth like . . .
A gerbil's toilet.

It's the best I can do in the time that I have.

Today is my first day at work, which I suppose is as momentous as having my first hangover, but I don't have time to write two poems.

To compensate for feeling so utterly crap, I shovel two thick slices of toast down my neck, piled high with lemon curd on top of peanut butter, and swig some orange juice straight from the fridge.

'I wish you wouldn't do that,' my mother says, padding into the kitchen behind me She's wearing her summer dressing gown, which is floral, short-sleeved and cotton, as opposed to her winter dressing gown, which is pale blue and quilted. Her mouth is set in a small tense line and she snatches the orange juice carton from my hand, pours herself a glass and then bangs two mugs down on a tray. 'As you may have guessed from the state he came home in, your father was out with bloody Tom last night. He's feeling absolutely terrible, I'm very pleased to say, and as a penance he shall be spending the day mowing the lawn and washing the car. Oh, and he'll be decorating your bedroom as soon as he's fit. I'm sick of those rolls of wallpaper cluttering up the pantry. I'd make him start on it today, but I don't think he's capable of hanging anything in a straight line.'

Poor Dad. Mum can be a fiend when she's got the moral high ground. Simon will be paying for his night out with Tom for the foreseeable future, fixing wonky shelves, tidying up the garden and finally, oh joy of joys, decorating my bedroom.

'Good work, Tom,' I mutter under my breath.

'Pardon, darling?'

'I'm going to work,' I remind her, and she gives me a sudden unexpected hug, recoiling almost instantly.

'Good Lord, Helena, make sure you clean your teeth before you go. Your father's got some Listerine in the bathroom; a quick gargle wouldn't go a miss.'

I stuff a change of clothes into a duffel bag for after my shift – a pink denim shirt and a slightly washed-out khaki skirt with appliqué rainbow patches on the pockets. If the weather holds, people will be hanging out in the square gossiping over Liza's party, and I intend to be there.

I feel a pang about Hermione, and I try and work out whether I actually want to see her again? I mean, what excuse can she have to let me down like that? After all, I did give her my phone number. If she wasn't going to come, she could have at least called.

I think about the party as I cycle to St Anne's. By the time I get to the Cravendale Hotel, I've more or less made up my mind that I won't speak to Hermione again. I shall be polite but distant, and in my mind's eye I picture myself in the middle of a crowd of laughing teenagers squashed into a booth in the Blue Monkey with Hermione outside staring in through the window looking miserable. I add rain to complete the picture and feel a bit more cheerful, but not much. It was fun having a friend for a while.

I leave my bike round the back of the hotel in a scruffy yard full of overflowing bins buzzing with blue bottles, and then I make my way round to the entrance at the front.

The walls of the foyer are covered in fake pine wallpaper and the rubber plant by the front door is plastic. As there's no one on reception, I press a plastic buzzer that is strapped to the desk with discoloured Sellotape. The place reeks of fried eggs and furniture polish.

A woman with dyed jet-black hair comes running through a bubbled glass door at the back of the hallway. Her smile vanishes when she realises that I'm not a paying guest and she shoos me to the rear of the hotel. On the way, we pass through a steaming kitchen where a fat man dances nimbly from stove to grill to serving hatch, spooning hot fat over bright-yellow yolks, turning rashers of bacon and ladling tinned plum tomatoes on to china plates. A couple of teenage girls run in and out with dirty crockery piled up on round silver trays, while a boy with acne stands with his elbows deep in sudsy water. Radio 1 belts out 'The Disco Stomp' at full volume. '*Everybody do the disco stomp, disco stomp, disco stomp.*' The pace is relentless. This already looks like hard work and I haven't even started yet.

Twenty minutes later, I'm wearing a burgundy Cravendale tabard and have been introduced to 'Beverley, who knows the ropes'. Beverley is a thin woman in her late twenties with greasy brown hair and rat-like features. I try and jolly her by saying, 'Be gentle with me, Bev, it's my first time,' but she just looks at me sourly and snaps, 'We haven't got time to piss about,' and my heart sinks as I follow her up the stairs.

The Cravendale is two massive Victorian red-brick houses that have been knocked into each other and extended over the years into an elaborate warren of corridors and staircases, half-landings and hallucinogenic carpets. Each room seems to hold a fresh horror. In room 309 on the top floor, someone has been sick in a wastepaper basket, while in the room next door, a condom lies slimy and knotted beside the bed.

I get a bit peckish around eleven. Fortunately, every room is supplied with a tea tray which includes a twin pack of shortbread fingers. As luck would have it, Beverley has put me on tea tray duty, and I manage to eat eight shortbread biscuits behind her back.

In room 209 (sea view on the second floor), Bev and I are remaking the double bed when I find a nightie under each pillow. Both are sensible cotton, ankle-length nighties in size L from British Home Stores.

'Lesbians,' mouths Beverley. 'It's not normal, two women sharing the same bed.' But I can't help thinking, I mean, really, what could be more normal than two large cotton nighties from British Home Stores? It's hardly the height of deviancy, is it?

I don't say anything. I just get on with making the bed, carefully refolding the nighties and moving on to the next room.

We finish at one. Beverly is furious. 'You'll have to speed up next weekend,' she informs me, marching us back to the corridor that constitutes a staff cloakroom. 'I'm usually out of here by half twelve,' she adds, and then leaves without another word. I flick V-signs at her narrow back, the nasty cow.

Retrieving my duffel bag, I decide to go round to reception again to ask for my money. The woman with the elaborately coiled, dyed black hair is perched on a stool on reception reading the *News of the World* and eating a Curly Wurly. Without taking her eyes off the paper, she slides a brown envelope over the counter and says she'll be asking Beverley how I got on.

Shit, Beverley hates me. Oh well, sod her, I think, gleefully shoving the brown envelope in my bag.

The sun is doing its best as I walk down the front steps of

the Cravendale, and I'm just thinking about picking up my bike and nipping to the nearest public toilets to get changed, when I realise that someone is waving frantically at me from the other side of the road. I squint short-sightedly, livid that only really rich people can afford contact lenses. Suddenly the traffic lights change and the waving person dodges through the stationary cars.

'Helena!' she yells.

'Hermione!' I yell back excitedly, forgetting in an instant that I'm not really speaking to her.

HERMIONE

Helena grins and waves when she finally sees me, but by the time I reach her side of the road, she has stalked off and I have to run to catch up with her.

'Helena, wait for me . . . I'm so sorry about last night.'

'I'm not actually talking to you,' she snaps. I knew she'd be pissed off with me for letting her down last night, but it's not like I can tell her the actual truth. I can't say, 'Sorry, Helena, but that party last night actually happened before I was born.' So I tell her the other truth, about having a load of family crap to deal with.

'It's Paul . . . His daughter turned up with this great big spud of a baby, and everything got really complicated.'

'You could have called me,' she says.

'I lost the envelope with your number on it,' I say, feeling awful as I say it. 'I looked everywhere. And I couldn't remember where the party was. My mum was in a terrible state. I couldn't just leave her.'

She listens quietly while we walk side by side. I have to work quite hard, but I can feel her thawing. I make her laugh by imitating the noise of the squeaking dinosaur toy on the stairs and how me and Mum just froze like musical statues. Then she tells me about bumping into her dad coming home pissed and how him being pissed took the heat off her being pissed. I ask her if he drinks a lot and she laughs and says, 'Nah, he's a lightweight, I've only seen him drunk about three times in my entire life.'

I couldn't begin to count the number of times I've seen my dad pissed. I've seen Casper pissed, stoned, high and once, when I was really small, actually hallucinating. We were in the kids' playground down at Camberwell Green, a crappy place at the best of times, but made much worse by my dad being off his head and thinking that the animal heads on the children's roundabout were alive. He kept pushing me round and round and while I got dizzier and dizzier, my dad had this long, involved conversation with a duck. I shudder slightly at the memory and ask about the party.

'Well . . .' says Helena with a grin, pushing me towards a bench, and I know that she has forgiven me. I couldn't be more relieved. I've got my friend back.

We sit gossiping on the bench like two old women as Helena describes every detail of the party to me, until I can see it like a film in front of my eyes, and I laugh at the image of the next-door neighbour screaming out of the window, Alex King's creepy older boyfriend with his tragic hip flask and his flashy car, and the impromptu game of music chairs, though I immediately stop laughing when she tells me about some Hell's Angel pushing himself on top of her.

'He did what?'

'He kind of pinned me down on the floor and was rubbing himself against me. I could feel his, you know . . . and I couldn't really breathe or move because he was so heavy.'

Helena is still sort of laughing as she says this until she sees the expression on my face. 'Helena, that's not funny.'

'Well, I was quite drunk,' she says, looking embarrassed. 'So I suppose it was my fault really.'

'No, it wasn't,' I tell her firmly. 'It was HIS fault. It's never OK for a bloke to do that, do you understand? Never. It's up to you to decide whether you like something or not, and it doesn't sound like you did. It's called consent. OK?'

She nods and says OK, but I'm not sure she really gets it. This girl has a lot of learn. I'm about to explain more when, with a sly smile, she says, 'It was Sticks who saved me.'

I raise my eyebrows, and she goes on, 'Yup, he kind of sorted it out and helped me up and held my hand, just for a bit.'

'Oh yes,' I say. 'And what did Liza have to say about that?'

She grins triumphantly at the memory.

'Well, she was throwing up in the toilets upstairs so what she doesn't know won't hurt her!'

We both fall about laughing at that, then Helena pronounces herself starving.

I haven't eaten either and suddenly my stomach growls. Paul is taking Mum, William and Lucy out for a carvery, but I managed to wriggle my way out of it. In any case, a carvery's wasted on me. I'm part vegetarian, sometimes, well, I was back in London, though right now I'd kill for a nice bit of pork crackling.

I offer to take Helena out for lunch, but she waves her pay packet at me and says, 'Let's go halves!' then she nips into the public loos to get changed.

'We could go to the Monkey?' Helena suggests when she comes out, looking a bit crumpled in a pink shirt and khaki skirt. I presume she attached the rainbow patches herself, because they're starting to peel off and I'm almost tempted to tell her those iron-on things still don't work in 2021, but obviously I don't.

There are loads of things I could tell Helena, about life in the future, about shops being open on Sundays and mobile phones, K-pop and TikTok, and computers, and Pret a Manger but I know I mustn't.

I don't want to go to the Monkey, I want an afternoon with just the two of us, and if we go to the Blue Monkey, I will have to share her and I'm not feeling that sociable.

'I know!' she suddenly exclaims. 'Let's go to Blackpool. We can have a slap-up Wimpy burger and chips with all the trimmings, then take a stroll down the prom afterwards. It'll only take us half an hour on the bus. I'll pick my bike up later.'

So that's what we do. I'm quite excited as I haven't been to Blackpool since we moved up here. Paul thinks it's a 'dump' but my mum's intrigued. She's always been a sucker for fairground rides and an amusement arcade.

As we get on the bus, I have a sudden flashback to my dad taking me and Mum to Southend. I remember once he spent all his money on the rifle range, trying to win my mum a massive green Orville, even though my mum was hopping up and down saying, 'I don't want a fucking duck.'

What was it with my dad and ducks?

Helena lights a slightly bent No.6 on the bus and turns to me with round, serious eyes.

'He does fancy me, Hermione, doesn't he? Sticks, I mean?'

'Yeees,' I say, working out how to put what I want to say next. 'But I'm not sure he's right for you. And he's seeing someone else.'

'Yes, but she's horrible!' says Helena.

'That doesn't matter though,' I tell her sternly. 'You don't want to muck about with other girls' boyfriends. Imagine if someone did that with your boyfriend.'

Helena looks at me, head on one side. 'See,' she grins. 'That's why I need you, Hermione. I can't talk to Gwen and Elaine about this sort of stuff. Gwen would probably tell me to ask God to show me the way, and Elaine only cares about rabbits, so would probably say, "Does he like eating lettuce out of your hand, Helena? Because there's no point having a relationship with someone who doesn't want to eat lettuce out of your hand." I mean, really,' and she does this funny voice which has me in stitches.

It strikes me that Helena has possibly outgrown these two. It happens. Some friendships are like old jumpers: they don't fit any more, but you can't bear to chuck them out.

Blackpool blows my mind. There are trams for starters, rattling down narrow metal tracks with bells that clang at every stop, and arcade after arcade, all the way down the promenade as far as I can see. We get off at Central Pier, which according to the posters and billboards promises 'The Very Best in Live Entertainment' and 'Fun for all the Family', with shows offering side-splitting comedy, world-class dancers, stars of stage and screen, TV impressionists and internationally renowned singers. Not that I've heard of any of them.

Down on the famously sandy beach, entire families brave the chilly wind on wooden deckchairs, with striped canvas windbreaks and tartan rugs. It's the first time I have seen string vests with my own eyes. I mean, what's the point in a vest that's more holes than vest?

The whole place is an old-fashioned postcard come to life. Kids ride donkeys, and a crowd gathers round a Punch and Judy stall. It's all true, all the stories of how life used to be are right there in front of my eyes.

The place is heaving. Pavements throng with lobster-shouldered holidaymakers and I can't help noticing how strange it feels not to see a single black, brown or Asian face.

My head spins with it all and my nose tingles with the scent of vinegar on chips. It's almost overwhelming. Blackpool is full of people trying to have the best time they can while wearing ridiculous shoes. Girls in massive platforms wearing kiss-me-quick hats cling to blokes strutting in stacked heels holding bottles of beer. It's all here, like a big stick of rock in your face, and above it all looms the tower, looking more like the Eiffel Tower than I ever expected.

'My mum and dad don't like me coming here,' admits Helena. 'They think it's a bit common and that I might get mixed up with the wrong crowd.' She laughs, as if she couldn't think of anything she'd enjoy more.

A couple of blokes in their thirties with tightly permed hair and moustaches wolf-whistle in our direction and Helena beams with pleasure. I wonder how long I would need to teach her the rudiments of feminism.

'Lunch!' I remind her sternly before Helena starts flirting with thirty-something sleazeballs.

'The Wimpy's over there,' she says, pointing to a side street on the other side of the prom, but there's too much traffic to cross before the matching moustaches approach.

'All right then, darling,' says moustache one, looming over Helena. 'How about a bounce on my knee in a bus shelter and I'll buy you a drink?' Helena goes pink and giggles, which is obviously the worst thing she can do. I decide to take control, grab Helena by the arm and inform the creep, 'Not right now, thank you very much.'

To which he retorts, 'I wasn't asking you, you frigid lesbian bitch,' which is charming. Fortunately at that moment I see a gap in the traffic and pull Miss Jailbait 1975 to the other side of the prom.

Helena thinks the incident is hilarious. 'You sounded like my mum when she goes to John Lewis and a shop assistant tries to show her some fancy new gloves,' and she does an impression, '"Not right now, thank you very much!"' and I can't help but laugh.

At the Wimpy's, we sit opposite each other at a shiny red table. An illustrated laminated menu offers the usual burgers and chips, but for a mere 35p we can get a full Wimpy Grill, which promises steak, chips and a tomato. Or if we really fancy pushing the boat out, there's the 'International Grill', which comes with the added bonus of a lettuce garnish.

A waitress comes over and looks expectantly at the two of us.

Helena says, 'I'd like the Wimpy Special Grill (fried egg included) and a Coke, please,' and then she nods to me. 'And my frigid lesbian bitch friend will have . . . ?'

I try not to laugh as the waitress looks at me with long-suffering patience. I decide there is no point being vegetarian in 1975.

'The International, please, and do you have any mayonnaise?'

'She means salad cream,' translates Helena. 'Honestly, Hermione, you're not in London now.'

Our meal is kind of terrible, but Helena seems to think it's brilliant. I think taste buds may have changed since the last millennium and I wonder what Helena would make of my favourite Wagamama chilli chicken ramen dish with a side of edamame beans? I manage to eat my burger, but I leave my soggy salad garnish and a handful of flabby chips, which Helena polishes off.

'I've got a brilliant idea,' she says. 'Let's go and see Gypsy Petulengro on the prom and get our palms read!'

And I agree, deciding not to mention the fact we don't really call people gypsies any more. Honestly, the 70s wouldn't know political correctness if it bit them on the arse.

HELENA

I'm having the best day ever. I mean, obviously this morning was rubbish, but right now I couldn't be happier. Hermione is the ideal mate to visit Blackpool with. For starters, she's never been before, so she gawps, properly gawps, her jaw dropping, at everything. One day I'll take her to the Tower Circus – that will makes her eyes pop out. My dad took me and Juliet once, ages ago, when Rosalind was a baby, but I still remember it, the lights and the sequined costumes, the girls in silver headdresses flying through the air and being caught by the ankles.

At the end, the circus ring filled up with water, and fountains spewed sparkling coloured water everywhere. It was one of the most magical things I've ever seen.

A few years ago, before Juliet went to university, I was telling Rosalind about how we saw an elephant wearing a fez and Juliet starts interrupting, saying there wasn't an elephant in the show, because how could they get an elephant halfway up the tower? We started fighting about it and she got really cross and kept shouting, 'You can't fit an elephant in a lift.'

The trouble with Juliet is that she has no imagination.

Blackpool is full of people that make Alicia wince. Everyone is too loud, too fat, too sunburnt, and most of the babies have dummies in their mouths. My mum thinks giving a baby a dummy is a criminal offence, and as for piercing their ears! So far today I've counted six babies with pierced ears. If my mum were here, she'd be saying 'they'll be tattooing them next'.

Other Blackpool sights my mum can't cope with include women with their hair in rollers, or women who nip out for a pint of milk in their slippers and then, wait for it, put the milk bottle on the kitchen table without pouring it into a jug. My mum doesn't really belong to 1970s Lancashire. She'd be far happier in Regency England living in a Jane Austen theme park.

I'm so glad I'm here with Hermione. She's the perfect best friend. I feel like I can tell her anything. She is so easy to hang around with, and she doesn't disapprove of me like Gwen does when I swear, and she doesn't go all peculiar when boys are around. She wears good clothes too. Gwen always looks like her mum has dressed her for a twelfth birthday party and Elaine seriously hasn't got a clue. I mean, she wears her school shoes at the weekend and doesn't mind. Today Hermione is wearing a blue and white striped T-shirt with a pair of jeans and the kind of pumps we wore at primary school, the ones with the elastic at the front. Suddenly it strikes me that I've only ever seen her in pumps or trainers.

'Don't you ever wear heels?' I ask her, and she rolls her eyes.

'I can't see the point in wearing uncomfortable shoes,' she says. 'Why make life more difficult than it already is? I mean, how many men do you see falling over in platforms?'

Well, quite a few in Blackpool, to be honest, but she's got a point.

'I don't subscribe to wearing heels,' Hermione continues, 'and I don't diet, because I refuse to get an eating disorder just because some stupid magazine tells me that a certain size is too big. Women have been kept small for centuries, in case we outgrow our "little woman" status. It's bullshit.'

'Yeees,' I reply, 'but then, you're not fat, so that's easy for you to say,' and she shrugs at that and says, 'Lucky genes. My dad eats complete rubbish and looks like a whippet in a leather jacket.'

Wow, imagine a dad with a leather jacket! I mean, Simon has leather patches on his corduroy teaching jacket, but a whole jacket made out of a cow; there's no way.

We link arms as we stroll along the Promenade. I have a vague idea where Gypsy Petulengro has her booth and it's more or less opposite Central Pier, next to a stall selling rock in all different shapes and sizes. Seriously, you can even get a full English breakfast made completely of rock, with a fried egg and everything. We pass a tattoo parlour on our way and Hermione tells me she's going to get one as soon as she's old enough. She wants an anchor or a mermaid, and as soon as she says this, I want one too. I want matching me and Hermione mermaid tattoos and I don't care how much it hurts and I laugh when I think about what my mum would say.

Helena says her mum can't mind because she's got three and that her dad is covered in them. Apparently, her mum has a bumblebee, a rose and a cartoon Daffy Duck, which Hermione

227

says is the height of naffness. Imagine having a mum with tattoos! If my mum had a tattoo, it would probably be a picture of a quill or a Shakespearian quote, something profound, not that she'd ever have one, not in a million years.

At Madame Petulengro's booth, a plump girl of about twelve with ginger curls sits on a tall stool next to a cash register. She tells us to come inside and wait while her great-grandmother finishes with a client. The walls of the booth are decorated in red and gold flocked wallpaper and lined with framed black and white photos of Madame Petulengro with various showbiz celebrities. Some of these photos are quite old, but I recognise Pat Phoenix who plays Elsie Tanner in *Coronation Street*, and Danny La Rue is also up there, all dressed up as a woman and on either side of Danny are Ken Dodd, with his idiotic tickling stick and the footballer Kenny Dalglish. Loads of girls at my school fancy Kenny Dalglish.

Hermione is rubbish at spotting famous faces. She even looks blank when I point out Mary Hopkin, and even blanker when I start warbling her Eurovision hit, 'Knock, knock, who's there, could this be love that's calling?'

Suddenly a red velvet curtain is pulled back and a woman in her late twenties comes out looking very pink and pleased with herself, obviously happy with the fortune she's been told.

'You can go in now,' says the adenoidal twelve-year-old on the door.

'You go first,' Hermione says, and gives me a little push towards the slightly grubby curtain.

Madame Petulengro is very small with very dyed black hair, which she has mostly hidden under a scarf. I think she's going bald and I try not to stare. She must be well into her eighties and her make-up reminds me of Nana Nancy when she goes overboard. A pearly pale-blue eyeshadow is smeared right up to her eyebrows and she's drawn a shaky line of liquid eyeliner along both the top and bottom lid. Her eyes are small and hooded, and they're probably brown, but they look black to me.

I don't think she's removed her mascara since 1952 and her eyelashes are reduced to tiny little stumpy clumps.

Madame Petulengro smiles, showing a perfect set of gleaming white dentures, and a web of deep creases breaks through a layer of orange panstick foundation. The rim of the china teacup on the table in front of her is smudged with scarlet lipstick, and she gestures at a price list, written out like a menu in a gold frame.

I realise I can only afford either a palm reading or the crystal ball. A complete tarot reading is far too much and there's something about tea leaves that I find a bit silly. They remind me of when Mrs Perks dressed up as a gypsy with gravy browning all over her face 'reading the cups' at a Girl Guide rally that Elaine made me go to.

'Just the palm, please,' I say, and Madame Petulengro nods. The air is heady with incense. She asks whether I'm left or right-handed. I say right and she takes that hand in hers. Her long, pointed nails are heavily nicotine stained and as curved as almonds. For a couple of seconds, she turns my hand this way and that, and a furrow on her brow deepens between her eyes.

When she starts talking, her voice is hoarse and her accent is more Liverpudlian than Lancashire. Without pausing for breath, she informs me ... that I like a good time, that I sometimes don't listen and that I can hurt people with my sharp tongue, but I forgive easily and that's a good thing.

She tells me I have many friends but some are far away, and I gasp, because she can obviously see them, Elaine and Gwen, in my palm. How mad is that?

Then still looking intensely at my palm, she says, 'You feel loneliness deeply, and you are eager for love. You can be impetuous and sometimes this will lead you to making the wrong choices. You must learn to . . .' Suddenly, her hand suddenly grips mine and her sharp little nails almost puncture my skin. She looks up at me. 'You must take care. You are very loved, your family is close, I can see arguments, but I see love, so much love.'

'I've got two sisters,' I offer.

'Yes,' she agrees. 'I can see that you have sisters; your sisters are here in your hand. And is there a dog?'

'No,' I respond, 'we haven't got a dog. I've got a nana though, Nana Nancy.'

'Yes, it's not a dog. I can see her now; she needs to take care of her chest.'

'Yes!' I agree. 'She wears a vest in the winter and rubs her chest with embrocation.' Madame Petulengro nods and coughs as if in sympathy.

I'm hanging on to her every word and so far she's mostly right, but it's all a bit vague, so I decide to risk a couple of questions. 'But will I be famous and will I find true happiness?' I blurt.

'There is a story,' she says, her eyes suddenly beady. 'You are in the papers . . . it's . . .' And then she suddenly stops.

Madame Petulengro's eyes meet mine and for a moment, hers seem to brim with tears. 'I cannot promise you the moon,' she says, 'and some things that are written in the stars are best not known. You have been born lucky. This hand shows intelligence and much laughter; it is a happy hand. What more can I tell you?'

I sense she's had enough, but I push for more information. 'Will I get married, will I have children, will I be rich?' The old woman laughs a phlegmy laugh, turns my hand over and pats the back of it. 'Yes, yes of course. He will be tall and dark and handsome, and you will be rich enough but not too rich, and I see three little girls.'

'Bloody hell, am I going to have triplets?' I gasp, and she laughs again.

'Not necessarily all at once. Now, that's your lot, young lady,' and with a last hard squeeze of my hand she dismisses me, turning to blow her nose hard into a red and white spotted handkerchief.

As I exit the inner sanctuary, she shouts something in a language I don't understand to the plump little redhead, who turns to Hermione and says, 'She'll be ready for you in a tick, miss. She just needs a couple of seconds right now.'

'What was it like?' demands Hermione. She looks a bit nervous.

'It was great,' I tell her. 'I'm going to be rich and famous and have triplets!'

Madame Petulengro calls out in the unfamiliar language again and the redhead nods at Hermione. 'She's ready for you now.'

Hermione disappears through the curtain while I have another look at the gallery of black and white framed photos. A once-upon-a-time Miss England is photographed outside the booth next to a younger-looking, less creased June Petulengro. She is wearing her 1967 sash and not much else. She looks bloody freezing.

Now and again, I can hear snippets of conversation coming from the other side of the curtain. I make out the words . . . *London . . . never been here before . . . no, never.'*

Feeling like I'm eavesdropping, I move away from the curtain, and step outside the booth.

Out on the prom, one of the massive carriage-pulling horses lifts its tail and drops three massive dollops of poo – one, two, three. I can smell the shit from outside Madame Petulengro's booth and I wonder if it drives her mad or if you get used to it?

HERMIONE

Madame Petulengro doesn't really know what to make of me. I give her my right hand and she flips it this way and that. She seems confused and at one point she reaches for a magnifying glass to inspect my palm more closely. After a lot of squinting and muttering in what I guess must be Romany, she starts speaking in a husky Scouse accent and I waver between thinking, 'This is utter bullshit,' to believing in her every word.

'Yours is a hand well travelled,' she begins. 'Tell me, are you local?'

I reply that I've recently moved from London and she seems relieved. 'This is why there is so much confusion in here,' she says tapping my palm slightly crossly. 'Nothing is settled and now is not the time to choose which path to take, but one day the direction will be clear and everything will make sense.' She takes a deep rasping breath and continues, 'There is happiness here and sadness too, a deep sadness that will shape your life for ever. But believe me, it's not your fault; you cannot carry the blame for something you couldn't prevent.'

I presume she means the complete fuck up of my parents' relationship and the great big mess of their separation, so I nod encouragingly, and weirdly she strokes my hand in the way a mother would soothe a kid, a kid with chicken pox or measles; not my mum obviously, but the kind of mum who would do that kind of thing, like Helena's mum probably.

Her hands are bony and together with those long, curved talons, that hooked nose and hooded eyes, there is something of the eagle about the old woman.

'Some things are hard to understand,' she mutters. 'Life can seem very unfair, but there is always light, and our job, while we are in this world, is to find the light.'

For some reason, the way she keeps staring at me is starting to make me uncomfortable and I think she can feel me squirm because all of a sudden she coughs and her voice becomes a lot more detached and businesslike. 'There is travel and a career ahead of you. I see books; you will study and you won't have to rely on any man.' She squints at my palm again. 'Something very important happens in the year 2006; it's a time of starting again.'

I swallow a laugh, because considering that 2006 is the year of my birth, she's kind of bang on.

She drops my hand and abruptly pushes her chair back. I think she may have misinterpreted my laugh. 'What you choose to believe is up to you,' she almost hisses, 'but before you go, I need to tell you to take care of your friend.' She nods towards the curtain. 'The blonde girl, something might happen to her, a bad thing.'

I stare at Madame Petulengro, but she refuses to meet my eye.

'Not every tragedy can be avoided,' she says under her breath, and then she slumps back in her chair with her eyes closed and I suddenly realise how very old she is. In fact, I'd say if she hadn't already got one, Madame Petulengro would be due a telegram from the Queen any day now.

Without opening her eyes, she rasps, 'Roberta will take your money. Tell her I offered you a two-for-one deal; it's the least I can do.'

Roberta's goldfish blue eyes widen in surprise when I tell her of this arrangement.

'She never does that,' she says. 'Two palms for the price of one? Never, not even when Cannon and Ball came in together from the pier and offered her free tickets for the show.'

'It's me and my lucky hand!' laughs Helena, wiggling it around as if it has a life of its own, like 'Thing' in *The Addams Family* and I force a smile and try to push the uneasy feeling away as we make our way out of the booth.

It's gone five but before we catch the number 11 back home, Helena pulls me into an amusement arcade. All the games look like something out of a museum and the noise is deafening, with the clack-clack of the pinball machines, the rattle and ding of the one-armed bandits and the constant sound of coppers dropping into metal slots all around us.

While Helena starts frantically counting out some loose change from her purse, I quickly nip over to the coin exchange to cash in my emergency twenty-pound note. The bloke behind the glass barely looks at my crumpled-up note. He just chucks it in a cash drawer and hands over a pile of mixed 70s currency, which might weigh a ton but thanks to the fantastic exchange rate between 1975 and 2021 will last me at least a week.

'OK, lady,' I say. 'Grand National or the rifle range?'

But apparently we're not here to play games and instead she drags me to a photo booth in the far corner of the arcade.

We reposition the stool to the correct height for the two of us and squeeze in together, an arse cheek each on either side of the stool.

Unlike the modern machines, this one only takes black and white photos, but that's kind of cool, like an arthouse movie.

Helena refuses my money; this is her treat, she says.

'So,' says Helena, feeding ten-pence pieces into the slot in front of us, 'how shall we do this? Are we doing sexy, goofy, serious or natural?' We decide to do all four, changing poses each time the camera flashes in the booth. We pout for the first; pull faces, sticking our tongues out and crossing our eyes, for the second; try (and fail) to compose ourselves for the third; before finally collapsing into hysterics for the last shot.

Ten minutes later, the still slightly tacky set of black and white photos slides out of the machine and Helena holds them carefully, taking care not to smudge our faces before they're completely dry and we both do some screaming and dancing around as we catch sight of our monochrome selves.

When I finally get to examine the photos properly, we are sitting on the top deck of the bus heading back to St Anne's with the late afternoon sun glinting through the windows. Helena's head rests on my shoulder as she slumps against me half asleep, and for a moment I feel oddly choked up as I stare at the two of us captured in the strip of small black and white images.

Helena is so Helena. Her personality radiates from the tiny images. By comparison, I look slightly self-conscious. I don't pull faces with the same panache as Helena. I'm not sure anyone does?

But it's the last photo that I want to keep for ever. In it the two of us are laughing, laughing so hard at each other that I can see Helena's silver fillings glinting. I don't think I have ever looked happier and I can't help wondering how long this magical summer of 1975 can last.

As we approach St Anne's, Helena begins to snore. Carefully I rip the strip of four photos in half and slide the two I like the best into my purse, tucking them safely away in the wallet bit where they can't get lost or damaged. Then I wake Helena, hand her the two remaining pictures and remind her she needs to get off at the next stop to fetch her bike. Helena flies down the stairs in a panic, yelling, 'When will I see you again?' but I don't have time to answer before the bus pulls away.

The bus takes me past sights that I know will disappear in the coming years. The postboxes will remain red, but the telephone box on the corner will disappear, as will the pet shop on the hill and Raymond's Electric Organ Emporium. It's like one of those spot-the-difference picture quizzes, and the more you look, the more differences there are.

As we pass by the secondary school that I'll be attending in September, I notice how small its current 1975 incarnation is. According to Paul, back in the 70s it used to be a right dump, but not now, not since they built the shiny new science and technology block with lottery funding a couple of years ago. It's got a new theatre space too, he told me and mum, 'all very state of the art'.

Everything back in 1975 is smaller and simpler. The petrol stations still have attendants waiting on the forecourts to fill your tank.

Part of me wishes I could stop time here, move my life to this decade, away from the complicated one I live in now, but I know that's not possible, and I feel a stab of sadness at the realisation that this is not my world, and Helena can't ever really be my friend.

As the bus rounds the corner towards my stop on Common Edge, I notice the front gardens are bursting with the same roses and hollyhocks that will bloom again in forty-six years' time, 2021.

It's just gone six and the sun is casting long shadows over the gravestones in the churchyard as I enter through the little gate. I'm not quite ready to face my real life yet and I feel compelled to stay here a little while longer. I wander all the way round to the rear of the church where the church grounds stretch back further than I'd expected and I meander right down to the far end where the moss-covered headstones tilt like crooked teeth. For a while I lose myself among the long-gone Victorian names – Edith, Albert, Percy, Agnes.

I notice how many people died too young, of war and Spanish flu, and all the babies who didn't make it beyond their first birthday.

I decide to leave before I get too maudlin and crunch around an unfamiliar gravel path that I presume will lead me back to the exit at the front of the church. The sun is dappling through the boughs of an oak tree. I haven't been down this way before. The graves are newer on this side, the inscriptions easier to read. Gordon John a dearly beloved granddad aged 89, RIP. It strikes me how much longer everyone lives these days and I'm thinking about the magic of modern medicine, of birth control and vaccinations, when a magpie catches my eye. I stop for second hoping to see its mate. I'm funny about magpies. It's my mum's fault. She's really superstitious, and over the years it's rubbed off on me.

The magpie seems to know I'm watching him and as he hops along the curved edge of a heart-shaped headstone, he suddenly stops, his head tilting down as if to read the inscription below.

Gold letters are carved into the white marble and suddenly my heart lurches. The magpie flies away, but it's too late, I've already read it.

Helena Treace
16th March 1960 – 2nd August 1975
Darling daughter and sister,
Much loved and missed for ever

My heart seems to stop and the world spins, the ground tilting away from me.

Helena has three days to live.

HELENA

THURSDAY

There's a postcard on the breakfast table when I get downstairs in the morning, which means that everyone will have read it before me. The picture on the front depicts one of those annoying seaside scenes, all yellow sand, blue sea and striped umbrellas. The writing on the other side is so familiar that I can see the two of them, Gwen and Elaine, sitting side by side, sharing the same multicoloured, push-up biro. Gwen writes first in blue ink –

Dear H, Elaine got so burnt on the first day that her back blistered up like a Dr Who monster and she had to be wrapped in damp towels for 24 hours like an Egyptian mummy. Also she forgot to pack her bikini bottoms. This means she has been showing all the French boys her flabby derrière, as they call it over here.'

I will not laugh; I will not laugh at these traitors. Elaine

240

writes next in green ink.

She lies. My derrière is not hanging out for all to see, but I have had to swim in my shorts. All is most excellent apart from the fact that we went to a restaurant where they were serving rabbit stew and I had hysterics in the car park. We have been pony riding and visited a few cathedrals too.

Thank God I didn't go then. If there's one thing that can put a massive blot on a holiday it's the inside of a cathedral. I can just imagine Mr Sanderson all puffed up in his Jesus sandals and socks, reading facts out of a guide book. At the bottom of the postcard, they have written in red (Gwen) and purple (Elaine) ink,

We miss you and we cannot wait to see you. Won't be long till we are back, don't expect a present hahaha! Xxx

Normally I would save this postcard and stick it on my wall, but with my new wallpaper ready and waiting to hang, I decide to throw it away.

Rosalind catches me as I step on the pedal of the bin. 'Why are you chucking that away?'

I decide to be honest. 'Because they went without me and to be honest, it feels like they're rubbing my nose in it.'

'That's daft talk,' says Rosy, doing an uncanny impression of

241

Nana Nancy and she reaches into the bin, digs the postcard out and makes me promise to keep it, even though it's crumpled and covered in tea leaves.

Suddenly I realise the sky outside is as blue as the postcard, and it occurs to me that it's going to be hot enough to brave the open-air pool. Now, I don't really know how I feel about this. On the one hand, I love swimming – obviously, because I'm a Pisces – but on the other, it means exposing myself for all to see. My mum would say at this point, 'No one's looking at you, Helena.' But Alicia doesn't understand what it's like to be fifteen and squeezing yourself into a bikini that was a bit tight last year. The alternative is to wear my Queen Anne's swimming costume, which is even tighter because I've had it since I was thirteen. It's also brown, which makes you look like you've been swimming in sewage, and designed to flatten any chance of a bust I might have, plus it's got my name tag sewn on the outside of a shoulder strap.

Now, obviously I don't want to go swimming by myself, because I don't want to look like a fat, friendless freak, but considering I still have no way of getting in touch with Hermione, I do something that takes me completely by surprise. I phone Alex King. I've had her number since we were both in the play at Easter and I dial it, half hoping no one answers. Calling Alex feels strange to me.

She sounds surprised to hear from me, but I put on my best *Jackie* 'fun friend' voice and burble on about being 'up for getting some tan lines and having a laugh' and I don't think she can think of any reason to say no.

'But I'll have to tell Paul,' she says, and I wonder why?

I mean, it's not like he's her dad.

Then she goes, 'Have you asked Liza?' and before I can stop myself I blurt, 'God no.'

There's a silence, so I fill it by doing my Mutley wheezy cartoon-dog laugh from *Wacky Races* and Alex says, 'Is that supposed to be Mutley from *Wacky Races*?' And I say, 'Yes, there's no end to my talents,' but she doesn't laugh back, she just says, 'OK, I won't call Liza. You and me can just have a nice girlie chat, unless that mate of yours is coming too, the weird one from London?'

I want to say, 'She's not weird, and if I knew her number, I wouldn't be calling you.' But I don't, I just say, 'She might see us there. Why don't we meet outside the pool at twelve thirty? I'll bring a packed lunch.'

'You and your grub fixation. Liza's right, you've got food on the brain,' responds Alex. 'It's too hot to eat anything other than ice cream.'

Well, I beg to differ, so I pack a Tupperware with peanut butter sandwiches, grab an apple and some crisps, and leave a 'gone swimming' note on the kitchen table. Fortunately for me, Mum has nipped out to the Co-op to do a quick shop. I breathe a sigh of relief. If she knew I was going to the lido, she might ask me to take Ros and I'm not cramping my style for an eleven-year-old kid.

For starters, I will want to smoke, and in any case, children and teens don't congregate in the same area. The teens, like me, head for the flat roof on top of the changing rooms, while the kiddies and families set up camp near the café and toilets. Those are the rules, but my mum wouldn't understand.

I join Alex in the queue outside the baths. As usual she looks amazing and I curse myself for not having a pair of pink heart-shaped sunglasses like hers. Honestly, she is so ridiculously pretty and her legs are the colour of tinned sausages in brine, all smooth and golden brown. She's obviously wearing her bikini under her gypsy blouse because I can see the tie of the halterneck. *Jackie* magazine said halterneck bikinis 'flatter most body shapes' in their seaside fashion special last week. Damn my rubbish bikini for not being a halterneck. Alex has a straw basket over one arm containing a striped towel, a small transistor radio, some Ambre Solaire, a packet of ten No.6, and a lighter. I have my duffel bag, which makes me look like I'm going swimming with the Guides.

It feels a bit strange, the two of us being together like this. It's as if we're trying each other on to see if the friendship fits. Personally, I feel like we aren't quite each other's size, colour or shape. All the time I'm talking to Alex, I'm thinking how much fun I had with Hermione yesterday, and how I wish she was here.

'So did you have fun at the party?' Alex and I are laying our towels out on the last unoccupied corner of the changing-room roof. Her bikini is red and blue check, with a wooden ring attaching the two triangles of fabric between her boobs. Boobs which I'm glad to say are quite normal in size, more poached egg, like mine, than hot-air balloon like Liza's. My bikini isn't as flattering as Alex's. It's pale blue with white flowers on it, only the flowers have faded and if I go in the water, the top half goes completely saggy. I arrange myself face down, which I think makes me look thinner than the other way round.

'Oh, the party,' I reply casually. 'Yeah, it had its moments.'

Alex's eyes narrow as she says, 'I saw Sticks playing the knight in shining armour.'

'Yeah.' I can't help but smirk. 'That Albie was coming on a bit strong.'

'I think you're reading too much into it,' Alex replies. 'He's shagging Liza's sister so, you know, I wouldn't get your hopes up.'

'I don't fancy Albie!' I protest. 'He's ancient.'

'He's not as old as Paul,' Alex snaps back, at which point I'd quite like to say, 'Yeah, what's that all about? He's a creep, with his old-man hip flask and car keys.' But I don't.

Instead, I ask how long she and Paul have been together and after thirty minutes of being bored senseless by Alex King telling me about every date she's ever been on with Paul Thursby, I begin to wish I had brought Rosalind. At least she's more of a laugh.

I can feel my eyelids drooping. It's really hot, and I'm almost drifting off when I hear her say, 'So that Hermione girl, who exactly is she?'

This wakes me up. 'Oh, she's just moved here from London. She's really cool,' I answer.

'Thinks a lot of herself if you ask me,' sneers Alex, propping herself up on one elbow and calling out to Susie Jones, who has just walked up the steps on to the roof. My heart sinks, but I notice my shoulders turning pink, so at least I'm getting a tan.

Susie Jones is wearing an orange bikini with beaded string ties and is fortunately even pudgier than I am. Her knees are dimpled and her ankles are thick. 'Legs like bottles,' Nana

245

Nancy would say, and I cheer up a little.

For a while we smoke cigarettes and Susie Jones slags everyone off, which is kind of funny but after a while gets as monotonous as Alex banging on about Paul Thursby.

I keep quiet, trying to retain some air of mystery, even though Susie Jones has known me since Brownies and once saw me cry because I failed my Brownie first-aid badge. Basically, I was nine and I got into a mess with a crêpe ankle bandage and Brown Owl saw fit to deny me the badge, the bitch.

Alex is obviously delighted to have Susie join us. Susie is much more on the scene than I am. I don't have access to all the latest gossip, I don't know half the people that Susie and Alex know, and I certainly didn't know about the gig that Sticks is playing at the Fairhaven Social Club on Saturday night.

I sit up and start really listening. Sticks is playing a gig; he's sitting in for a drummer who's been sent to borstal, the young offenders institute.

I feel the hairs tingle on the back of my neck. Oh my God, not only is Sticks playing an actual gig this weekend, but also I know people who know people who have been sent to borstal! This is possibly one of the most exciting moments of my life.

'Who's been sent to borstal?' I enquire casually. This is actually the first time the word 'borstal' has ever dropped out of my mouth and it feels kind of exciting.

'Oh, you wouldn't know him,' says Susie, who seems to think I'm still nine years old.

Alex, however, can't resist adding more detail. 'Thommo Thompson. His older brother Gordie is a mate of Albie's and everyone's saying he dropped Thommo in it.' For the first time since we arrived at the lido I am genuinely interested in what Alex has to say. 'Turns out,' she continues, 'Gordie and Thommo were doing a robbery on an off-licence – not a big job, cash and fags – only a cop car on patrol spots something fishy and Gordie does a runner on his Harley leaving Thommo up against a wall with five hundred Benson and Hedges and the contents of the cash register stuffed down his trousers – and bingo, he's gone down for six months. So Thommo plays drums in a band called The Ravens, who play Eagles and some Led Zeppelin covers, and anyway, because Thommo's gone down, Sticks is sitting in for him, like literally. He's going to do the drumming at this gig on Saturday and if he's any good then they might take him on for the full six months.'

'Only thing is,' interrupts Susie Jones, 'it's like a really big thing for Sticks, and Liza can't be there, because she's got to go back to Brum for her nan's actual funeral, and she's gutted.'

Alex looks at me slyly. 'We'll all be there, of course.'

I don't say anything, but my mind is racing,

Sticks is playing a gig in St Anne's on Saturday night and Liza is stuck in Birmingham. And I know that whatever happens, I'm going to be at that gig and with any luck Hermione will be there with me.

HERMIONE

As soon as I wake up, I remember what I saw yesterday and instantly I feel terrified. The words 'Helena's grave' seem to echo in my head and when I close my eyes, I see it all over again – the magpie, the heart-shaped headstone, a headstone that is engraved with Helena's name.

As if for reassurance, I glance over at Helena's handwriting on my bedroom wall, the biro scribble that has become so familiar to me. The words are so Helena, so alive, so funny, she can't possibly be dead, it can't be true, none of it is, the whole thing is a . . . a what?

A mirage is the closest I can come up with. We learned about them once in geography, how travellers in the desert could be tricked into seeing what looked like a real-life oasis, when in fact it was just an optical illusion. Could that gravestone – or perhaps all of my experiences this week – be some kind of mirage? A world of make-believe, a three-dimensional optical illusion?

Something very dark pricks at the back of my mind, something about my dad's mum, how she had mental health

248

problems until she died about ten years ago. The word schizophrenia looms into my brain and won't budge. What if that's what's happening to me? Apparently, she had visions and saw people who didn't exist. What if I'm just as sick as she was, and made Helena up? Maybe *I* wrote the stuff on the wall? Maybe I fabricated the whole experience, the Blue Monkey, weeing behind the bushes in Ashton Gardens, the terrible meal in the Wimpy Bar?

But deep down, I know I didn't make it up and I have evidence – small black and white squares of proof that it actually happened, me and Helena, laughing fit to burst, and my heart tightens.

Helena cannot die; there must be something I can do to change the course of fate. As long as I'm with her, then I can stop anything bad from happening. I will look after her, I won't let her die.

I look down at my hands and realise I'm trembling. I have to pull myself together. Falling to pieces isn't an option. I need to get back to 1975 and find out if there is anything I can do to prevent this tragedy.

Madame Petulengro's face flashes in front of my eyes and I try to block out the memory of her voice saying, 'You cannot carry the blame for something you couldn't prevent,' as I force myself out of bed.

The house is quiet again, after the invasion of Lucy and Will. They'd gone by the time I got home last night. Apparently the trip to the carvery had been a raging success and even my mum was in a really good mood, but then Tess does love a bit of pork crackling.

'Three types of meat, Hermione,' she'd boasted when I got in. 'You'd have hated it, nothing for veggies and the best Yorkshire puddings I've ever had in my life.' Paul showed me some photos on his phone and there was even one of Tess, smiling with Will on her knee. Wonders will never cease.

Mum is in her bra and pants on the back lawn and Paul is pottering about with a hose. It's weird but they do seem kind of content together, and I have to admit Paul has never been anything less than kind to her, and my mum really needs that. Fat pink roses have bloomed overnight and two yellow butterflies flit among the lupins.

I manage to get some cereal down me, then run back upstairs to shower and get dressed. It's really hot today, so I pull on shorts and a Debbie Harry sleeveless vest before realising that in the UK she doesn't have a hit until 1979 so I quickly I swap it for a faded old grey number with Mickey Mouse on the front. Mickey's been around for ever. To finish the effect, I put on some vintage Persol sunglasses that used to belong to my dad and as I do I realise I haven't thought about him in ages. I've had two texts from Casper since I've been here and considering the last one referred to me as Trevor, it's safe to assume only one was intentional. Mum says we'll hear if he's in trouble, and I can't help noticing that when she talks about my dad, her face looks ten years older. Since we moved in with Paul, she's less tense. She's even trying to cut down on the fags and has started vaping instead.

I pack my bag with everything I might need for a day out in 1975 – sunscreen, loose change and a bunch of pound notes, which have been out of circulation since before I was born.

I tuck an extra fiver into my purse for emergencies and set off, praying that my usual short cut through the graveyard will perform its time-travel magic. Whatever happens, I'm not going round the side where I saw Helena's grave. I never want to see that thing again.

As I cut through the churchyard, it suddenly strikes me that just because it's a glorious day right now, back in 1975 it could be pissing it down. But I'm in luck. The century might have changed as I exit through the funny little wooden gate into the last millennium, but the weather is exactly the same. It is midday on a gloriously hot day on 31st July 1975, which, according to the inscription on that awful heart-shaped headstone, is just two days before my friend dies.

I dig my nails into my palms and think, *not on my watch*.

Upstairs on the top deck of the bus, all my favourite seats are taken, so I sit halfway down the bus on the left-hand side, behind a mum and her little girl.

The sun shines through the window and the little girl's hair ripples like a river of gold and I have to stop myself from leaning forward and touching it. She is going into town to buy some shoes.

'Can I have red ones?' she asks her mother.

'*May* I have red ones,' her mother corrects her. 'Let's just see what the shop has to offer, shall we?'

She has her arm around the little girl and is softly stroking her shoulder, and for some reason I get a lump in my throat. 'Only I got blue sandals last year and it's nice to have something different.'

Her mother laughs. 'You'll be asking me for wedges next like

Helena,' and the little girl laughs back.

I gasp and they turn their faces. This must be Helena's mum and sister, I realise. Alicia and Rosalind. I pretend I'm having a choking fit, which inevitably turns into a real choking fit and the little girl offers me her last Spangle from a slightly grubby packet. 'Ooh, a red one,' she says. 'That's lucky.'

I take the sweet and thank her. Her face has some of Helena in it, but there is a dreamy gentle quality about her that Helena doesn't have. Helena is all mischief and fun. 'There now,' she tells me when I stop coughing. 'That's better,' and it is.

I would spend the rest of the journey eavesdropping on the pair of them but I can't listen to them without feeling like crying. The thought of that little girl losing her sister, her mother's grief, their entire world falling apart, I can't bear it.

So I move downstairs and sit among the old women with fat freckled arms in sleeveless summer frocks, thinking, *Where are you, Helena?*

There is a real holiday feel to the town today. Not only are the locals out in force, but the square is inundated with tourists too. Pensioners fill every bench, kids traipse out of Woolworths with brand-new buckets and spades, and the queue for the ice-cream van is beginning to snake around the corner.

I decide to check out Helena's regular haunts, starting with the Blue Monkey, though I can't imagine why anyone would spend a day like today in that stinky hole.

Inside, a small bunch of grimy-looking Hell's Angels, trying not to look hot in all their leather gear, are lounging around on the banquettes, adding a whiff of BO to the usual stench of fag ash. I stay long enough to listen to a Rolling Stones number my dad used to play all the time when I was a kid, knock back a dismal cup of milky tea, then when Helena doesn't show up, I get up to leave.

As I head for the door, one of the Hell's Angels decides to block my way, and when I make an attempt to push past, he asks me why I'm in such a hurry.

I decide to be honest. 'I'm trying to find a friend. Her name's Helena.'

The bloke smirks and yells over his shoulder. 'Hey, Albie, where's that little schoolie?' Then he looks me in the eye, rubs his crotch and says, 'We've got a sweepstake going on that one. First one into her knickers wins a pint.'

'Oh for fuck's sake,' I snap, barging past.

Bitchy Sandra shouts after me, raising her voice, so that I can hear her over the guffaws and back-slapping. 'Ashton Gardens or the lido, love, if she's got any sense.'

Of course, I think, the lido, then immediately afterwards I panic. Oh god, what if she has an accident at the swimming pool? What if she drowns? But then I remember she's still got two days to live. Still, I want to get to her as soon as I can, just to be safe. *Hang on, Helena*, I think. *I'm coming.* I'm kicking myself for not packing my bikini before I left home. Sod it, I can't go back now, and I don't have time to start choosing new swimwear. I can sunbathe in my bra and shorts. I need to find Helena.

The lido is packed and instinctively I follow a gang of other teens up some concrete steps on to what seems to be the roof of the changing rooms.

Helena spots me and starts waving frantically, and I'm so

253

relieved to see her. I'm also pleased that she's set up camp far enough away from the edge of the roof not to be in any immediate danger. By time I reach her, I can see that her shoulders are burnt.

'You should put your T-shirt on,' I say. 'You're going red.'

She rolls her eyes at me, but does as she's told and budges up so that I can share her towel.

I strip off my T-shirt, relieved to be wearing a lime-green sports bra that can almost pass for a bikini top. It's obvious no one's been swimming, which is fine by me. The only time we did life-saving at school it involved a pair of pyjamas and a rubber brick.

I've already met Susie, so Helena introduces me to Alex.

'Oh, so you're the famous Hermione,' she drawls, checking me out, judging my thighs, my boobs, my hair.

I lie down next to Helena, shutting my eyes but keeping my ears as wide open as is physically possible.

The big topic of conversation, in fact the only thing these three seem capable of talking about, is this gig at some club on Saturday night. Apparently everyone's going to be there because Sticks is playing the drums for a band called The Ravens.

I glance at Helena. Her cheeks are bright pink and her eyes are shining. It might be the effects of the sun, but I know that it's more than that. Helena is plotting something and no doubt it has something to do with Sticks's gig on Saturday night, and whatever she is plotting, I'm going to have to stop it. Because Saturday is 2nd August which, according to the gravestone, is the day that Helena is going to die.

HELENA

After the lido, Hermione and I walk back through the square and Hermione suggests we stop and have a cup of tea in the Pavilion Café in Ashton Gardens. It makes a change from the Blue Monkey, I guess. For starters, the milk comes in a jug, no one has touched the sugar cubes and we can gossip without anyone overhearing.

I'm, like, bursting with excitement over the gig. 'Imagine,' I say. 'Sticks is actually going to be on stage playing drums for The Ravens!'

Hemione makes a face.

'What?' I ask.

'Alex said they play Eagles covers,' she says.

'So?'

'Well, why would you even want to go to the gig when you don't like that kind of music? We could just stay in! Have a girlie night . . . put on face packs and paint our nails?'

'Erm,' I say, 'because Sticks is playing? He's going to be on stage? In a band? We can have a girlie night any night.'

'I guess,' she says, not looking me in the eye. 'I just don't really like American rock music.'

'It isn't really my thing either,' I protest, 'but that's not the point! Anyway, it could be worse. At least it's not Cliff Richard or The Rubettes! Though don't let Gwen hear me say that.'

But she doesn't laugh like she normally would. In fact, she looks kind of sad.

'What's wrong?' I ask.

'I'm a bit distracted, that's all,' she says.

I try to get her to understand how important the gig is to me, how St Anne's isn't like London, how I never get to see live music, how amazing it would be to go with her and see the boy I fancy up on stage, but she's barely listening, she's not herself, she seems nervy and on edge, and I wonder if maybe her period's due?

Or maybe that's not it. Maybe she's just too cool for this gig? Hermione is so worldly-wise, she's seen loads of bands, mostly at gigs in parks, sort of mini outdoor festivals, as she's explained to me before. Apart from the Radio 1 Roadshow, all I've seen is a brass band playing in the bandstand in the park with Nana Nancy and her friend Madge, who got there early to make sure they got us a good seat on the nearest bench.

I guess it's not surprising Hermione doesn't really want to go. Then just when I'm beginning to feel really down, she suddenly sighs loudly and says, 'All right then.'

'All right then what?' I say, not daring to hope.

'All right then, let's go,' she says, and I squeal and leap up to give her a massive hug.

'And we should probably go into town tomorrow too and

find something nice to wear,' she says, smiling again at last.

I tell her I've already more or less spent my skivvying wages, but she says, don't worry, I've got this. Trust me.

So I can hardly say no to that, can I?

Suddenly I remember I promised my mum that I'd be home at five today because she's got a last-minute appointment with the hairdresser and she wants me to mind Rosy. It's their anniversary and my dad's taking her out for dinner. They'll probably go to The Cherry Tree in Wrea Green, and my dad will have the steak, because he always does, and my mum will have the fish of the day and regret it, because that's what she always does.

Hermione says she's got some things still to do in town, so we say goodbye and agree to meet outside Woolworths tomorrow morning at ten.

When I turn back to wave, Hermione doesn't see me. She is looking deep into her tea, like a mini Madame Petulengro, as if she might find a message in the bottom of the cup.

HERMIONE

I sit outside the café for a while, worrying about whether I should have insisted on going home with her, but instinctively I know if anything is going to happen to her, it's going to happen on the day of the gig, the date on her headstone, not today.

Just the thought of that headstone makes my stomach flip and I shudder, feeling a sudden chill despite the hot summer afternoon.

I can't stop her going though. I tried, but there's no way. Helena is determined that she is going to watch Sticks play those drums, so all I can do is stay by her side and make sure that she has the best time ever, for as long as she has left on this earth.

So that's why I've decided to do what I'm about to do. I want to give Helena the time of her life and I've figured out a way of doing it.

I noticed the shop a few days ago. It's funny how the symbol for a pawnbroker hasn't changed since Dickens's time.

The necklace is the last Christmas present my dad gave me, a silver chain with a Tiffany heart-shaped charm with a tiny little diamond stud in the middle. I know exactly how much he paid for it because I checked out the price online. It cost just over four hundred quid. I have no idea where he got the money from, and right now, I don't care.

I didn't actually get the necklace until just after New Year. Casper was meant to meet me in Nando's in Camberwell on Christmas Eve, but he never showed up. It's my only piece of proper jewellery, but it also reminds me that my father never keeps his promises, so I don't wear it very often.

I've had it tucked in the bottom of my bag for a while now, while I waited to pluck up the courage. It's still in its original box, so it should be worth a bit. If they ask any awkward questions, I'll say it was a gift from a rich relative in the States.

Only they don't ask any awkward questions, because the bloke who runs the place couldn't care less. His eyes light up as soon as he sees the necklace, but then he goes immediately into disinterested mode. 'Twenty quid,' he offers, and I almost laugh. 'Twenty-five,' he ventures, and I find myself agreeing. I don't really want the necklace; I never did. I wanted my dad to meet me at Nando's like he said he would. The necklace itself is worthless.

I love my dad and I will always forgive him, but I've finally realised I can never rely on him. When he did finally give me the necklace, his right hand was heavily bandaged, and he had a black eye.

For a split second I can almost understand what Tess sees in Paul. He might wear repulsive shorts and hideous socks, but he

259

reminds her to put her seatbelt on and he takes her a cup of tea in bed in the morning.

The truth is, I don't believe that my dad went into Tiffany the week before Christmas when other dads were buying their daughters presents; I don't believe he chose and paid for the necklace himself. He'd have bartered for it in a pub or swapped it for some coke. God bless Casper but he has never put me first and right now Helena is more important to me than my father.

HELENA

When I get home, I discover to my utter amazement that my dad has actually hung the fabulous purple floral wallpaper and my room is now fantastic.

Well, it will be once I get some new bits of furniture and a lava lamp and a beanbag, though my mum says those will have to wait for Christmas, the big meanie. I've decided that until Juliet gets back, I'm going to borrow her purple needlecord beanbag, because it goes really well with my wallpaper. Honestly, I can't wait to see Juliet's face. She's going to be livid. Even Rosy, who doesn't really do jealousy, is really jealous, and I can't wait for Hermione to see it. I mean, it's ridiculous, we're like best friends and she still hasn't been round to my house. The thought of us getting ready to go out on a Saturday night in our new outfits to see a boy I fancy play in a band is almost too exciting to bear.

For dinner Rosy and I eat fish fingers with Smash instant potato, peas and ketchup in front of the telly.

My shoulders itch from too much sun, and at the moment

they are bright pink, but hopefully in the morning I'll be a bronzed goddess.

HERMIONE

Of course, two hours later, as soon as I'm safely back in 2021, my phone tings signalling a new message, and who should it be but Casper.

> I seem to be in Chile, digging the empanadas, hope the North isn't driving you nuts, ha-ha, catch up when back in Blighty, Dad x

I reply immediately.

> How, why, when are you coming back???
> Miss you, love you.

But he doesn't text back, and I sit there on the bed trying to come to terms with the fact that I've just flogged the only thing my dad's ever given me to pay for what might be my best friend's last 24 hours on earth.

Tess yells up from downstairs. 'Paul and I are going to the pub for dinner,' she says. 'It's Thai night at The Blossoms. Do you want to come?'

'No,' I shout.

'Suit yourself,' she bellows back, and seconds later I hear the front door bang.

HELENA

FRIDAY

Hermione is waiting for me outside Woolworths with a big bag of pic 'n' mix.

Together we sit on the bus, eating sweets and gossiping. In some respects, Hermione is my Madge, who was the only person who could get Nana Nancy out of bed when Poppa Hubert died. I tell this to Hermione, who says, 'awww'.

'Apparently Nana Nancy went from full mourning to playing bingo twice a week within a fortnight,' I tell her. 'Nowadays there's no stopping the two of them. They even go ballroom dancing together.'

'Both my nanas are dead,' says Hermione, and she suddenly looks a bit upset, so I let her have the last Fruit Salad in the bag.

We go to Miss Selfridge first, which is situated at the top of the escalator in John Lewis. It's like walking into a cave, all dark with neon lights and pop music. Disco Tex and the Sex-O-Lettes are belting out, 'I wanna dance wit' choo'. Hermione doesn't know the words. It's weird. I know she loves music, but she seems to know nothing about the charts.

I adore everything about Miss Selfridge, and even Hermione looks knocked out. 'It's all so authentic,' she sighs.

In the end, there's too much choice and the only dress I really want to try on, a little blue and white spotty number with a contrasting long white collar and red buttons, is far too expensive, but Hermione buys some love beads, and a purple suede belt with loads of fringing.

I'm starting to panic about not finding anything, but Hermione decides we need to keep calm and have lunch, so we have poached eggs on toast in the British Home Stores café.

Afterwards we cross the precinct to Chelsea Girl. Honestly, it's like Hermione has never been to Chelsea Girl before. She keeps muttering 'this is so cool' over and over. Maybe the branches in London don't look the same? This one in Blackpool is quite small and poky and my mum always says they keep it deliberately dark so that you can't see how shoddy the hems are – like anyone cares about hems! The assistants are always the prettiest, scariest girls you've ever seen, and none of them ever want to help you find anything. They just sit on stools looking beautiful and bored. They don't even pick up clothes that have fallen off hangers; they just leave them lying on the floor. Honestly, if I could ditch my rubbish chambermaiding job and get a job in Chelsea Girl, then I'd do it like a shot. They've even got joss sticks burning on the counter and some new-fangled eyeliner, called kohl, which is based on what the ancient Egyptians used.

I have to admit that it's quite hard to find anything that might be both nice and affordable, because it's too dark to read the prices, never mind the sizes, but Hermione suddenly grabs me and pushes me towards the communal changing room. She is holding two identical dresses, one is black and the other bright red.

'I can't wear red,' I hiss, and Hermione smirks and says, 'I know. The red one's for me.'

We strip off and slip into the dresses. To be honest, they're not something I would have noticed. They're very simple cotton cross-over numbers with a belt that ties at the back and a bit of what my mum would call broderie anglaise trim around the flared sleeves and hemline. The neckline is V-shaped and weirdly flattering, and somehow the way the belt is attached makes my waist look loads smaller than it really is. For a second, neither of us say anything, because we both know it – we look great. Hermione, with her shaggy dark hair, looks brilliant in the red, while the black, even though I say it myself, really complements my blonde hair, and even though my legs aren't as brown as Alex King's, they look perfectly fine. I blush as we catch each other's eye in the mirror and the two of us burst out laughing.

'Right,' says Hermione, 'that clinches it. We're having them.'

Under the dressing-room lights, I catch sight of the price tag and my heart sinks. I can't possibly afford mine. I don't know what I was even thinking trying it on. I can't even afford a little box of kohl eyeliner.

'I'm sorry, Hermione,' I say. 'There's no way I can buy this. I haven't got nearly enough money.'

But she just shrugs it off and says, 'My treat. I'm buying both of them. It's not a big deal, so don't even think about saying no.'

I'm so thrilled I could hug her, but considering she's just

taken off the red dress and is standing in her bra and knickers, I don't, because it would be weird. Instead I do something entirely different but equally weird – I burst into tears. Hermione laughs, but she looks a bit teary-eyed too.

'You and me,' she says. 'We're going to be the belles of the ball.'

She hands over some notes to a girl at the till, who can hardly be bothered to put our dresses into bags. 'We'd like a bag each, actually,' Hermione tells her, and the girl blinks very slowly but does what she's told.

As we make our way out of the shop, I do an impression of Hermione saying 'we'd like a bag each actually' in a really posh voice and we both crack up.

Out on the street, I catch sight of our reflection in the shop window and I have one of those 'glad to be alive' moments, when your heart feels like it's going to burst with happiness. I am walking down the street in the sunshine with my new best friend and a new dress in a brand-new Chelsea Girl bag and I swear other girls on the street are looking at us and I can help thinking they must be livid with jealousy.

'What now?' says Hermione.

And as soon as she asks, I know.

HERMIONE

Helena frogmarches me across the promenade and we join a short queue of mostly middle-aged couples and young families at the base of the famous Blackpool Tower.

'I'm taking you to see something magical,' she informs me, and I wonder for a second if she thinks aquariums are my thing? Because apparently there's one in the basement of the tower and my heart sinks at the prospect of seeing a load of miserable-faced fish trapped behind glass. When we reach the cashier, she pushes me to one side.

'This is *my* treat,' she grins, paying the woman behind the ticket counter.

I follow Helena to the top of a set of wide shallow stairs, where a woman in a uniform takes our tickets and ushers us through a set of heavy wooden doors and into . . . the most beautiful room I have ever been in in my whole life. And then it dawns on me, of course. This is the famous Blackpool Tower ballroom, as seen every year on *Strictly*, which my mum loves. I hadn't really known what to expect, but this beats anything I could ever imagine. It's like stepping into a film . . . everything is golden, like the inside of a really posh West End theatre crossed with a really fancy box of chocolates. It's so over the top and extravagant that all I can do is stand and blink.

In the middle of the stage someone is playing an organ. It sounds like the kind of thing you'd hear in a cathedral, only the man playing it is wearing a white suit with silver rhinestones on the back, and instead of hymns, this great beast of an instrument is belting out dance music. The sound is deep, as if it comes from the belly of the tower itself, while above our heads, huge crystal chandeliers spill a Hollywood glamour over the place.

I'm a tiny bit winded. Groups of chairs and tables surround the dance floor and for a while, we sit quietly, our Chelsea Girl bags on our knees, just drinking it all in. Suddenly Helena nudges me. 'Over there,' she hisses.

I follow the direction of her finger and there, in the middle of the dance floor, are two women in their seventies, twirling each other around.

'I had a feeling they might be here,' Helena says. 'That's Nana Nancy and her friend Madge.'

I guess instinctively that the taller, grey-haired woman is Madge and the shorter, rounder woman with the very obviously dyed auburn hair and a leopard-skin chiffon scarf around her neck is Nana Nancy. The two of them are having a ball, literally, in this most beautiful of ballrooms. I'm not sure of the dance they're doing, all I know is that it's too quick to be a waltz. 'They're foxtrotting,' Helena whispers when I ask. Gradually, as my eyes get accustomed to what I'm seeing, I realise that Madge and Nancy aren't the only same-sex couple on the dance floor, but that no one is batting an eyelid. I'm guessing this is one of the only places in 1975 where such behaviour is acceptable, and I love it so much that I suddenly feel really emotional and I really wish I knew how to do these funny old-fashioned dances so that I could ask Helena to dance with me.

When Madge and Nancy come off the floor 'for a breather', we make our way over to their table and Nancy is so delighted to see Helena that I feel myself getting all choked up again. There is something about this place that makes me ridiculously emotional. It's so beautiful and Helena is so happy here, that the thought that tomorrow could be her last day on earth is unbearable.

It can't be, it mustn't be.

Madge goes to the bar to buy us all a cup of tea and comes back with some really weird cake things, which are basically marshmallow covered in chocolate and shredded coconut.

'Ah, snowballs!' breathes Helena hungrily. Nana Nancy eyes me up and down, and bombards me with questions.

'London, you say? Madge and I went on a trip a few years ago. Saw a show didn't we, Madge?'

'Mmmm,' Madge says.

'What was it called? *There's a Girl in My Soup*, was it? Ooh we did laugh, didn't we, Madge?'

Madge doesn't say much, she just smiles and nods.

When Helena nips to the loo, Nancy leans right over to me and says, 'She's my favourite. I don't love her any more than the others. I love all three of my granddaughters, but Juliet can be a bit like her mum, snobby, and the little one, well, she's the sweetest girl you ever did meet, and when she was ill, it nearly killed me, did Helena tell you?'

271

I nod, and she mouths, 'Leukaemia,' and taps at her heart as if it might be in danger of stopping. 'The doctors say she's doing very well, but she's not out of the woods yet. They're monitoring her, God love her.'

'God love her,' echoes Madge.

'But Helena,' continues Nancy, 'she's been making me laugh since she was born.'

'Lights up a room,' mutters Madge, and I smile and say, 'I'm very lucky to be her friend.'

At which point Helena comes back complaining of no toilet paper in the ladies'. 'Well, I hope you didn't do a poo!' says Nana Nancy, and I laugh until I feel a bit faint.

Before we leave, Madge and Nancy have a last waltz across the floor and Helena looks at me and says, 'Promise me when we're seventy-five we will come back here and dance.'

'Of course,' I say, 'and let's wear the dresses that we bought today,' and the two of us chuckle at the idea of a couple of pensioners in their Chelsea Girl finery, but under the laughter I'm so very close to tears, because I know that even if I do manage to save Helena's life tomorrow, this can never happen; we will never be old ladies together.

On the bus home Helena turns to me and with big round pleading eyes says, 'Hermione, will you come round to mine tomorrow – before we go out I mean – so we can get ready together? Please, Hermione, you've got to see my room. Please Hermione, please say yes?'

And I do, of course I do. We arrange to meet in the Blue Monkey at three then go back to hers for tea, because right now I would do anything for her.

HELENA

I've given Mum strict instructions about what she's allowed to cook for tea: no garlic and no fish. She tells me she is thinking of making garlic baked trout, which isn't even funny. Simon's been warned that he can't wear shorts, or ask Hermione if she plays any musical instruments because it's none of his business. I've also threatened to behead every single Barbie Rosalind possesses if she does any snooping or door-listening.

'Why would I be interested in you and your stupid friend?' she snipes back. She looks pale today and the shadows under her eyes have that worrying purple tinge. She had a bad night apparently, a 3 a.m. nosebleed. Alicia looks kind of stricken when she tells me this. Rosalind had nosebleeds before, when she was ill; that's how they found out she *was* ill. Mum thought she might be anaemic and took her to the doctor and he did some tests and . . . But then again, some perfectly healthy people have nosebleeds. I remember going ice skating for Gwen's birthday when we were twelve and one of her drippy maths-wiz mates had a nosebleed all over the ice. When her mum came to pick her up, she just said, 'Oh, Elizabeth is a terrible bleeder, it happens all the time: weak nasal capillaries. I normally make her carry a spare top.'

See, it's nothing to get your knickers in a twist over.

A postcard arrived from Juliet this morning, so that was annoying. Mum read it out at breakfast. According to Juliet's postcard, the villa and the pool are fab, she's the brownest she's ever been, and when she comes home next weekend, she's going to cook some amazing Italian dishes for us all. Big bloody deal. The last thing I need is more pasta making me even fatter.

I spend the rest of the morning making my bedroom look as trendy and grown-up as I possibly can. Not only do I nab my big sister's beanbag, but I also swap a few kiddie books from my bookshelf for some more grown-up stuff of Juliet's. Basically, I swap my *Just William* collection for *The L-Shaped Room*, *Love Story*, *Jonathan Livingston Seagull*, *The Picture of Dorian Gray* and *Madame Bovary*.

I dither for a while over which posters to put back on my gorgeous floral walls. In the end I opt for the Biba poster and my *Diamond Dogs* pride and joy. Ideally, I'd like a new roller blind and bedspread, but even so, I have to admit that I'm really lucky, my room looks great, and I decide to buy my dad a Walnut Whip next time I'm at the shops, because they're his favourite and he deserves a treat.

The weather is weird today. Although it's hot, the sky is a strange yellowish grey. My mum says she can smell thunder. She always says this, like she's some kind of witch. Mind you, she's usually right and she usually gets a migraine too. Well, she'd better not get one tonight. She needs to make sure the house looks nice and that me and Hermione get a decent non-garlic, non-fishy supper.

HERMIONE

Before I set off to meet Helena at the Blue Monkey, I pack everything I need for the evening in this little vintage vanity case that I bought from a charity shop last summer. I'm feeling a bit panicky as I think about the day ahead, but I try to control my breathing and stay calm. I can't crumble now.

Part of me has no idea whether I'm going to be able to cross the divide back into Helena's actual house, which is of course my house – well, not my house, but Paul's.

In some respects, I'm intrigued to see what it looks like in the 70s. It would be weird to see Helena's wallpaper, which is currently in shreds all over my bedroom floor, freshly hung on the walls.

As for her parents, I've already met her mum and sister, not that I ever told Helena about the bus incident, and I doubt Alicia and Rosalind will remember me. I was just some random girl coughing her guts out on the number 11.

For the first time since I've been time-travelling, the weather between the two zones is quite different and the atmosphere in

1975 feels fraught with tension, as if something needs to happen to clear the air.

Helena is already giddy with excitement when I get to the Blue Monkey, which on this clammy, overcast day is even more fetid than usual.

I'd like to drag her to the park instead, but she loves this place. I think it's because she's one of three girls and goes to a single-sex school, so boys are still a massive novelty. I've always been to mixed-sex schools, so I'm used to the fact that guys are idiots. Helena laps the idiocy up though, she can't help it, she laughs at any old laddish nonsense.

But that's fine. Today's not about me. Today is about one thing and one thing only and that's keeping Helena safe. If I can just get her to midnight without anything going wrong then maybe I can break the spell?

HELENA

Apparently the band are already at the venue, doing sound checks and practising, and a thrill of excitement goes through me. This time last year I wouldn't have even known what a sound check was and for the first time since I broke up from school, I realise that I'm actually really glad I wasn't invited to go on holiday with Gwen and Elaine. Because if I'd gone to France, I wouldn't have met Hermione and I wouldn't be going to this gig.

It's really too hot to be stuck inside the Blue Monkey, so a load of us go and sit on the patch of grass in front of the café. Bitchy Sandra moans about us taking her crockery outside and says she'll swing for us if so much as a spoon goes missing, but no one takes any notice and everyone just lounges about and a girl with red hair does a cartwheel, which is a bit annoying and showy-offy, and then she does a handstand and goes over into a crab, which is pretty amazing.

I'm a bit furious that I didn't try harder in gymnastics because if I had, I might be the one scuttling around the patch of grass like a super-flexible crustacean, getting all the attention. Crab-girl seems to have set off some kind of weird, competitive reaction. Some of the lads start doing press-ups and girls are chanting, 1, 2, 3 . . . until the boys collapse on to their faces. Then Gazza and Jezzer arm-wrestle and everyone's laughing only someone says the wrong thing and Gazza suddenly whacks Jezzer in the face, so then Gazza punches him back and within seconds the little front garden with its border of begonias is just a seething mass of scrapping lads, all elbows and fists, and the next thing I know Hermione is hauling me out of the throng and dragging me away.

HERMIONE

Helena can't believe I'm dragging her away from the Monkey madness, but then I explain that if we get caught up in the fray, we run the risk of ending up with black eyes for tonight, and that seems to do the trick. In reality, I just think she deserves better. After all, this could be her last . . . Oh God, don't say it, Hermione, don't even think it.

As we walk to Ashton Gardens, the sky turns metallic grey. Helena slags off the red-haired girl.

'Who does she think she is, the Fylde Coast's answer to Olga Korbut?' Olga Korbut I presume is some kind of 70s female gymnast, but I refuse to get drawn into a bitch fest, so I just don't say anything until she's run out of steam and is kind of trotting to keep up with me, and saying, 'Do you think I'm just jealous?' and it's so blindingly obvious that she's hit the nail right on the head, we both laugh.

In the gardens we sit on 'our' bench with my vintage cherry-red case between us and Helena admits that jealousy is her big problem, that she's jealous of her sister, because Juliet's thinner and because she's got friends with 'places in Italy' and that she's jealous of Rosalind, because Rosalind isn't jealous of anyone. 'Oh,' says Helena, looking over my shoulder, 'and I'm jealous of her.' She stands up and waves at a smiling, tanned girl who is approaching us with two boys who I recognise as Jimmy Simmonds and the yet-to-be-gay Greg.

Sally dashes over to say hi to us. I immediately like her. She has shoulder-length, shiny brown hair and fantastic teeth. She and Helena don't hug – apparently hugging your friends is so not done in 1975 – but I can tell they are happy to see each other and comfortable in each other's company.

'This is Hermione,' Helena says, and the pride in her voice almost makes me teary. 'She's from London.'

At this point I feel I should do something very London, but apart from suddenly adopting a heavy Cockney accent and singing 'Any old iron' I can't think of anything, so I just grin and say, 'Hi.'

Sally has been to Torremolinos, she says, hence the tan.

Thunder rumbles in the distance and we all head to the empty bandstand in case it starts raining. The scent of roses hangs heavy in the air and there's a sense of stillness before the storm.

Helena asks if they're going to see the band tonight and Sally says of course they are, isn't everyone, and Jimmy kind of winces and says, 'She twisted my arm.'

'And mine,' adds Greg, because he's like an echo of Jimmy, and I wonder what eventually will make him realise that Jimmy likes girls and he doesn't.

Sally has a cousin who lives in South London, and she starts chatting about places I might know. At one point I make a rookie mistake and mention the Millennium Wheel, which obviously doesn't exist in 1975, but fortunately at that moment a massive fork of lightning illuminates the sky and we all scream, except for Jimmy, and count the seconds until the thunder cracks.

'Let's get home before it pisses down,' shouts Helena, and we make a dash for the bus stop.

HELENA

We get on the bus with Sally, Jimmy and Greg. Greg is weird but hilarious. Apparently he likes musicals, and saves up to go to matinées of things like *Cats* in Manchester with his mum.

It's a bit painful seeing Jimmy with Sally. They obviously really like each other and twice on the bus I saw him kiss the bare skin of her shoulder. There is something gentle about the way he treats her. He's got what Nana Nancy would call 'lovely manners'.

Sally looks fantastic too. No wonder Jimmy can't keep his hands off her. She's got a proper tan, which makes her eyes seem brighter and her smile loads whiter. She and Hermione get on really well, and I think how nice it will be in the future to have this little gang to hang out with.

Then I remember that what I really want to do is get off with Sticks. Tonight is my chance, I can feel it in my bones. Something big is going to happen. I hope I get to snog him.

As the bus pulls to a stop on Common Edge, there is another fork of lightning followed almost immediately by a violent roar of thunder. It sounds like it's coming from directly above us, and as we step down from the bus, fat raindrops are already splatting down hard on to the pavement.

'Run!' I yell, and me and Hermione leg it, shrieking and laughing down the back street and through the back gate to my house.

HERMIONE

I feel like Alice in Wonderland as we enter the garden. It's weird because while it's the same as Paul's, it's completely different. The lawn and some of the rose bushes are in the same place, but an ancient greenhouse has since been replaced by Paul's patio and gas-fired barbecue area. In 1975 a riot of sweet peas run across the back wall and something green with tendrils curls up a series of bamboo canes in what looks like a vegetable plot. Ducking our heads under a washing line hung with sodden tea towels, Helena bursts through the back door, yelling, 'We're home,' and I get this strange feeling, because I am home, sort of.

The kitchen is smaller than Paul's. At some point a wall must have been knocked down. Cooking smells emanate from the oven and the walls above the kitchen surfaces are covered with these vivid bright-orange tiles. There is something arty and welcoming about the place.

'I love these tiles,' I tell Helena.

'Well, considering I made them, that's a good start,' says a woman's voice, and there, through the open doorway, sitting at a pine table in the next room and filling in a crossword puzzle, is the woman I saw on the bus. Helena's mother looks at me as if trying to place my face, but it's Rosalind, reading a comic on a cushioned window seat, who recognises me instantly.

'It's choking girl!' she announces, and with that the ice is broken.

There's a pot of tea on the table and Helena fetches two more mugs, both of which I'm told were handmade by Alicia, and we drink tea while Rosalind tells Helena how she gave me her last Spangle on the bus. Alicia bustles in and out of the kitchen. 'It's quiche,' she tells me, 'with salad, baked potatoes and peas.'

The house exudes this family from every room: Alicia's pottery, Rosalind's Barbies and comics, Simon's jumper slung across what is obviously his chair in the sitting room.

Upstairs, Helena shows me quickly around her parents' and sisters' bedrooms, before, beaming from ear to ear, she reveals the pride and joy that is her own room. It's so weird to see the wallpaper that I've been scraping off my own walls freshly hung. The yet-to-fade pinks and purples are dazzlingly bright, and I notice the bed is exactly where I have my bed.

Helena says supper will be at six and that we should leave at seven thirty to get to the gig for eight. She puts Ziggy Stardust on the record player, and I'm mesmerised by the spinning vinyl and the album covers in her record collection.

'I bet you've got loads of records,' she says.

'Not as many as you'd think,' I reply, thinking about Spotify and all the millions of songs just sitting on some cloud in the ether, 'but my dad's got a great collection of sixties Motown.' I feel a tiny pang when I mention my father, but I shrug it off, because what's the point?

'My dad's a classical-music nut,' says Helena, 'and he likes jazz.' We both roll our eyes at each other.

I unpack my dress and hang it next to Helena's in the wardrobe so the creases have time to fall out, and Helena sits on the bed, which is made with sheets and a blanket instead of a duvet, while I settle on the beanbag and we paint our nails and chat and I have to work hard to make sure it's not all about Sticks.

I'd stay here all night if I had the choice. If we could just stay in and not go out, then maybe I could keep her safe? After all, it seems unlikely any harm could come to her in her own bedroom, not while I'm around anyway.

Alicia calls us down for supper and we blow on our nails to make sure they're properly dry before taking a seat around the pine table.

Helena's dad and Rosalind are already in situ. Rosalind introduces me as the 'choking bus girl' and Simon asks if I play any musical instruments, at which point Helena goes mad, but then everyone laughs.

The quiche is watery and the potatoes are a bit hard, so I cut mine in half and slather on a load of mayo, and when Alicia apologises I accidentally say, 'Oh don't worry, my mum's a really crap cook too,' which makes everyone laugh again.

We are having our pudding, fresh strawberries and cream, when Rosalind suddenly sighs, turns the colour of alabaster and starts dripping blood into her bowl of strawberries.

The result is weirdly shocking as the blood slowly stains the cream a gruesome pink. For a second we all freeze, as if someone cast a spell over the table, then Alicia runs for ice and Simon puts Rosalind on his knee, pinches the bridge of her nose and instructs the girl to tilt her head forward. They are very calm, but Rosalind is weepy and Helena gives me a look as if to say, *let's leave them to it*, so we do.

'She's crying because she's embarrassed,' Helena tells me as we return to her room, 'because you're here and she wants everything to be perfect for you. That's the kind of kid she is.'

I decide to seize my chance. 'Maybe we shouldn't go out?' I say. 'Maybe it'll be less worrying for your parents if we just stay in and have a quiet night? I don't mind.'

Helena looks at me as if I'm mad and gasps, 'You must be joking! What about the dresses? Hermione, I am going to this gig if it's the last thing I do.'

Outside the rain threatens to break the window.

HELENA

In the end, because the weather is so filthy, my dad offers us a lift to the social club. My mum has given us one of Nana Nancy's left-behind umbrellas so that we don't get drenched getting out of the car. Alicia looks tired, the lines around her eyes suddenly deeper.

'I'm going to see how she is after a good night's sleep,' she says. 'She's resting on the sofa now if you want to say good night.'

I pop in to see Rosy before we leave. She's dozing but when I kiss her cheek, she immediately opens her eyes and pulls a face at me. So I guess she can't be feeling too bed then, which is a relief.

I'm itching to get to the venue, but every traffic light is against us and each time we stop, Simon asks Hermione another ridiculous question. 'So what O levels will you be taking next year? What does your mother do? Is your stepfather a keen golfer?'

I mean, what sort of question is that?

I'm squirming with embarrassment in the front seat, but Hermione doesn't seem to mind. She just chats away and when we finally reach the social club, she gets out of the car and says, 'Thank you so much, Mr Treace, it was really kind of you to give us a lift.'

The pair of us make a beeline for the queue lining up beside the building, and I put up Nana Nancy's hideous purple brolly while we wait in the pissing rain to get our hands stamped.

Inside the social club, the first thing I see is the drum kit set up on the stage in front of a metallic curtain made from what looks like strips of silver ribbon. A painted black bird takes flight across the face of the middle drum, 'The Ravens' written in swirling letters beneath its wings. There's also a microphone set up centre stage. Apparently, a comedian is going to be warming up for the band.

There's a small dance floor directly in front of the stage and then a load of tables and chairs reaching all the way to the back of the room, where the cash register behind the bar is already ringing like crazy. A DJ with decks set up on the far right-hand side of the stage is playing chart hits and above it all a mirror ball spins, reflecting different-coloured lights around the room. Everything about the place reeks of promise and excitement and I love it.

After some discussion, Hermione and I grab a table right at the front, though a bit to one side, so as not to look desperate (Hermione's idea) and soon Sally, Jimmy and Greg join us, which is good because now it looks like we're one of the popular tables.

We all decide to drink gin and orange juice, as that seems

like the right drink for this occasion, and Jimmy and Greg head over to the bar to see if they can get served (though we've all heard this place isn't too fussy).

As the place gradually fills up, I recognise loads of people from the Blue Monkey and do lots of flitting around saying hi to people and getting loads of compliments on my dress.

Soon the place is buzzing and it's clearly a full house tonight. There's a big group of bikers standing around the bar at the back, steaming slightly in their rain-soaked leathers, holding pints in big, tattooed fists. Filling the tables in front of the stage are a load of us Monkey regulars, while a number of social club regulars, who probably came for the cheap drinks and the comedian, sit at banquettes round the side.

At last, at about eight thirty, the lights go off and the DJ introduces the comic from his booth at the side of the stage and everyone whoops and cheers and claps and takes their seats. His name is either Benny or Bernie Eggers, and he does a funny walk from the wings up to the mic, at which point a woman behind me becomes semi-hysterical. Once he reaches the mic, he starts quacking like a duck, which seems to be his trademark 'thing' but not everyone's getting it. One of the bikers at the back yells 'tell us a fucking joke' so he does, he does all these jokes, about Pakis and fat women and the mother-in-law and Jews and poofs and Hermione's face turns to stone. After about three minutes, she leans over and says, 'I can't really deal with this,' and heads for the toilets.

I follow her into the ladies' where she is splashing her face with cold water.

'Imagine,' she hisses, 'how it must feel listening to that shit, if you're fat or Black or gay or Jewish, or maybe all those things? It's so hateful.' Her eyes are blazing and I try and calm her down by saying, 'It's only a bit of fun,' but she won't have it. 'It's because of people like that, that boys like Greg have to pretend not to be queer.'

'What?' I say. 'You don't know that . . .' I protest, but she snaps back, 'I've got eyes, Helena, and something called a gaydar, which you'll understand one day. Anyway, I'll just stay here until he finishes and then I'll come out for the band, only if I go out there, I'm going to start heckling.'

HERMIONE

Helena grins mischievously at me, swigs at her gin and orange, lights a No.6, winks and disappears back into the audience.

I sit in a cubicle for a while trying to calm my breathing, waiting for the hideous comic to finish his foul act, while above my head the rain beats relentlessly against a grimy skylight.

I shiver. *Just stick with Helena*, I remind myself, forget the stupid comic; the only important thing is to make sure she's safe. That comic probably had a heart attack by the time he was fifty, judging by the state of him.

I'm just about to exit the cubicle when I hear the door to the ladies' toilets open. An instant whiff of sour beer riding in on a wave of noisy applause hits me. I push the cubicle door ajar with my foot and glance in the mirror opposite. Instinctively I shrink back inside the cubicle because I've caught sight of who just came in. My heart starts hammering. It's Liza Branwell. She isn't meant to be here, and right behind her is Alex King, in full gush mode.

'I can't believe you're actually here, Liza. I thought it was your nan's funeral?'

'Cremation,' Liza throws back. 'Twenty minutes, in and out, sausage roll and a Cinzano at the local pub, then me and our Tina got the train back. My mum's not talking to us, says we're a disgrace, but I'm not missing out on seeing my boyfriend playing drums with The Ravens, so, here I am.'

I need to warn Helena, I think. I flush the toilet and emerge really casually, heading for the sinks to wash my hands. Liza Branwell is smearing an ointment-pink foundation around her face and feverishly dry-shampooing her hair. When she sees me in the mirror, she refuses to move over but Alex shifts to one side so that I'm standing between them as I run the taps. She addresses me in the mirror. 'Oh look, if it isn't little Miss London.'

Alex looks embarrassed, but I plaster on a sickly smile and say, 'Oh, hi, Liza.'

She checks me up and down, smirks and says, 'I see you and your mate are wearing matchy-matchy dresses. So sweet. I used to do that with my sister when we were about eight and six. Shame she's had to leave so suddenly.'

My blood runs cold. 'What?'

Liza carries on doing her make-up, as if she hadn't just dropped a bombshell.

'Why? Where did she go?'

My brain has gone into overdrive. Surely she can't have turned tail just because Liza turned up, not without telling me? I can feel the panic rise in my chest.

Liza shrugs. 'Yeah, she freaked out after me and Tina told

294

her we'd seen an ambulance outside her house. Just ran out.'

'Fucking hell,' interjects Alex King.

'Yeah, we were passing her place in a cab from the station and there it was, *nee na nee na*, all lights blazing, so I told her and she just went to pieces. Don't worry though,' Liza says, 'Albie, Tina's boyfriend, offered her a lift home on his Harley.'

Before she's even finished, I'm running out the door, pushing my way back through the club to the exit. One thing I know for certain, whatever happens, Helena must not get on the back of that motorbike.

At the door, a bouncer stands blocking the exit. 'Not another one leaving so soon. Listen, darling, if you don't like it in there, you can always keep me company.' I don't have time to tell him to fuck off, I just hurl myself out of the door and into the pissing rain.

It's raining so hard, I can barely see, and I've no idea which way to go . . . If she's got on the bike, it's too late, I'll never catch her. I just have to hope . . .

And that's when I spot her, round the side of the club, getting on to a massive silver and black motorbike.

'Helena!' I scream, but she doesn't hear over the sound of the engine.

'HELENA!'

I scream at the top of my voice. At last she turns and sees me. She taps Albie on the shoulder, and the engine stops.

'Get off that bike NOW!' I scream, running over to her.

I realise when I get to her that I'm crying and when she gets off the bike I can she is crying too, crying and shivering. She clutches at me. 'I'm sorry, I have to go, Hermione. Something's happened to Rosy . . . There's an ambulance . . .'

'You can't get on that bike, Helena . . . he's been drinking, it's raining, it's not safe . . . you haven't got a helmet.'

'What if she's dying, Hermione? My sister, my Rosy-Posy . . . I HAVE to go.'

I try and calm her down. 'Why don't we ring home?' I say. 'Let's just check first.'

Albie's getting annoyed at this point. 'Look, do you want the lift or not, love? I'm not waiting around in the rain for ever . . .'

'The phone in the club is out of order,' says Helena. 'He's going to give me a lift home, it's the quickest way.'

Albie goes to start the engine again.' Come on, darlin', and remember to hold on tight.'

'No!' I yell. 'Listen to me, I can't explain why now, but just trust me . . . you cannot do this, there has to be another way.'

She stares at me. 'She's my sister.' Her tears mingle with the rain running down her cheeks.

Albie revs the engine, almost drowning me out, and I have to grab hold of her dress to stop her getting back on that terrifying machine.

I pull her to the side of the building, where the overhanging roof offers some protection from the weather and I will her to listen. In the background, Albie drives around on the Harley, making slow, menacing figures of eight on the sodden tarmac, waiting for Helena to change her mind. 'Helena,' I say, 'listen to me very carefully. I'm going to phone your house and we are going to see what's going on, so you must just trust me.' And slowly I reach into my bag.

Helena eyes me carefully. 'What's that?' she says, as I pull out my mobile phone.

'I'll explain later,' I reply. 'Just tell me your number.'

Up until now I've always been so paranoid about anyone seeing my phone, but right now I don't care. I don't even know if it will work in 1975, but as I hold down the 'on' button, the glass screen illuminates in my hand.

I look at Helena, and she starts reciting her number. Barely daring to breathe, I press in the numbers, and . . . Simon answers. I thrust the phone into Hermione's hand.

'Dad?' she says. 'Is Rosy OK? Why is there an ambulance—'

I watch her expression carefully and within seconds her faces changes and although the tears and snot continue to streak her face, my heart leaps because I can tell that now she is weeping with relief.

When the conversation is over, she passes the phone back to me, and I hang it up for her and drop it into my bag again.

'It wasn't for our house,' she gulps. 'The ambulance. It was the old bloke next door, he fell down the stairs and broke his leg, Rosalind is up and playing Kerplunk with Mum, Dad's watching the telly, it's fine, they're fine. Oh, Hermione . . .' And she collapses on to me, hugging me tight and as I hug her back, the rain brings out the scent of her shampoo and in that moment I know that's it, I did it, it's over, Helena won't die tonight.

Helena pulls out of the hug and looks at me.

For a second we just stare at each other, smiling, but I see the questioning in her eyes.

'Please don't ask me,' I say. 'Please just trust me.'

'Is it your stepdad's?' she asks. 'Is it a police thing?'

'Something like that,' I say, 'but you mustn't tell anyone. I could get into awful trouble.'

'Of course,' she grins. She doesn't care; her sister isn't in an ambulance.

Just then, the sound of a drumbeat travels through the night air towards us.

Helena's eyes grow wide. The band has started.

As we head back inside, we pass Tina standing in the corridor with her hands on hips, shouting at Albie, 'What are you playing at, Albert Greencock? I'm your girlfriend, you stay here with me, do you hear?'

Inside the bar, The Ravens are playing up a storm and people are dancing. All the girls take their handbags with them to the dance floor and make moves in circles around them, which makes me laugh. Everything is funny now, everything is perfect, a great weight has lifted from my heart. If they brought the comic back on, I'd probably even laugh at him, though that's possibly going a bit far.

HELENA

The band are AMAZING! Sticks is a brilliant drummer, that's obvious, and he looks so painfully cool up there on the stage that I can't help wishing Liza wasn't here. Once or twice when I dance near the stage, I catch him looking at me, but Liza is always there, zooming in as close as she can, wiggling and jiggling her tits around, trying to disguise the fact that she's a crap dancer.

Hermione comes up to me and shouts in my ear. 'Forget about him! Why is he flirting with you when he's got a girlfriend? He's not good enough for you!' And suddenly I know she's right.

So I drift further back away from the stage and decide to just enjoy myself boogying with my mates instead. Greg is a brilliant dancer. He and Hermione are pulling off some really excellent moves when that red-haired gymnast girl who was doing the crab walk on the Monkey lawn comes over and kind of takes over. Hermione isn't fazed, she just dances with me instead, and for a moment I get this feeling of pure happiness – me and my best mate Hermione dancing in our fabulous dresses. Who cares about Sticks and his whiffy armpits and skinny little nicotine fingers.

Then just at that very moment, these two lads kind of sidle up and start dancing with me and Hermione. Is that how this works? Do they only come over when you're having fun without them? And as I think it, Hermione winks at me – she is so clever!

Hermione's one, Lucas, is quite weird looking. He's about nine feet tall and really thin with long, auburn curly hair and he's so white his freckles are like cinnamon on his face, but he's a good dancer and Hermione looks happy enough. My one is called Nick and he has thick shaggy blonde hair, a bit like Jimmy's but with normal-coloured eyebrows, and he's taller and kind of tanned-looking and when he smiles he's got a dimple in his cheek and he's the most gorgeous thing I've ever seen. We dance for ages and finally, when the band have played their encore and the DJ is playing some end-of-the-night smoochy numbers, I realise that Nick is kind of holding me around the waist, and halfway through Roberta Flack's 'The First Time Ever I Saw Your Face' he's leaning down and I'm looking up and for a moment I'm not sure which side my nose should go, but our faces fit together like a slightly squidgy jigsaw puzzle and, oh God this is it, we are snogging!

When I eventually come up for air, the music has stopped and a horrible bright striplight is flickering overhead.

The band is clearing their stuff off the stage. Sticks catches my eye, but I turn away, thinking, 'Ha.' Liza loiters, watching him hungrily. She can have him as far as I'm concerned.

People are picking up their jackets and bags and the empty dance floor is covered in empty bottles and fag ends. Over at the bar, the comedian is arguing with the metal grate which is closing in his face and separating him from the beer pumps.

Nick writes my number on a beer mat and promises to phone, before leaving with lanky Lucas. Honestly, I can't wait to ask Hermione if she snogged him.

Oh God, this has been the most perfect night.

HERMIONE

I didn't snog him, possibly because even though I quite fancied him (Lucas is, after all, completely my type), I couldn't stop thinking that back in my real time zone he would be in his sixties, bleurgh, and that kind of put me off. But I told Helena we had more of a friends vibe going on and she dropped the subject. After that it was all Nick, Nick, Nick.

While we're hanging around outside the venue, trying to decide how the hell we're going to get home, Greg admits his mum is coming to pick him up and points to a tiny mustard-yellow Mini, parked up at the gates of the social club.

Helena and I squeeze into the back of the car and Greg's mum is delighted to see us, although she does ask which one of us is his girlfriend. I tell her that neither of us are good enough for him and Greg chucks me a quick glance of gratitude in the rear-view mirror.

By the time 'call me Joan' drops me and Helena off at the corner of the back alley Greg and his mum have sung several numbers from the musical *Oliver!*, which fortunately we did at my old school in London a couple of years ago. Having played one of Fagin's gang, I was able to sing along for once, as did Helena, who is hilariously tone deaf.

We climb out of the car with Joan insisting we 'come over for tea very soon' and we sit side by side on a low wall by the entrance to the alley, neither of us wanting the night to end just yet. The rain has finally stopped and above us the moon shines pale gold and perfectly round.

There is silence for a couple of seconds and then she says, 'That silver thing, the magic hand telephone; is Paul a spy? Only I was thinking it's a kind of James Bond thing.'

I laugh, I can't help myself. The idea of Paul being a bit 007 is so ridiculous.

'Tell me . . .' she demands, and she looks me right in the eyes. So I do.

HELENA

She tells me she's from the future and that she lives in 2021, that somehow when she walks through the graveyard of the church on the corner, she travels back in time. She says that fate threw us together so that she could save my life, and that after tonight, she's got a feeling she won't see me again, but that doesn't mean I'm not her best friend, I am and I always will be, no matter what.

I stare at her for a minute. Then I burst out laughing.

'Yeah, right,' I snort. 'Good one. You can tell me the truth when you sober up tomorrow,' and I check my watch. Shit, nearly midnight.

'I'd better go . . .'

HERMIONE

We stand up and hug each other, even though friends don't really hug back in the 70s, and as we pull away, I find I'm fighting back the tears.

'Thank you for tonight, Hermione,' she says, looking at me seriously. 'It was the best night ever.' Then with a big grin she adds, 'And you will always be my best friend too.'

And with that she waves and disappears down the little street that leads to our back gate.

Helena thinks she will see me again, but I know she won't.

I take my usual route home via the churchyard and as I walk through the arched wooden gate, I can feel the elemental shift in time. The air is suddenly warmer and the streetlights are a different shape. A car cuts through the pub car park opposite, 'Butter' by BTS blaring from the stereo, placing me firmly back in 2021. Helena would love K-pop. So many pretty boy-band members to fancy.

Instinctively I walk around the back of the church, retracing the steps I took that night after seeing Madame Petulengro. I'm terrified to look, but I need to know if it worked.

In the shadow of the church, away from the streetlights, the moon acts as a torch, glowing down on the gravestones and the final resting places of the dead. I pass Gordon John's grave (dearly beloved granddad aged 89, RIP) and Annie Morgan's ('fell asleep' age 101 in 2003) to where the heart-shaped grave used to be, but when I get there . . .

It isn't here, Helena's grave is not here.

She didn't die.

I feel dizzy with relief and have to sit down for a minute on a nearby bench and I laugh and cry until the clock strikes midnight and even Tess will be getting worried.

So I walk home and I let myself in soundlessly and creep up the stairs. My mum whispers, 'That you?' and I whisper, 'No, it's your local friendly burglar,' and together we chorus, 'G'night!' then Paul snores and we both giggle.

Suddenly I realise that deep down I'm pleased for Mum. Paul might not be my idea of God's gift to women, but he's been nothing but decent to my mum and she deserves to be happy, so if he makes her happy then what's the harm. My dad's certainly not going to do it, is he?

Who knows, maybe I can be happy here too? Maybe it's time to give the place a go?

I close my bedroom door, sit on my bed and turn on the bedside light. Helena's handwriting dances on the wall in front of me. I trace her name with my finger. Oh, Helena, my sweet, jealous, lovely, funny friend.

I take out the photo-booth picture of us taken in Blackpool

just a few days ago in 1975 and slip it under my pillow, smiling to myself.

Then before I can change my mind, I pull the bed away from the wall, prise the lid off the tin of paint and tip some of the fiery orange mix into the tray that's been sitting there waiting for a week.

Then I load up the roller and begin to paint.

Thanks to my family,
my editor Polly Lyall-Grant,
my manager Richard Allen Turner
and to number 49,
the house where I grew up.

Also available as an audiobook

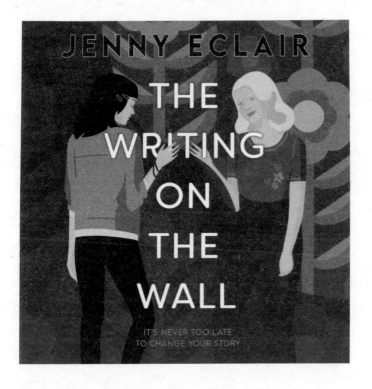

Narrated by Jenny Eclair

Want to be the first to hear about the
best new teen and YA reads?

Want exclusive content, offers and competitions?

Want to chat about books with people who
love them as much as you do?

Look no further...

bkmrk

Find your place

@teambkmrk

SNEAK
PEAKS

BONUS
CONTENT

OFFERS
AND
GIVEAWAYS

See you there!

bkmrk.co.uk